The Faith, Family, and Friends Series

Book One:

The Faith of Ella Reed

By:

Lynn Hobbs

The Faith, Family, and Friends Series
Book One

The Faith of Ella Reed

LARGE PRINT

Lynn Hobbs

Published: 2026

LARGE PRINT

Scripture quotations are taken from the Holy Bible, King James Version (KJV).

Published by: Proof Productions – Moundsville, WV 26041

Cover Art by: Jeff Brannon

First Edition: April 2026

ISBN: 10-978-1-969004-07-0
13-978-1-969004-07-0

Acknowledgement

First of all, I give God the glory for this book being completed and published.

I always pray for His direction before and during each time I write.

I want to thank my son, Jeff E. Brannon…it was his idea for me to start writing a new Christian Fiction series.

And his encouragement on how I have a gift for writing them…that prompted this new book and new series!

I also want to thank him for creating my book cover, formatting, editing, publishing …and all of his time involved in all of that!

And I thank my daughter-in-law, Miranda Brannon, for her support and encouragement.

I thank my granddaughter, Jessica Todd for her skills in editing and all of her time spent helping with that, and her encouragement! Special thanks for the illustration she surprised me with…so unique!

Thanks also to my son, Mike Brannon and my daughter-in-law, Kathryn Brannon, for being so supportive!

And to all of my family for being so happy when I complete another book…☺

To God be the glory!

Dedication

Blessings come in so many ways, and yes, I am so thankful for each one!

One way that stands out to me as a writer…is to have the right people, at the right time…in their extremely busy lives…to be those extra eyes…editing with timely insights!

And so it is with my son, Jeff E. Brannon.

He took time out from his job, his podcasts, his own writing, and time spent with his wife Miranda…to edit my book!

And so it is with my granddaughter, Jessica Todd.

She took time out from her job, her own writing, time spent with her husband Charlie, and time out raising their daughter, Cora…to edit my book!

You are both such a blessing to me, and I give God the glory for both of you!

I thank you both tremendously for your time and effort in helping make this book possible!

When it all comes together… God has His hand in it!

I pray this book will be a blessing to all!

UNDERWOOD

The Faith, Family, and Friends Series
Book One

The Faith of Ella Reed

LARGE PRINT

Lynn Hobbs

Table of Contents

Chapter One

It began so innocently, on a beautiful day in downtown Dallas.

The sky was bright and clear, stretching wide without a cloud in sight, and a warm breeze gently moved through the busy streets. It carried with it the faint scent of food from nearby cafés and the occasional hint of car exhaust, a familiar blend that somehow belonged to the city.

People were everywhere.

Some walked quickly with purpose, their eyes fixed ahead, while tourists slowed their pace enjoying the bustling city, and the rhythm of the day.

Cars passed steadily along the street, engines humming, and every so often a horn sounded in the distance.

The sidewalks were alive with conversation.

Laughter, phone calls, greetings between strangers and friends alike.

Ella Reed walked along the sidewalk, her purse resting comfortably on her shoulder.

A thirty-year-old woman, a professional, with a day off work.

She smiled to herself.

For once, she felt at ease.

No rushing through hospital halls hearing code blue.

No switching compressors.

No beginning CPR.

No pressure weighing on her shoulders.

Nothing going wrong to instantly fix.

Just a day off.

The dedicated surgeon in a different environment.

"I couldn't have picked a better day," she said softly, almost as if she didn't want to disturb the moment.

Until the force of a rough shove sent her face first into the side of a building.

"Ooh!" Groaning, she rubbed her forehead and cheek and stumbled to stand erect.

The guy sprinted away, knocking into others as he passed them.

They too, grumbled.

Just a nuisance you sometimes encounter.

Her hand shook as she straightened her long hair and smoothed it back in place around her shoulders while entering The First National Bank.

The bank had its own quiet rhythm. The soft tapping of keyboards. The low hum of printers. The occasional shuffle of papers sliding across the counter.

Hanging lopsided on the ATM machine, an 'Out of Order' sign appeared to be a permanent fixture.

She hurried to the long counter and stood in line.

A teller greeted her with a bright smile as she made it to the front of the line. "Good morning, ma'am! How can I help?"

"I'd like to take out three hundred, please." Ella slid her driver's license and debit card under the protective glass. Her cheeks pinkened as she pictured the rest of her day. "It's been too long since I've had a good shopping day."

"You and I both." The woman laughed. She automatically pushed her glasses up on her face as she entered Ella's information into the computer. "You know, Macy's is having a sale right now on the most comfortable slippers you've ever worn."

"Really? I'll have to stop there first!"

A rosy daydream suddenly showed her tossing her keys onto her bedroom dresser after a long day at work, a day like yesterday, and gliding into shoes that hugged her feet like pillowy clouds. Before Ella realized it, the teller was counting out her money and slipped it into an envelope with her two cards. She handed it to Ella.

"I hope you enjoy them, if they're not sold out when you get there!" She chuckled.

"Oh, I'm going to." Ella set the contents of the envelope between her purse and the teller. She visualized a map of the local area as she set her driver's license and cash into her wallet. "You can never be too comfortable, especially for someone who works on their feet every day."

"Can I throw that envelope away for you, ma'am?" The teller spoke up. "I usually ask if customers want an envelope, I'm sorry."

"No, it's fine! Go ahead." Ella smiled at her. Lifting her purse over her shoulder, she slid the envelope under the glass. "Thanks for the recommendation. Have a great day!"

"You too, ma'am!"

Pushing past the heavy bank doors, she left.

People on the sidewalk were like ants scurrying about after their mound was damaged. Left and right simultaneously.

Stepping into the crowd's chaos, she mindlessly began to weave through the people, heading towards Macy's.

"Comfy shoes here I come! I can't believe I never thought to get slippers before."

A chuckle bubbled up from her chest as she examined herself. *"Am I getting old now?"*

Her eyes sparkled at the amusing thought while rummaging through her purse and instantly stopped.

"Wait…what? Where is my debit card? Don't tell me I dropped it!" She cringed and searched through her wallet and side compartments of her purse.

Rushing back to the bank, worse case scenarios flooded her mind…

"Did someone find it on the sidewalk?"

"Is my checking account horribly overdrawn now?"

Panic set in.

Sweat beaded on her forehead and the back of her neck.

Ella caught her breath at the bank door.

She leaned against its heavy door for only a moment before she caught the curious gaze of a security guard standing off to the side. She flashed a quick smile towards him.

The guard did not return her courteous smile.

Ella glanced around the room before she found the teller she had talked to earlier and approached her stall.

“Good morning, again.” Ella gave an awkward chuckle.

“Oh! Ms. uh…Reed, right?” The teller offered a friendly wave. “Is everything alright?”

“I think I left my debit card. It’s not in my purse.”

“Well, nothing’s been turned in but…let me look.” The longer the teller pilfered around her desk, the more anxious Ella became, and the quicker her fingers tapped on the marble counter.

“Oh!” She exclaimed, and out of the trash came Ella’s debit card. “Here it is. I’m sorry I didn’t catch it. Here.” The teller slid the card under the glass. “If it helps you feel better there’s only paper in there.”

“Oh, thank you!” Ella beamed and snatched her card off the counter like a winning lottery ticket. “Praise God, I was so worried.”

"Hey, even if we couldn't find it here, we could just shut down the card and print you a new one. No need to worry."

"That's the memo of the day, I guess." Ella breathed a sigh of relief and slid her card into her wallet. "Thanks again and have a great rest of your day!"

Leaving the bank in a hurry, her heart finally stopped pounding in her ears… once she was outside.

With each step to Macy's her excitement returned…and grew.

It had been years since she'd shopped in person at the store. Online purchasing saved time with her work schedule.

And she arrived!

Lights flashed from the window displays as she neared the store's entrance. Excited to browse at leisure, her eyes sparkled from brilliantly lit showcased perfume and jewelry to lavish clothing ensembles. She entered with a child's amazement of approaching a gigantic toy store.

She made a few purchases, and was headed toward the shoe department, when she heard someone call her name.

"Ella Reed?"

The voice stopped her.

Ella flinched and turned.

Two police officers stood behind her. Their faces were serious, their posture firm. Not unfriendly, but not casual either.

"Yes?" She asked, glancing from one to the other.

"Ma'am, we have a few questions for you," one officer said. "We need you to come with us."

"Me?" Ella gave a small, uneasy laugh. "There must be some mistake. I haven't done anything."

"We just need to confirm a few things," the second officer replied. "For now, you need to come with us."

Ella looked around.

People continued walking past them.

No one stopped.

No one seemed to notice.

A couple walked by laughing.

A man checked his phone as he passed.

Life continued as if nothing unusual was happening.

But for Ella, everything shifted.

The sounds around her seemed to fade, inside and out. Even glancing through the store windows, the street remained just as busy. People still walked past. Conversations continued. Cars moved along the road. Yet it all felt distant, as if she were no longer fully part of it.

Her heart began to beat faster, each pulse stronger than the last. She could feel it in her chest, in her throat, even in the slight tremble of her hands.

"For what?" She asked, her voice tightening. "I need to know what's going on."

The first officer looked directly at her, his expression unchanged.

"You've been seen entering and exiting the First National Bank building several times this morning. We're investigating a robbery."

"A robbery?" Ella's voice dropped, barely above a whisper. "No…that's not right." She shook her head, trying to gather her thoughts. "I was just there to—"

"Ma'am," the second officer said, steady and controlled, "we can sort that out. But right now, we need you to come with us."

Ella swallowed hard, her mouth suddenly dry.

For a brief moment, she looked around again, almost hoping someone would notice; that someone might step in and say there had been a mistake.

But no one did.

Her fingers moved to the small cross around her neck, pressing it lightly between her thumb and finger. The cool metal grounded her, if only slightly.

A quiet stillness settled over her, not peace, but a moment of surrender.

She nodded slowly.

"Okay."

The officers stepped beside her and began guiding her down the sidewalk. Their presence on either side of her felt heavy, closing in, making each step feel more deliberate than the last.

Ella's mind raced as they walked.

A robbery?

That didn't make any sense.

She had only gone to the bank to withdraw some money.

Nothing more.

Nothing unusual.

And yet somehow…she was standing here.

The three walked together.

No smiles.

No small talk.

"What if the teller doesn't remember me?" Ella thought wildly. *"I really was at the wrong place at the wrong*

time…Lord, please help me!" Her mind continued at record speed.

They soon entered the bank, and Ella pointed to the bank teller who had waited on her.

"There. She helped me. Ask her."

They approached the teller, and Ella instantly exclaimed, "Ma'am, you waited on me earlier, will you tell these gentlemen? My name is Ella Reed…"

One of the officers quickly interrupted her. "Ms. Reed, I'd like to see your I.D. again to compare the information with what's on your debit card."

She opened her purse and pulled out her driver's license with trembling hands.

"Here it is." She handed it to him wide eyed.

"And your address is?" He questioned.

"The same as what's on the license, Hollybrook Apartments, Apartment 30, on Interstate 20."

"Did you help someone with her debit card named Ella Reed today?" He addressed the teller.

"I remember this lady's face." She pulled her glasses down and looked over the rims.

Sorting through a few transactions, she pulled one out. "Yes, debit card by Ella Reed."

Lifting a single eyebrow, she passed it to an officer.

Both officers examined the entry and glanced at each other.

"Ms. Reed, I can't see anyone using their debit card before robbing a bank. We'll get back to you in the future if needed. You can go, and I do apologize for the intrusion; but under the circumstances it was necessary." He smiled.

"I completely understand, officer." She took her driver's license back and walked out of the bank still nervous.

The excitement of the day was gone, and Ella still felt shaken.

Her hands had not quite steadied, and her thoughts continued to circle back to what had just happened. The questions, the looks from the officers, the word robbery still echoed in her mind.

She knew she needed to do something to calm herself down.

Taking a slow breath, she looked around and spotted a nearby coffee shop.

"That might help," she thought.

As she walked, a bright green billboard caught her eye advertising plants and fruit trees for sale.

A sigh escaped her. "*Oh…I'd love to have a garden. Not happening at my tiny apartment, though…as if I had time…maybe someday a relaxing patio…with a barbeque pit, tall plants scattered about, a fire-pit area, a greenhouse…*"

Ella pictured the restful area.

"…and today is a new day."

She could still hear her father's voice join her thoughts as she recalled… *'And I will rejoice and be glad in it!'*

Holding onto that encouragement, she made her way toward the coffee shop, her steps not as slow now, more deliberate, as if she were trying to keep herself grounded.

Slipping inside, instead of ordering her usual drink, she paused.

"I think I need something without caffeine," she thought.

"A calming tea, please," she ordered.

The café was filled with conversation and the soft clinking of cups against saucers. The rich aroma of coffee and tea lingered in the air, wrapping around her as she sat down. A machine hissed behind the counter as a fresh drink was prepared, followed by the low murmur of a name being called out.

Ella wrapped her hands around the warm cup, letting the heat settle into her fingers.

It felt grounding.

Steady.

Outside the window, people continued moving along the sidewalk, unaware of what she had just been through.

Inside, everything felt calmer.

But she wasn't quite there yet. Ella felt slightly removed from it all.

She took a slow sip.

Across the room, she noticed a woman reading a book. The cover showed a small-town diner.

Ella smiled faintly.

"I would enjoy living in a small town…maybe someday…"

She stretched her legs under the table and took another sip.

"Mind if I sit with you? All the other tables are full."

Ella flinched slightly and looked up.

An older woman stood beside her, smiling.

"Of course not. Be my guest," Ella said.

"Thank you. I don't often sit with strangers, but this is a public place," the woman said as she sat down. "The coffee is amazing here."

"Yes, it is. I agree."

"I'm Lucille Davis."

"Ella Reed. Nice to meet you."

"Same here! And what a peaceful place to rest. When my son Ted was in the service, it was referred to as R & R. Rest and relaxation."

"It still is," Ella said, smiling.

Lucille nodded.

Both remained reserved, not sharing anything personal at first.

Casual conversation passed between them; the weather, the crowd, and how busy the city seemed for such a pleasant day.

"It's nice to just sit for a while," Lucille said, glancing around the café. "Everything moves so fast these days."

"It really does," Ella replied. "Sometimes it feels like people don't even stop to think anymore."

Lucille nodded. "Especially with everything going on in the world."

Ella tilted her head slightly. "Yes… and depending on where you hear it, you get a completely different version of the story."

"That's the truth," Lucille said, leaning forward just a little. "It's hard to know what to believe anymore."

Ella lowered her voice. "You almost have to sort it out for yourself."

Lucille briefly scrutinized Ella, then gave her a small smile.

"Well," she said, taking another sip of her coffee, "I refuse to be manipulated by propaganda!"

Ella felt a flicker of surprise, then nodded. "And I won't be swayed by either side of created chaos."

Lucille laughed. "I agree, and isn't it wonderful we can sit here and talk freely? If this were social media, we'd be banned immediately!"

"Oh yes," Ella replied. "I've seen it time and again. It's either their way or the highway."

"Amen to that!"

Ella studied her for a moment and smiled. "We seem to agree on everything. Thanks for the conversation."

Lucille stood and shook her hand. "You are welcome and thank you for the hospitality."

She left.

Ella sat back, feeling calmer.

Maybe the day wasn't ruined after all.

And maybe…she could still enjoy it.

Chapter Two

"Not again!" Ella groaned as the news commentator announced the breaking news.

"First National Bank of Dallas was robbed for the second time in two days. Authorities have set up a perimeter surrounding the area and are even considering this to be an inside job."

Focused on the news, she could hear her phone ringing in the distance.

She hurried to the phone as the announcer continued. "Stay tuned as more details unfold."

"Hello?" Ella pushed the speaker phone option.

"Uh, Ella? It's me, Sybil." Her voice quivered. "Could you cover for me for surgery this morning? It's Joey Tapani's tonsillectomy, and it's scheduled for 8 AM." Her voice broke and she let out a whimper.

"Oh, Sybil! What in the world has happened?" Ella blurted.

Sybil moaned. "I'm at the police station, of all things!" Her emotion-choked voice rose in volume as she rushed on and on. "It's about a bank robbery and they have detained me for questioning. I may have to hire a lawyer. I don't know how long I'll be gone. I called my son Grady and told him what's going on…he can't believe it either…Ella, I need your help!"

Ella heard her friend trying to suppress a sob…

"Sybil! Of course I will, I'm off all day. I can't imagine you robbing anything or anyone! I'm so sorry this happened. The authorities even questioned me yesterday!"

"What?"

"It's a long story. I used my debit card to get some cash at the bank, and it got robbed minutes after I left."

"Oh my, that is so scary!" Sybil gasped.

"Be careful, Sybil, and I'll be praying for you. And don't worry about work. I'll take your place today."

"Thanks, Ella! I knew I could count on you. I've got to run. Bye."

"Bye."

Glancing at the wall clock, Ella ran to the bathroom and accidentally dropped the tube of toothpaste from her hand. Frowning as it slipped to the floor, she grabbed it and her toothbrush hurrying to brush her teeth.

And proceeded to knock over the plastic bottle of liquid ivory soap.

"I might as well throw everything on the floor." She grumbled angrily.

She continued and washed her face vigorously with soap and water.

"What a way to wake up! Six o'clock! Got to hurry to the hospital!" Slipping on her clothes, she said a silent prayer for Sybil, and rushed outside waving at a taxi to stop for her.

And got one.

Climbing into the available taxi, she smiled at the driver. "T & P Hospital, please."

"Yes ma'am." He swung the car back into traffic and accelerated.

She eased her back against the seat and her mind whirled. Reality hit her with full force. Her friend had to be in serious trouble since the police were questioning her at the station. A sudden surge of high blood pressure raced through her body as a warm flush enveloped her from head to toe. Her nervous stomach twitched.

"Calm down…you can't help her by getting sick." She spoke under her breath, and sighed.

"Ma'am?" The taxi driver glanced at her in the rear-view mirror.

"Oh, it's nothing. Just talking to myself, getting my day lined out." She gave him a brief smile.

He nodded and they soon arrived at the hospital. Ella handed her debit card to the driver telling him to add a twenty-dollar tip to the amount owed.

"Thank you! Lady, you're starting my day off supercharged!"

He grinned and returned her card from his machine.

"Have a blessed day," she replied, stepping out of the taxi.

Approaching the hospital entrance doors, she barged inside routinely as she'd done a thousand times.

But this time was different. This time she was in control of the upcoming surgery but could do nothing to help her friends' son.

"Ms. Reed?"

Ella turned and came face to face with the hospital Administrator.

"Mr. Vaughan. Good morning, sir."

"Good morning. I thought you had Tuesdays off."

"Yes sir, I do. I'm helping Sybil this morning; taking over her surgery."

"I was not informed. You and Sybil both know procedure on that." He frowned.

"Oh, I'm sorry. I figured the paperwork was ready for me to sign, I guess you haven't heard what happened."

"No ma'am, I haven't." He crossed his arms over his chest and eyeballed her sternly.

"She phoned me earlier this morning at the police station. She's an emotional wreck. She is being held for questioning in a bank robbery."

"I imagine she is an emotional wreck! I'll personally get written permission for the surgery from the patient, or guardian, and of course I'll sign off on it. Go scrub up, papers will be ready for you to sign in a few minutes."

Ella nodded and rushed to the surgery department. The air wafted of strong cleaning supplies and astringent hand sanitizer as she hurried down the hallway, but she didn't notice today. An impersonal monotone voice paging people from the intercom didn't faze her either.

She entered the prep room and plucked the patient's clipboard from the wall. Joey Tapani's file lay numb in her hand. She looked over his medical history and previous surgeries. At the bottom of the note she saw 'Primary surgeon specialist Dr. Sibyl Ponder' and Ella's chest tightened.

The uneasiness never left as a nurse handed her the new surgeon documents to sign. Signature in place, the nurse left, and Ella changed clothes.

Only when she finished scrubbing, and the sound of rubber gloves being snapped on did reality sink in.

She was taking Sybil's place because of a robbery.

The coldness of the room seemed to alert her to a new depth of seriousness as her stomach churned.

And it was the seriousness of what Sybil was experiencing that worried her…not the surgery.

One hour later, Joey Tapani was wheeled into recovery, still sedated. The surgery was a huge success.

An assistant followed Ella out of the surgical room smiling from ear to ear.

"Congratulations. That was great work! How about going for a coffee?"

Ella gave her a weary smile. "Thanks, some other time I'd love it. I'm so ready to go home. It's been a roller-coaster day."

"Doctor Reed, paging Doctor Reed. You are needed in the Administration office, Doctor Reed to the Administration office." The intercom announced the message as the assistant and Ella both raised their eyebrows at each other.

"Raincheck on that coffee." Ella remarked as she pivoted and hurried down the hallway… until she turned the corner.

Mr. Vaughn was standing outside the door of the Administration office clearly waiting for her.

He wasn't smiling.

Ella felt the uneasiness return to the pit of her stomach and tried to smile.

"Ms. Reed," the Administrator held the door open for her, and followed behind her into his office. "Please, have a seat." He motioned to the chairs in front of his desk, as he walked behind the desk and sank into his chair.

"I've recently learned some disturbing news. Sybil Ponder has been arrested for robbery and is being held without bond…"

"Oh, no!" Ella's hands covered her mouth and her eyes instantly watered. "My poor friend! She wouldn't do anything like that!" Ella exclaimed and looked directly at the Administrator. "I may never see her again!"

"I'm sorry to be the one to tell you, but we're all shocked, Ms. Reed. It's inconceivable this is even happening! I brought you in here to point out the police said she is not allowed visitors and can only talk to her attorney. Hospital procedure requires her to be placed on leave until she is found not guilty."

"I understand." Ella's hand trembled as she wiped away tears.

"It's all over the news." He grabbed the remote from a desk drawer and turned on the TV screen attached to the top of one wall.

Sybil's son is seen leaving the police station when reporters stop him.

"Is it true your mother is a surgeon at T.& P. Hospital here in Dallas?"

"Yes, in fact she had a friend sub for her in a scheduled surgery today that she should have done."

"Can you prove that, or is this your effort to try and bring credibility to your mother as a respected, professional person?"

He frowned at the camera, obviously annoyed.

"Yes, I can prove that!" He bellowed. "Her surgeon friend, Ella Reed, took her place." He shoved the reporters away as he maneuvered towards his car.

Mr. Vaughn turned the TV off.

His face sagged as he glanced at Ella.

"Be extremely careful if you do talk to the reporters, and I personally advise against it."

"Yes sir, and thank you for informing me." She took a deep breath trying to calm herself.

He cleared his throat. "You are welcome. You can go now, Ms. Reed."

She pulled herself up from the chair.

He gave a kind smile.

"Thanks again." Ella reached and shook his hand as she left the office.

The hallway was unusually empty while she ambled to the nearest exit.

Groaning, she instantly rubbed her hand across her stomach… all the turmoil had built into a nervous spasm.

"Oh, poor Sybil, Lord help her!" She thought to herself.

Nearing the exit doors Ella spotted the reporters outside and her blood pressure shot up.

Looking all around, there was no way of escaping them. She could hear her heart pounding in her ears as fear overwhelmed her in waves that flushed through her whole body. Her leg muscles tightened and her body tensed ready to run. She shoved the door open and pushed through the scattered reporters on the sidewalk.

"I've got to get home!"

A quick scan at the traffic, and she waved her arms at an approaching taxi.

He pulled over and she jumped in, giving him her address.

Within minutes, he had her in front of her apartment.

She paid and felt her adrenalin rush calming down.

"*I made it.*" Her breath burst in and out as she stood in the foyer. Tears of relief suddenly fell down her face, and she stumbled to the kitchen.

"*This is a nightmare…my poor friend, Sybil. She must be going through much worse than I encountered. Lord, comfort her!*"

Taking slow sips of water and calming down, she opened her computer and started scrolling through YouTube videos to take her mind off of everything.

Startled, a loud knock on her door interrupted her video.

"I'm coming. Wait a minute." She stretched her arms and stood momentarily then shuffled to the front door.

"Who is it?"

"Lieutenant Griffith, ma'am, of the Dallas Police Department."

She flung the door open and gazed wide-eyed at his face.

"Yes, sir. What can I do for you?" She noticed a movement near him as another officer came from behind him and walked towards her.

"Are you Ella Reed?"

"Yes sir, I am."

"And are you friends with Sybil Ponder?"

"Yes. We work together."

"We need you to come down to the station for questioning."

"Of course, anything to help my friend." Ella smiled. "Let me lock up and get my purse."

The ride in the patrol car would have been silent except for abrupt, loud static from a two-way radio.

Ella stared out the window wringing her hands.

"I'll be so glad when this is all over." She gazed out the window… not focusing on anything… as possible scenarios ran through her mind…

… Sybil being in a courtroom facing a judge…

… Sybil and her son Grady both standing in front of a judge…

"Ma'am?"

Ella flinched as the courtroom scene disappeared from her thoughts.

They had arrived at the police station and one of the officers was holding the passenger door open for her.

Ella smiled and left the car, and for the second time in her life, she walked again with an officer on both sides of her. They entered the station and proceeded to an interrogation room.

After informing her she was being recorded, and having her state her name, they gave the date and time, and Ella breathed a sigh of relief, appearing relaxed.

"Ms. Reed, is it true you are friends with a Ms. Sybil Ponder?"

"Yes, I am."

"And is it also true you know her son Grady Ponder?"

"Yes, I do."

"Have you been in contact with Sybil during this last week?"

"I talked to her today when she wanted me to sub for her at work, but before that we only talk occasionally at work. We did go out for coffee though last week."

"Do you know why Sybil or her son would want to rob a bank?"

"No, I don't."

"A guard saw you running back to the bank out of breath, what was that about?"

"I was halfway to Macy's when I realized I didn't have my debit card. I was hurrying back to make sure I didn't just drop it somewhere."

"Grady called you out by name on the news, was that a planned strategy?"

Taken back by the question, she put her hand to her chest.

"Absolutely not. Who do you take me for? I'm not some criminal!"

"Ms. Reed, is it true you were in the First National Bank of Dallas twice on a day it was robbed?"

"Yes…well, actually it was …"

"Ms. Reed, you are under arrest for the robbery of the First National Bank of Dallas. You have the right to remain silent. Anything you say can and will be used against you in a court of law. You have the right to an attorney. If you cannot afford an attorney, one will be provided for you. Do you understand the rights I have just read to you?"

Ella gulped and stuttered, "Ye…yes!"

The officer continued in a monotone voice.

"With these rights in mind, do you wish to speak to me?"

"No, sir, it sounds like…like I need a …a lawyer." She burst into tears and promptly fainted.

Chapter Three

Ella blinked and stared at the light bulb on the ceiling surrounded by a metal cage. Voices came and went over the intercom as the faint sound of keyboards clicking roused her senses.

Struggling to rise from the hard cot she lay on, someone's hand instantly pushed into her chest and stopped her.

"Good evening, Ms. Reed. I need to take your vital signs." A nurse grabbed her finger and stuck it in a small device. Nodding, she typed the information into her electronic tablet. "Pulse is good."

"You can sit up now." The nurse wrapped the blood pressure sleeve around her arm and began pumping the machine to tighten it.

Ella heard the air release in the machine, and the nurse pumped it up again squeezing the arm even tighter.

After the third time, the nurse typed the results into her tablet and quickly scanned an automatic thermometer across Ella's forehead. "No fever." The nurse remarked.

"I'll let them know you are okay; they can take you to booking now."

"What? I…"

"You were arrested here inside the Dallas police station and fainted today. They will take you for fingerprints, mug shots, inmate clothes, and then to your cell. Standard procedure."

"Could I make a phone call?"

"Not now, but later. And if you follow instructions, there won't be any problems." She added.

The nurse spoke a code number into her phone and soon a loud buzzer went off as two female police officers came and escorted Ella to the booking area.

Ella seemed to be in a daze and went through the motions of whatever was required of her.

Finally booking was over and she was escorted to a new area. Walking with officers and waiting for locked gates to unlock at each entrance to each hallway, they made their way into a large, circular room with cells made of thick, concrete block walls. The door of each cell only had a 1x1 foot window to see out of, and it had heavy metal bars across it.

"Sybil might be in one of these cells." Ella immediately thought as she walked past several cells.

"Here comes a new one!" One prisoner shouted. Another one laughed in a rude manner, then cooed, "Oh, ain't she sweet?"

Several others yelled back and forth at each other.

The ruckus continued as they passed a wall of cells.

"Hmm," Ella thought, *"the officers aren't getting onto the yelling prisoners; I might as well try it."*

She opened her mouth for the first time, "Sybil!" Ella yelled loudly.

The officers instantly stopped.

"You do not incite violence. Do you understand?"

All of the prisoners quickly shouted from their individual cells at the same time, and far back in the background she heard Sybil's voice.

"Oh, Ella!" Sybil moaned and instantly fell silent.

"Yes, ma'am, I understand." Ella replied to the officers and felt her heart pounding in her chest. *"Sybil heard me, she knows I'm here!"* Ella thought as adrenaline raced through her veins.

A cell door was soon unlocked.

"Here you go." One of the two officers said.

Ella entered the cell and heard her stomach growl as it quivered.

The officers locked the door behind her.

She stared at the bars over the tiny window and noticed the iron bars were shiny in places where hands had gripped them.

And shuddered upon hearing the steel mechanical doors sliding shut as the officers' footsteps echoed along the hallway… leaving her.

She sat in a rigid posture on a cot that was firmly fastened to a wall and stared at the four concrete walls.

Some inmates had carved crude words on the walls, while others wrote names and phrases that appeared to be nonsense but clearly had value to the writer…

Her stomach drew into another knot as the odor of prisoner's sweat filtered into her cell.

And she heard them whispering to each other…sometimes becoming vulgar. She cringed and closed her eyes in an effort to remove herself from their world.

It didn't help.

Absentmindedly running her finger back and forth across the rough material on the cot, Ella's worries intensified.

"What's going to happen to me now, and how long will I be here?" She wondered. "…*And Sybil…Can I ever see her again?... What will happen to her?"*

A sob caught in her throat as she realized nothing in her life would ever be the same.

She took a deep breath. *"I'm going to need my strength to get through this…I'll rest when I can."* She recited Psalm 91, and Psalm 23 out loud from memory, and then tried laying on the cot, changing positions to get comfortable. The saggy mattress had no back support. Ella twisted her lumpy pillow in half placing it under the small end of her back. Folding her arms under her head, she fought back tears, and even with the prisoners bellowing out disgusting remarks at each other…she finally dozed off.

Lucille Davis and her boyfriend Frank Haden strolled down the center of the shopping mall in Longview, Texas in absolutely no hurry. Laughing, Frank glanced at Lucille and shook his head.

"I thought you were going to buy that gaudy dress the salesgirl was pushing off on you."

"Now that's funny! I was only being polite; she took it the wrong way." Lucille explained. They laughed and he reached for her hand. She took it and they held each other's hand while roaming in and out of several shops.

As they approached a store displaying a row of television sets, "BREAKING NEWS" was suddenly splashed across the screen of each one.

Frank and Lucille paused.

"What's this about?" Frank muttered out loud.

The announcer spoke excitedly. "We have Captain Arnold Richardson, Chief of Police, with the latest update on the First National Bank of Dallas robberies. Stand by, please."

A solemn man approached a microphone and stood tall with great posture.

"Citizens, we are confident both robberies have been solved. Detectives are still uncovering more evidence currently, but we have arrested two suspects. They are being held without bond."

A reporter barged into the camera's view.

"Sir, are they local people or from out of town?"

The Chief of Police frowned at him. "I am not taking questions at this time. However, I will release their mugshots."

The screen switched to the mugshots of two women.

Lucille gasped.

The Chief continued. "Sybil Ponder is the woman with blonde hair, and the brown-haired woman is Ella Reed. Both are known to be acquaintances with each other, and both are surgeons at a hospital here in Dallas. That is all."

He nodded at the camera and left.

"Oh my gosh, Frank! I know the brown-haired one; Ella Reed!"

"How could you possibly know a bank robber?" He blurted.

"Sh! I'll tell you later." Lucille whispered.

The announcer stared at the camera and rapidly spoke into the microphone.

"Our own investigation team has discovered the name of the hospital where both suspects worked. It was verified to be the T. & P. Hospital here in Dallas."

He raised his eyebrows and leaned forward at the camera. "As standard procedure of that hospital's policy, both surgeons have lost their jobs; not on a leave of absence as some guessed."

The second announcer looked wide-eyed at his co-worker. "It looks like they might have known each other for a long time."

"They could have planned this, I mean, who would think a surgeon would rob a bank?" The first announcer laughed.

"True, but they are presumed innocent until proven guilty. This is Duke Lassater, and Bennie Wells from KJYK in Dallas, Texas. We now return you to your regularly scheduled program."

A commercial came on with a cute jingle about a Louisiana attorney getting it done.

Frank gawked at Lucille.

"Okay, how do you know Ella Reed?"

"It was a mere coincidence during my trip to Dallas. I slipped into a coffee shop for a latte, and the place was full. She sat at a small table with an empty chair. I asked if she'd mind if I joined her. She was friendly."

"What did you two talk about?"

"Oh, we were just talking politics, and the news. None of it lasted over five minutes. Nothing to it."

"Okay. You must be careful; you never know what someone is up to."

"Oh, Frank. I do admire your being cautious, and you are so right! But don't worry; I'm not the naïve young woman I was years ago."

"Just looking out for you, my dear." He grinned.

"And I appreciate it." She squeezed his hand. "Thank you!"

They left the mall and listened to the radio as he drove her home.

They caught the end of a local newscast and heard Ella Reed being mentioned. Lucille turned up the volume.

"Regarding the bank robbery in Dallas; it was reported the suspect Ms. Ella Reed has hired an attorney. A guard stated she remains quiet and withdrawn. The other suspect, Ms. Sybil Ponder also has an attorney and both have pleaded not guilty in court today."

Music soon resumed and Lucille glanced at Frank.

"I can't help but feel sorry for her. I honestly don't think she did it."

"She may not have…time will tell."

Chapter Four

Ella carefully assessed her court-appointed attorney, Jack Rogan. Fresh out of law school,

determined to make a name for himself, he stood five foot, five inches tall with the confidence of

a bull about to charge into a courtroom.

"This is case number 28384. The State of Texas versus Ms. Ella Reed," the clerk announced.

"Mr. Jack Rogan representing the defendant, and Mr. Bill Langford representing the State."

Judge Otto Hemming looked down from the bench.

"Ms. Reed, how do you plead to the charge of robbery?"

Jack placed a steady hand on Ella's arm.

"Not guilty, Your Honor."

"So noted," the judge replied. "Counsel, you may proceed."

Bill Langford stood.

"Your Honor, the State intends to show that Ms. Reed was knowingly involved in the robbery of The First National Bank of Dallas. We have surveillance placing her at the scene, as well as witness testimony connecting her to Sybil and Grady Ponder."

He sat down, and all eyes turned to Jack.

Jack stood.

"Your Honor, my client was in the wrong place at the wrong time. She had no knowledge of any robbery and no involvement in it. The evidence will show there is no credible link between Ms. Reed and this crime."

He sat.

The Judge nodded.

"Call your first witness."

"Your Honor, the State calls Mr. Monroe Stevens."

Monroe Stevens took long strides to the stand. After being sworn in, he sat stiffly, hands folded.

Bill Langford approached.

"Mr. Stevens, did you see the defendant on September 28th near the bank?"

"Yes, sir."

"Can you identify her?"

"She's sitting right there." He pointed toward Ella.

"And what did you observe?"

"The first time, she walked into the bank like anyone else. The second time, she came running in… out of breath."

Jack stood. "Objection to characterization."

"Sustained. Stick to what you saw," the Judge said.

"She ran into the bank out of breath," Stevens corrected.

"No further questions."

Jack rose and approached calmly.

"Mr. Stevens, did you see Ms. Reed commit any crime?"

"No."

"Did you see her with Sybil or Grady Ponder that day?"

"No."

"Thank you."

Stevens stepped down.

Langford stood again.

"The State calls Ms. Ella Reed."

Jack leaned toward her.

"Stay calm. Just answer what's asked."

Ella nodded and walked to the stand. Her legs trembled, but she steadied herself. She raised

her right hand and took the oath in a firm, clear voice.

"You may be seated," the Judge said.

Langford approached slowly.

"Ms. Reed, are you friends with Sybil Ponder?"

"Yes, sir."

"And do you know her son, Grady Ponder?"

"Yes."

"You were at the bank twice on September 28th?"

"Yes, sir."

"Why?"

"I went in to withdraw cash. I prefer using cash to stay on budget. When I got to Macy's, I

realized I didn't have my debit card, so I rushed back to the bank to find it."

Langford studied her.

"You weren't scouting the bank for a robbery?"

"No."

"You didn't plan anything with Sybil Ponder?"

"No, sir."

"Did you have any knowledge that a robbery would take place that day?"

"No."

Langford paused, then nodded slightly.

"No further questions."

Jack stood.

"Ms. Reed, did you participate in any robbery?"

"No."

"Did you communicate with Sybil or Grady about committing a crime?"

"No."

"Were you anywhere in that bank for any reason other than your personal business?"

"No."

"That will be all, Your Honor."

Ella returned to her seat, her heart pounding.

"Mr. Langford, your next witness?" the Judge asked.

Langford stood—

—but before he could speak, the courtroom doors opened.

"Your Honor!"

A man hurried forward, speaking quickly to the bailiff. A folder was handed to the Judge.

The courtroom fell silent.

Judge Hemming read carefully, his expression tightening.

"Counsel, approach."

Jack and Langford stepped forward. A quiet exchange followed. Jack's brow furrowed, then

lifted slightly as he listened.

The Judge leaned back and addressed the courtroom.

"Let the record reflect that the court has received newly reviewed surveillance footage and a supplemental report from the State."

A murmur spread through the room.

He continued.

"This evidence does not place Ms. Ella Reed in participation with the robbery beyond her presence as a customer. There is no indication she communicated with or assisted the suspects before or during the crime."

Ella's breath caught.

Langford stood.

"Your Honor, in light of this development, the State acknowledges that it cannot meet its burden of proof against Ms. Reed."

Jack closed his eyes briefly, relief washing over his face.

The Judge nodded.

"The law requires more than suspicion and proximity."

He looked directly at Ella.

"Ms. Reed, this court finds insufficient evidence to proceed."

A pause.

Then—

"All charges against you are dismissed."

The gavel struck.

Gasps echoed through the courtroom.

Ella's hand flew to her mouth.

"…dismissed?"

Jack turned to her, voice steady.

"You're free."

Before the noise could rise again, the Judge continued.

"This ruling does not affect the State's case against Ms. Sybil Ponder, which will proceed

separately."

That sentence hung in the air.

Ella's relief came in waves… but something didn't sit right.

Sybil…?

No.

Something about this still felt wrong.

Reporters scrambled from the room. Voices rose and overlapped.

Ella was immediately released from her handcuffs, and Jack gently guided her to her feet.

"Come on," he said quietly. "Let's get you out of here."

A bailiff stepped forward.

"Ms. Reed will need to be returned to holding for release processing."

Ella nodded faintly, still trying to grasp what had just happened.

Jack gave her a reassuring look.

"I'll meet you out front."

She walked with the guard through a secured hallway, the heavy doors opening one at a time with sharp metallic clanks. The familiar buzz of the locks echoed around her.

Back inside the holding area, everything felt different.

She wasn't staying.

She was leaving.

A few minutes later, a guard called her name.

"Reed. You're being released."

Those words hit harder than the gavel.

She followed the guard to a small processing room where her belongings were returned—her purse, her phone, her clothes… pieces of a life she thought she might not get back so soon.

She entered the dressing room and changed quickly.

"It feels strange…" she said softly as she stepped back out. "Wearing my own clothes again…even carrying my purse…"

"You'll get used to it," the guard replied.

They led her to the final gate.

The locks disengaged with a loud, mechanical snap. A buzzer sounded, and the door slowly

opened.

Freedom.

Jack was waiting just beyond the exit.

He smiled the moment he saw her.

"Told you," he said.

Ella exhaled, almost laughing, almost crying.

Jack escorted her to his car and drove her to her apartment.

Waiting for her to enter it, he drove off as she waved from her front door. She quickly went inside and locked her door.

"What a privilege to lock your own door…and no one locking you in…"

She ran into her bedroom and threw herself across her bed.

"It's so good to be home!" She expressed out loud and gathered the soft comforter

around her like a blanket.

"And Sybil's sleeping on a hard, rough cot…"

Ella whimpered thinking about her friend still in jail and dozed off, exhausted.

Tossing, and her mind on Sybil; she awakened from the brief nap and said a silent

prayer for her.

"Sybil would want me to get on with my life, but I'll keep praying for her life too."

Later, she took a frozen brisket steak-burger from the freezer…char grilled to

perfection… and placed it in the microwave. Lathering mayonnaise on two pieces of

bread, her mind went to the bland food at the jail and she shuttered. Meat patties in the

jail were called brake pads and faintly had the taste of meat.

This brisket steak-burger had juice running out of it and was thick and tender.

Her entire apartment was soon filled with the aroma of meat cooked over a charcoal fire

outside on a summer day!

Ella prayed over the meal.

"Yum! This is the best!" She mumbled between bites, wiping the juice from her chin and

fingers… and proceeded to eat all of it.

After a long, warm soak in the bathtub, she yawned and happily went to bed. In the

quiet privacy of her room, laying on her bed, she reflected on everything she had

experienced. In her nightly prayers, she prayed how thankful she was to be out of jail

and that she had a home to go to. She also prayed for Sybil, and as she drifted off to

sleep, she added something else to her prayer; "I'll never take anything for granted again…"

Chapter Five

"Eight o'clock? I can't believe I slept until eight in the morning!" Ella shouted and smiled sleepily and snuggled into the covers for a while. "But I don't have to look at that clock now." Lazily rolling over, she enjoyed minutes of sheer bliss until her mind was flooded with details of why she wasn't going to work.

…*"Standard procedure…I'm fired at the hospital…horrible…so unfair!"* She bit her lip as tears filled her eyes. *"And all charges against me have been dropped…"*

Tears silently rolled down her face. *"And my name is being drug through the mud…"*

"I've got to fix that situation…I can't lay here forever…that won't pay the bills…" she grunted under her breath as her feet hit the floor. "Heavenly Father, I thank you for another day, and I pray for you to bless those in need, heal those who are sick or injured either in body or mind, forgive me of my sins, and protect my family, my friends, and me from evil and keep us safe. I pray for those who are lost to want to receive You

as their Lord and Savior, and I pray for Your help so I can return to work. In Jesus Christ's holy name, I pray, amen." Standing, she stretched her arms and began her morning routine; bathroom, kitchen to plug in the coffee pot, and living room for the television's morning news.

Football scores were on and she had to laugh to herself. *"Seems like I get to watch something different!"* The coffee pot chugged out the last of the hot brew and she went after a cup. Returning to the living room, she slid into the recliner and stretched out her legs crossing them at her ankles. She took a sip and watched an incredible pass made by the quarterback and laughed to herself again… the young sports announcer seemed more excited describing it than the exuberant fans rooting for the player.

Another sip and world news was next.

"So now the announcers become solemn faced and give their one-sided version of the news without informing the public of everything that happens…in most stories…watching the news is like putting the pieces of a puzzle together…deciding what is true and what they edited out of the story." She thought to herself and knew this was a fact.

"But we need to be informed!"

A commercial showed happy people dancing who were taking a new medicine being promoted by a medical company. It did list the many side effects of taking their drug.

"No, thank you…" She uttered to herself.

She took another sip. Her coffee was cold. Sighing, she went to the kitchen to reheat her coffee.

She soon sipped her hot, delicious brew and calmed down.

Ambling back to the living room she caught her breath as she heard the announcer mention the latest on the Dallas, Texas two robberies of the same bank.

Ella hurried to sit in the recliner, slowly took another sip, and stretched her feet and toes on the recliner.

"And now for an update on the Dallas bank robberies; in a recent development, suspect Sybil Ponder, who was identified as the robber by an eyewitness, has just been sentenced to ten years in prison for the robberies.

He paused and caught his breath. "And the former suspected surgeon in the robberies, Ella Reed, has been cleared of all charges. This is Bennie Wells from KJYK."

Ella turned the television off and ran her hands over her face.

She moaned out loud, "... I still don't think Sybil would do anything like that! But there goes our reputations...all over town...and our jobs..."

She sank into the recliner.

Vivid memories flooded over her; the courtroom, Judge Hemming, the jail; and the horror of all of it.

"...Stop! Enough! I have got to eat...can't let that get me down..."

Forcing herself out of the recliner, she made the effort to take control and put the worst behind her.

Leisurely she went through the motions and fixed breakfast, ate, showered; even dressed for the day.

And it worked...she chose to go forward.

No longer stressed, she decided to Google, NOAA, the national weather service, anytime she wanted the weather and bypass television entirely.

"And I'll find a different source for news…" She hummed a tune and began a list of priorities that needed to be done.

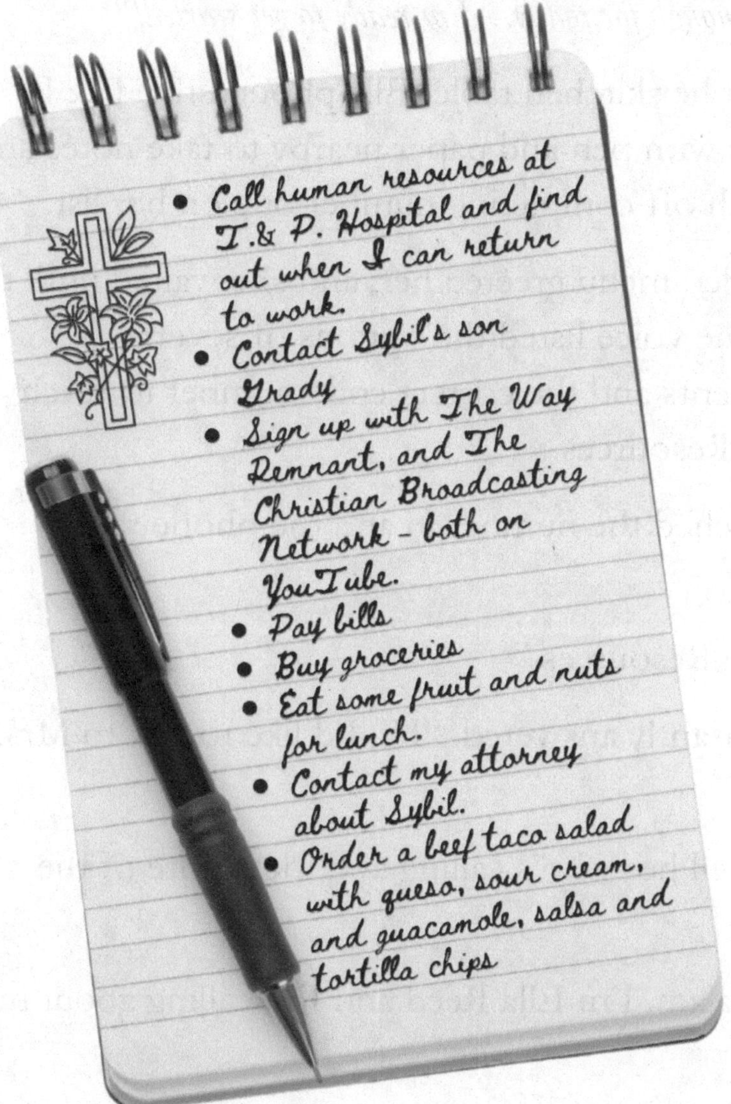
• Call human resources at T.& P. Hospital and find out when I can return to work.
• Contact Sybil's son Grady
• Sign up with The Way Remnant, and The Christian Broadcasting Network - both on YouTube.
• Pay bills
• Buy groceries
• Eat some fruit and nuts for lunch.
• Contact my attorney about Sybil.
• Order a beef taco salad with queso, sour cream, and guacamole, salsa and tortilla chips

"That's enough for today…I'm ready to get started!"

Sitting at her kitchen table, Ella phoned the T.& P. Hospital with pen and paper nearby to take notes and to scratch off completing number one on her list.

A recorded menu greeted her, and she waited until the monotone voice listed the options of several departments and the correct code number to reach Human Resources.

She punched the number in and the phone rang instantly.

"Human Resources."

Ella pleasantly answered. "Hi, I'd like to talk to Mrs. Padgett."

"May I tell her who's calling and the nature of the call?"

"Yes, ma'am. I'm Ella Reed and I'm calling about my job."

"One moment, please."

Ella waited patiently as background music played. Finally, a brief pause and Ella was connected.

"Ms. Reed?"

"Yes, ma'am. I'm calling to find out when I can return to work."

"Oh, I am sorry but that is against hospital policy."

"But you don't understand…"

"Ms. Reed, once an issue happens, our sponsors and donors to our hospital programs…some who are on the board of directors…refuse to let anything controversial interfere with the hospital's ability for profit."

"And I am controversial, is that it?"

"Your reputation is, Ms. Reed. I am sorry, but you aren't allowed to practice medicine here at T.& P. Hospital. If there is nothing more I can do for you, Ms. Reed, I must go, and I do wish you the best."

"Well, I do not agree. Goodbye, Mrs. Padgett."

"Goodbye, Ms. Reed."

Ella ended the call and clenched her teeth together.

Lost in thought, and a long, deep breath later, she groaned as the painful situation hit her with full force;

"And thank you, T.& P. Hospital for 8 years of service to you, and for 8 years of never being late." Her voice cracked, "And yes, thank you very much…"

She felt her muscles tense and called her attorney.

No answer.

She left a message and blew her nose.

A quick walk to the bathroom and she splashed cold water on her face. Her eye make-up smeared with tears as she mumbled to herself. *"Okay, this is the last time I give in to feeling sorry for myself! It stresses your insides up and you're a mess all over! I will be positive with my faith in my Heavenly Father, and nothing can stop me!"*

She returned to the living room and laid on the recliner. Closing her eyes, she considered her options and decided to start over in another town… a quiet, peaceful, small town.

Her phone rang.

Caller ID showed Jack Rogan, attorney.

In a better mood, she answered it pleasantly.

"Hello, Mr. Rogan!"

"Hello to you too, and how are you doing, Ms. Reed?"

"I've had better days, Jack, and they're about to get even better."

"I'm listening…and Ella, I hope I can help make them better."

"Thanks, so do I. I'm considering moving."

"May I ask why?"

"T & P won't let me return."

"Let me investigate. I don't think they can keep you from practicing in Texas, just at their own hospital…"

"Either way, it's a slap in my face. T & P's Human Resources thinks my reputation is bad for their hospital's image. How can I go forward with my life if I constantly must explain I was not involved in a bank robbery…all charges were dropped..makes for a bad resume. Not a good way to work burdened by a doubtful reputation!"

"I agree."

"I want to locate to a nice, small town in the country…away from city noise…and live there."

"May I recommend East Mountain, Texas? It's between Longview and Gilmer. Longview has two great hospitals, and Gilmer is nicknamed the attorney capital of Texas! I've had legal business in Gilmer often, and I think the whole area is just what you are looking for."

"Thank you, sounds like a great area."

"It is. Check it out. And I'd like to keep in touch. If you need help moving, I can recommend reliable people, just let me know."

"Thanks, I'd like that."

"Don't be a stranger."

"I won't, goodbye."

"Goodbye, and chin up."

Ella ended the call. Closing her eyes and tipping her head back, a wave of peacefulness surrounded her as her agitation left in that calming moment.

A soft smile slowly spread across her face. *"Thank You, Heavenly Father. I no longer feel like it's me against the world! I pray for Your continued guidance, Your will, and Your blessing on this move I am considering...and thank You for Jack...how nice to have a friend to engage in meaningful conversations!"*

Revived, she grabbed her priority list and studied it.

"Time to get up and get it done!"

First, she called Grady, Sybil's son.

His answering machine came on with a strange voice instructing you to leave a message.

"Hello Grady? This is Ella Reed, a friend of your mother's..."

He interrupted the message instantly. "Hello, Ms. Reed. I've had to screen my calls...for obvious reasons."

"I understand. How are you holding up?"

"It's a daily thing. It's tough knowing she's incarcerated...and will be for ten long years..." His voice broke and he choked on a sob.

"I pray for God's peace for you, and for this turmoil to stop. Grady, I wanted to reach out to you and let you know I will always be here for you. If you ever need me, just call."

"I appreciate that, Ms. Reed. There's not many I can talk to about all of this."

"Same here. That's kind of why I'm wanting to move."

"What happened?

"T. & P. said it's against their policy to employ controversial people."

"Mom would be so upset if she knew!"

"Yes, and Grady, I still don't believe she did any robbery at all."

"Neither do I. Thanks for calling me."

"Okay, take care and call me anytime."

"I will, goodbye."

"Goodbye."

"Hmm, so he thinks she didn't do it either…"

Ella turned on her desk computer. She had recently begun following The Way Remnant, Jeff E. Brannon's online ministry, after several fellow believers recommended it. She had already read two of his books and was looking forward to his newer ones, available on his website and Amazon. She also subscribed to his YouTube and Substack channels to catch his teachings. Afterward, she opened the Christian Broadcasting Network for news from a Christian perspective and signed up for their programs on YouTube.

"Another priority done!"

While she was online, she paid her bills. All that was left to do was buy groceries and eat.

She leaned back with her arms stretched wide, exercising in her chair...followed by a brief rest from the tasks at hand.

Invigorated, she quickly wrote a grocery list. And double checked the food in the fridge, adding more items to her list.

Locking her front door, she hurried down her front steps as only a thirty-year-old could do…fast, yet cautious, and waved for a taxi.

Minutes later, she arrived at Powell's Grocery with all its hustle and bustle. Kids screaming for candy, and customers grumbling for more checkers, when someone dropped a glass bottle of apple juice in front of checkout lane number three.

It was quickly blocked off.

Lines were backing up at the other two open lanes, and tempers were rising.

Ella made her way through the chaos and pushed her buggy towards the other end of the store. At first, she thought she heard someone yelling at her about something…and then she realized they were yelling about her.

"Hey, there goes that woman…you know…the one on T.V. caught robbing a bank…"

Ella, determined to show them a Christian reaction, did not get angry or yell at anyone. She finished shopping for her groceries and smiled courteously ignoring their remarks.

Trying to be pleasant, she soon paid for her groceries and left the store.

And felt their eyes on her as she left.

She kept walking…with both hands holding grocery bags.

On the next block she saw a beauty supply store that specialized in wigs.

"A wig? Yes, I could go wherever I want without being recognized." She thought excitedly, and taking a deep breath, entered the store.

Amazed at the floor-to-ceiling display of wigs along one wall, she was mesmerized looking at them. Short hair, long hair, every color you could imagine. One stood out among the variety offered for sale.

Blond, but not too bright or artificial. A common shade of blond with shoulder length hair.

Almost light brown.

"Hmm…"

"May I help you, ma'am?"

An older saleswoman approached her from behind, and Ella pivoted showing a beaming face.

"Yes, I'd like to try it on!" She pointed at the mousy blond wig.

"Certainly. I'll get it down for you."

Ella didn't see any customers in the store besides herself and hummed along as upbeat music softly flowed from the store's intercom.

She tried not to stare at the saleswoman's hair. It was obvious she wore a wig. The hair was entirely too thick for a woman her age …most had thinning hair …and it was too dark and curly for her light skin tones.

The saleswoman soon removed the blond wig using a long wire with a hook on one end. Talking non-stop, she handed it to Ella. "If it's not your size, we have more in the back room. This one is made with a weave that lets air circulate…so you are more comfortable."

Ella took it and stood in front of a mirror gently pulling it over her mop of brown hair.

"How does it fit?"

"It's snug." Ella replied, "but not too tight." She adjusted it by tugging at the back and slightly pulling it down.

"Oh, that style looks good on you," the saleswoman paused, "but how about a different color? Maybe a strawberry blond shade?"

"Thanks, but I really like this, the color seems to go with the shoulder length style better."

"Okay."

"How much is it?" Ella asked.

"Hand it to me and I'll look."

Removing it from her head, Ella gave it to the saleswoman and waited.

The saleswoman found the tag sewn inside the crown of the wig. "Here it is, this one is $219.99."

"What? That seems a bit high priced to me." Ella stuttered.

"Well, dear, it is synthetic, and they are cheaper. The wigs with actual hair are much higher." A smirk appeared on her face as she held the wig in her hand. "Have you changed your mind?"

"No, wrap it up. I want it."

"Certainly."

Ella paid with her debit card and left the store.

Obtaining a taxi was easy. She piled her grocery bags in the back seat and pictured herself wearing the wig.

… *"Less stress for me…"* She sighed.

Arriving back home, she phoned in an order and soon had her savory taco salad with all the extras on its way.

Slipping out of her sneakers, she turned on the five o'clock news and enjoyed lounging in the recliner.

"What a day…" Tilting her head to one side, she stared solemnly at the television.

"I hope I'm not on here again…"

A cool draft swept over her from the ceiling fan, and Ella's hand reached out to clutch her comforter. She pulled the covers to her neck and changed positions.

The double-paned window could not keep the noise out. Horns honked, a siren approached, and Ella's forehead began to ache.

Someday I'm going to move [illegible] away from [illegible].

She rolled from the bed. The chaos outside seemed to amplify louder. From the bedroom window, she gazed over a [illegible] all were [illegible] in traffic, and some [illegible] and their [illegible] from the windows in anger [illegible] to blast the [illegible] again.

Yep, it's time...

With her laptop, hot coffee brewed, and she sat at her desk computer reviewing options available [illegible] from realtor websites for small town locations.

Nothing was [illegible] considered [illegible] she had to leave [illegible] her own home.

Chapter Six

A cool draft swept over her from the ceiling fan, and Ella's hand reached out to clutch her comforter. She pulled the covers to her neck and changed position.

The double paned window did not keep the noise out. Horns honked, a siren approached, and Ella's forehead began to ache.

"Another all-too-common city traffic jam in all its glory…"

She burst from the bed as the chaos outside seemed to amplify in her room. Glaring out the bedroom window, she gave the area a quick survey. Not one car moved, all were stuck in traffic, and some occupants waved their arms out the car windows in anger…pausing to blast their car horns again.

"Yep, time to move…"

Within an hour, her coffee brewed, and she sat at her desk computer reviewing options available in Texas from realtor websites for small town housing.

Renting was not considered. She had always wanted her own home.

"Okay, what do we have here?" She mumbled to herself and clicked on a small house not far from the main section of a small town.

"Nope, too much square footage. The smaller the house, the smaller the utility bills…yep…I did learn the hard way… last year's cute and way too big apartment was a monthly nightmare… "

She saw another house that looked promising, clicked on it and began reading what it had.

"Nope, I will not buy an all-electric home…not with power outages increasing…"

Another house caught her attention.

"Hmm. One thousand, two-hundred square foot house with a garage, storage building, fenced yard, covered patio, and natural gas. Two-bedroom, one full bath. And how old is the home?" She scrolled down and checked out the facts.

"Built in 1968, annual taxes of $1,930.00, block foundation, vinyl siding…sounds exactly like what I want…but no…too much acreage…too big for me!"

After googling two other small towns, Ella continued her search.

"Nope…flood risk is increasing…"

'Nope, looks like a drainage problem…"

'This is not as easy as I thought it would be…" She gave a half-hearted shrug.

Pushing her chair away from the desk, she stood uttering, "I'll keep on trying later…"

Quickly dressing for the day, Ella grabbed her keys and left her apartment.

The mail room in the apartment complex was always busy. The small, locked boxes inserted from floor to ceiling into the walls was awkward to maneuver…people were constantly getting in your way.

Several neighbors unlocked their mailboxes and stood sorting through their mail. Some tossed most of it into a trash can. Ella unlocked her box and pulled the contents out. Mostly junk mail. She did notice a letter from an attorney.

"*…looks official…"* Ella glanced at the address and didn't notice two of her neighbors staring boldly at her.

"That's her alright." One woman stated.

"Yes, and she asks nonchalant…like nothing shocking happened." The other woman replied.

Ella froze, concentrating on her handful of mail.

She cringed.

"I won't let them see how this affects me, and I won't let them steal my joy…"

Returning to her apartment, she shut the door still hearing the women muttering.

Their whispers were interrupted by her phone ringing.

The tiny screen began to illuminate the name and title, Jack Rogan, Attorney at Law.

"Hello Jack!"

"Well hello to you too! Sounds like your day is going fine." He chuckled.

"Actually, I was verbally attacked by two noisy neighbors in the apartment's mail room, but it's over now." She laughed.

"Sorry, that happened. I'm sure you weren't laughing then." His tone turned solemn.

"No, but I wasn't about to trade the joy in my heart to walk around in their poison all day! It wasn't worth it."

"I like that. And you are right, Ella; it is a choice."

"Thanks. So, tell me, how is your day going?"

"Now I'm not used to hearing that! But thank you, ma'am. So far, so good."

"Well, get used to it. Friends, okay?" Ella inquired.

"Yes, friends." Jack replied.

"Amen to that."

Jack continued. "Yes ma'am, and I checked out a property for you in East Mountain, Texas. Recently inspected and passed all safety codes. I think you might be interested."

"I looked everywhere but there all morning." Ella remarked. "Thank you so much!"

"I'll be in court all week, so leave a message if you need to contact me. I wanted you to hurry and drive down there while it's still available."

"Good idea. Who's the realtor?"

"He's the local Realtor in Longview, Texas. Google it for the phone number.'

"Okay, I will, and Jack, thanks again."

"No problem."

They ended the call and Ella hurried to her desk computer.

Placing her fingers on the keyboard, the memory of a billboard advertising plants and fruit trees flashed across her mind…

"…Maybe I'll get a relaxing patio after all…"

She prayed for God's help and felt hope return to her life.

Typing in the search engine, "Houses for sale in East Mountain, Texas" showed only one entry.

Ella stared at the picture of the property, grinning.

"And Jack was right!" She gushed out loud. "This could be it!"

She checked the crime rate in the area, and it almost didn't exist, especially compared to a city. Hospitals, grocery stores, shopping malls, restaurants, etc. were all nearby in either Longview or Gilmer.

She considered life in the city and made her decision.

"… I certainly don't have to pick from bad or worse as a choice on where to live in the city...I can live here in the country…and enjoy it…and I will!"

Locating and calling the realtor, she made an appointment for the following day. It would take a four-hour drive. They agreed to meet at the house after lunch at 1:00.

Ella rented a car and packed it for a three-day trip, and at the last moment she placed the blond wig on her head.

"Nice…" She said gazing at the house as the realtor addressed her.

"A front porch, cozy and inviting; welcoming you to the 3-bedroom, 2 bath, 1,700 sq ft home with a .40-acre lot. Garage, fenced yard, storage building, and new appliances with both electricity and natural gas. Central air and heat. City water. Septic tank recently pumped. Come on in." He stepped aside as she entered.

Ella was sold.

She made an offer, and it was accepted. Ella paid for the house and would soon obtain the title free and clear.

She phoned Jack.

Left a message.

"I got the house! I'm in East Mountain! Thanks for the tip!"

Ella hired a moving company to bring her belongings to East Mountain, then mailed her housekey to the apartment manager in Dallas with her not having to return at all. She paid the money on ending her lease and was officially out of the city.

The rental car had to go next.

Jack phoned leaving her a message of congratulations, and that he was still tied up in court for at least another week.

She called him back leaving a message that the cellphone company she used said she could keep the phone number she had; so, it would be the same number.

They might be unknowingly playing phone tag, but at least they were keeping in touch.

Ella drove to Longview, Texas and bought a new car; a 2025 Toyota Rav4 Hybrid All Wheel Drive with a midnight blue color that sparkled in the sun. Then she had the salesman drive it and follow her to return her rented car to the nationwide Enterprise Rental Company that was also in Longview. She drove him back to the car dealership; content with peaceful but busy days!

And she continued to wear the blond wig.

For two days she unpacked boxes, put her bed together, placed floor lamps, and unrolled rugs. Kitchen utensils, dishes, pots and pans were distributed in their new places. Although exhausted, Ella hummed along as each task was completed.

On the third evening, plopping into her recliner in the living room, she sighed happily.

"I can relax here…anytime…my private place…and all mine…" She stretched her legs out and glanced at the room. *"And I'm almost through spending…except for a green house, some plants, and a nice barbeque pit, an umbrella patio table, and chairs …and a fire pit for this winter…and after that I'm done…I'm really done spending."*

She closed her eyes and prayed.

"Dear God; Yehovah my Heavenly Father, I thank You for my being here in East Mountain…for Your Guidance and Your will in my life. I couldn't make it without You, and I do not want to disappoint You. Please forgive me of my sins, and I pray to be a light to others for them to know You through my actions. It's so peaceful here, this is such a blessing, thank You Lord, in Jesus Christ's name I pray, Amen."

Ella woke up the next morning still wearing her tennis shoes and still stretched out in the recliner.

Chapter Seven

And time marched on…

Ella reflected on her move to this small town, and the events that brought her here.

"Everything happens for a reason."

"And here I am!" Ella declared. Smiling to herself, she glanced over her back yard.

A slight breeze lifted her hair, and she raised her head toward the sky.

"Thank you, Heavenly Father, for my home…and for it being in the country…"

She scooted her patio chair closer to the table and sipped on her iced tea. The umbrella tilted just enough to keep the sun out of her eyes, and she couldn't wait to turn on its tiny lights tonight. Living in a city apartment for years did not offer the experience of a patio umbrella with solar lights under it.

And the plans for the patio area, and entire back yard were coming together well.

A contractor had poured concrete and built a roof in a 20 x 40-foot area where the patio furniture was set. He laid a stone path to the firepit area, and the path to the newly constructed greenhouse he built. He also built the circular firepit using stone with a raised 2 feet high wall around it, and a circular seating area around the outside wall. Ella concentrated on filling the greenhouse.

She finished her iced tea and closed her eyes.

'Patio plants would still be nice, and I could scatter large ones around…maybe get some dwarf fruit trees and watch them grow…and have fruit! I'll have to check out what I can get and stay within my budget. I do want seed starter kits and good potting soil with fish emulsion to use as supplies in the greenhouse…and Heirloom seed packages…"

Raising from her chair, Ella sauntered to the house.

"Okay, girl…let's get this done…an oasis is waiting to be created!"

She slipped on her blond wig, picked up her purse and keys, and quickly headed out the door.

Arriving at Longview Lawn & Garden, she selected a picnic table, several chaise lounge chairs, and six Adirondack chairs to be delivered that afternoon.

And drove immediately to the She Shed Emporium.

She parked close to its entrance and, humming a cheerful melody, walked across the parking lot.

There she strolled through a variety of plants and fruit trees, picturing what she wanted …and could afford…around her patio.

A four-foot-tall fig tree caught her attention…and it was already growing figs.

"And only one left…" Ella thought as she read the tag attached to it. "*Self-fertile, container friendly, full sun…*"

"Excuse me, sir? Could you help me with this fig tree?"

The young man nodded and brought a load bearing cart towards her. "Yes, ma'am."

"Thank you! I'd like this one and could you show me dwarf fruit trees? For a patio? I'd like to have the right size pots for them and if it could all be delivered this afternoon, I'd love it!" She grinned.

"I'd be glad to, and there is a delivery fee, but your plants are guaranteed to be delivered in good condition."

"Perfect!"

He loaded the fig tree and showed her other self-fertile trees, and some flowering plants. She selected one dwarf pomegranate tree, one ice-cream banana tree, one large, yellow blooming hibiscus plant, and one large, pink blooming geranium plant. Pots were added to repot the trees and flowering plants. Packages of heirloom seeds, four seed starter kits, three 50 lb. bags of Organic potting soil, one 20 lb. bag of rocks, a water hose, and gloves completed the order.

Her eyes sparkled as she paid the cashier.

"I can't wait to get this done! This has been a dream of mine for a long time!" She gushed.

The cashier handed her the receipt and beamed.

"I'm happy for you, this ought to be nice! All we need now are delivery instructions."

Ella gave her the address. "Is it possible to deliver this after lunch today?"

The cashier typed on her tablet. "Let me check the schedule…uh yes…we can do that." She glanced at Ella and smiled.

"Awesome! Oh, do you recommend anyone to help repot the trees, and plants?" She asked the cashier.

"We also offer that service. I can add the charge now, if you like."

"How much?"

"We charge $25.00 an hour. One hour paid in advance. And the remaining time spent working for you will be automatically charged to your credit card."

"Fair enough."

Ella paid for the extra service and received another receipt. Stuffing both in her purse, she left the garden center and was on the sidewalk when she heard it.

And instantly stopped.

The shrill squealing of metal clanging into metal filled the air as a car collided with an ambulance.

It was only yards away in the parking lot.

The sound of the impact was horrific…like a train suddenly applying its loud brakes.

"Call 911!" Someone pleaded.

Another yelled, "Is there a doctor here?"

Ella instinctively rushed to help, shoving bystanders out of her way.

"I'm a medical doctor." She shouted.

Swinging into action, she immediately snatched the medical bag from the ambulance and headed toward the crushed car. An older man was thrown from the vehicle with an obvious broken leg. It bled uncontrollably and Ella squatted onto the pavement applying a tourniquet that stopped the bleeding.

He was alert. She took his pulse and offered him assurance he would soon be okay.

An ambulance driver lay several feet away and was making rasping sounds trying to breathe. Ella ran to him and gently felt he had a broken collar bone. Blood seeped from scraped wounds hitting the pavement…road rash some called it. He was lying on his left side on the pavement wide-eyed gasping loudly.

Ella carefully put her arm under his shoulders and placed him on his back. She cleaned his neck, retrieved sterile instruments from the bag and performed an intubation on the man. He instantly sucked in air and continued steady breathing.

Ella scooted to the second ambulance driver, also lying on the pavement.

His pulse rate was slow. He was bleeding from his chest. Ella examined him and told him he had internal injuries but would be fine and try and be calm. He stopped breathing and Ella performed CPR. He began breathing on his own when Ella heard a distant siren approaching.

Ella stopped and noticed the crowd for the first time.

They were watching her and some even videoed her with their phones.

The alarming thought flashed through her mind… *"I'm being videoed…"*

Ella groaned in agony as the sirens grew louder.

The crowd focused on the injured as the new ambulance arrived.

Ella stayed by the injured as the EMS officials took over their care. They quickly took charge, telling her that she did a great job.

"I'm a doctor, and I had to help them." She explained.

They nodded as the police sirens were nearing.

"The police…and I may be operating without a license! Dear Lord, I don't want to go back to jail…" She scanned the area again and quietly slipped through the crowd heading to her car.

All eyes were on the EMS and the injured.

Ella drove out of the opposite entrance…away from the approaching police sirens… heart pounding in her ears.

With each mile bringing her closer to home, she took short breaths, inhaling and exhaling slowly to calm herself. Before reaching East Mountain, she said another prayer.

"Heavenly Father, I meant well helping those people, and I pray they all improve. I pray for Your protection and safety, and I fully trust You. I pray for Your continued guidance and Your will in my life. I pray that no weapon formed against me shall prosper. I give You all the glory, honor, and praise. In Jesus' holy name I pray, Amen."

She pulled into her driveway with a sigh of relief.

And hurried inside; she headed to the kitchen for a bottle of ice-cold water and ambled to her recliner in the living room. Sinking into it, she gradually relaxed, trying to convince herself no one would recognize her in that blond wig.

"The blond wig! They were videoing me with it on!"

She snatched it off her head and promptly hid it under the recliner. Glancing at the wall clock, she noticed it would soon be time for Longview Lawn and Garden to deliver her order. She went to the bathroom and combed her mop of brown hair away from her face. Brushing the bangs from her forehead, she pulled them to the side with a large hair clip.

Nice and neat.

No messy frantic appearance of suddenly removing a wig.

"I'm trusting my Heavenly Father: God, please stop doubt from entering my mind…"

She sighed again and remained calm.

And Longview Lawn and Garden pulled into her driveway to unload the additional lawn furniture.

Directly behind it came a huge box car.

The workers from the She Shed Emporium had arrived.

"Thank You, Lord Jesus! Perfect timing to take my mind off that wreck!"

She nearly bounced outside to meet the delivery men.

And did they deliver!

Two helpers unloaded the She Shed order using heavy commercial size dollies with the trees strapped to their metal side bars.

Ella bolted across the concrete directing where each item went.

And the guys were an amazing team.

One distributed the bag of rocks into the bottom of the five main pots covering the drainage holes.

Another opened the potting soil and added just enough soil for the trees and plants to sit on. Trees were placed next, soil added around the sides, then soil in the pots for the blooming plants.

The two plants looked exquisite!

And the yellow and pink blooms added a brilliant pop of color.

Fast work!

And clean!

They placed the rest of the order on a pallet in the back yard while the three-man crew from Longview Lawn and Garden began unloading the additional patio furniture; a picnic table, and several chaise lounge chairs. They also delivered six Adirondack chairs to sit around the circular fire pit.

It didn't take them long at all. They even swept off the patio area before leaving.

Ella admired the finished results as the other workers completed their job. The two men glanced at the patio and lowered their voices as they talked.

Ella tried not to eavesdrop. Even by turning her back to them, she could still hear their conversation.

"It sure would look good there, and it would last a long time…"

"Well, tell her!"

Ella cleared her throat. "Excuse me, I couldn't help but hear…tell me what?"

"Well, my uncle is a lawyer, but he also makes fantastic barbeque pits… with or without an attached meat smoker. Each one is heavy duty, and that would make this whole patio area perfect! Do you barbeque?"

"Oh, I want to! I'd like one! But what about the price?"

"I can't say for sure, but I promise you they are more than reasonable. He makes all sizes."

Ella nodded. "Do you have pictures on your phone of what they look like?"

"I can do better than that. Let me get my uncle on the phone, and he can show you real ones for sale in his shop."

"Well, it can't hurt. Go ahead."

He phoned and instantly placed his uncle on speaker phone.

pits."

"Thanks, let me talk to her."

"Okay, she's Ms. Reed, here she is…"

He handed the phone to Ella.

"Hello, Uncle Sam?" Ella laughed.

He laughed then, "Sam Baldwin, ma'am. Martie says you are interested in a barbeque pit."

"Yes, I am. Where are you located?"

"Well, I'm out of Longview in the small town of East Mountain."

"Really? I just moved to East Mountain!"

"Great! You're more than welcome to drive over and see what's available. I'll be here until 5:00. I have one to deliver this afternoon to a customer in Longview."

"Okay, I'll check it out. Justin can tell me how to get there."

"Sounds good. Thank you, ma'am."

"Okay." Ella repeated excitedly, handing the phone back to Justin.

"It's about two miles from you, ma'am, on Medlin Road. We go right past it on our way back to Longview. You can follow us, if you like."

"Yes, I will, and thanks for the suggestion. Are you about done here?"

"Yes ma'am."

"Well, you did excellent work, all of you. Let me lock up, and I'll follow you. Wave at me or honk or something when we get there."

He grinned. "We will. It won't take long."

Ella hurried inside, snatched up her purse and keys, and locked the door on her way out.

The guys from She Shed Emporium had turned around, and stopped halfway down her driveway waiting for her. She pulled behind them and honked as they took off together.

Within minutes, they traveled past wooded areas, and pastures. A few homes were seen a distance from the main road. Suddenly, the She Shed vehicle slowed, and arms stuck out of both windows pointing to the house they were approaching.

She honked and waved at the workers and pulled into Uncle Sam's driveway.

Ella chuckled to herself. "I'll always want to call him Uncle Sam."

A lengthy concrete driveway stretched through the center of the property, branching into two separate paths about halfway along its course. On the left it circled in front of a massive shop situated near the side fence displaying barbeque pits, lawn mower trailers, metal gates, and personalized metal signs. On the right, the driveway graced the front of a huge brick two story home with a well-manicured lawn.

The house and shop were on at least two acres of land.

Very impressive.

She parked in front of the shop, opened her car door, and stood.

The man approached with his hand extended.

She smiled and almost stared but quickly shook his hand.

"You must be Ms. Reed."

"Yes, and I'm tempted to call you Uncle Sam!" She grinned.

He laughed again. "Whatever works!"

It was a pleasant stroll the short distance to the barbeque pits when an exciting thought came over Ella.

"Oh my gosh…are you single" …flashed in her thoughts.

She glanced at his wedding ring finger and noticed no ring there. Her face flushed, and she tried not to grin.

Dismissing the intrusion, she squinted at Sam Baldwin in the afternoon sun. "I wanted a good, quality barbeque pit and wasn't interested in the flimsy ones for sale in Longview."

"Those don't hold up well. I think you'll like the ones I make. And they come in all sizes."

He pointed to one that had a meat smoker attached to one end. "This is a nice size. Do you just grill or grill and smoke meat?"

"I do both, though I haven't done so in some time."

He smiled. "It's like riding a bike, once you learn, it stays with you."

She nodded and instantly noticed how beautiful his brown eyes were.

Trying to focus on the conversation, she pointed to the barbeque pit with the smoker attached. "Mr. Baldwin, how much for this one?"

"That one is $349."

"Are you set up to take a debit card?" She asked.

"Yes, ma'am!"

"Good, I've recently moved here, and I'm trying to get everything situated."

"No problem." He answered.

"Oh, how much to deliver?"

"How far away do you live?"

"About ten minutes from here." She replied.

"Well, since you're new here, and close by, I won't add a delivery charge."

"Oh! Thank you. I'll take this one then."

She handed him her debit card and smiled.

"I'll make out an invoice for you and be right back."

He eased toward his shop with a long stride.

Ella scanned the grounds and house again.

And it was all gorgeous.

Evergreen gardenia bushes lined the driveway on each side. While the property could have centered on that feature, the huge azalea bushes around the house were stunning and unusually pink.

"So inviting and so pleasant; someone obviously put a lot of thought into the landscaping. Hm…possibly this Uncle Sam?" She pondered to herself.

"Even the gray and white brick combination on the house accented both the azalea and the gardenia bushes…"

He returned with the written invoice and her debit card.

"Here you are." He handed both to her, and offered a brief, courteous smile.

"Thanks, I'll be enjoying it soon!" Ella beamed.

"Great! If it's okay with you, I can deliver it today about 4:00 before my delivery at 5 in Longview."

"That will work."

He extended his hand again.

She shook his hand and smiled. "Thanks again."

"Thank you!"

She turned and strolled back to her vehicle. Upon entering it, she peeped into her side mirror and saw him still standing where they had stood.

He waved at her, and she flushed.

"Oh no…he saw me looking back at him…how embarrassing..."

Ella hurried home and sat outside in the new patio area.

'He'll be here soon…now where should the barbeque pit go ...I sure don't want to call him back to move it …

She decided on the perfect spot and went inside to freshen up.

Reapplying her lipstick, she raised both eyebrows and stared at herself in the mirror.

"I'm ready…"

At four o'clock a truck stopped in front of her house, and Sam Baldwin rang her doorbell.

Ella answered the door looking prim and proper. She wore a sleeveless turtleneck top paired with wide, floor-length trousers, so only her head and arms were uncovered.

"Hello, Uncle Sam!" She grinned.

He flashed a wide smile. "Well, hello!"

She never gave him a chance to talk.

"If you take your truck around to the side, it will be easier to unload the pit."

"Thank you, ma'am. Will do." He smiled again and returned to his truck.

She walked to the fence unlocking the gate to the patio, and he backed his truck up to the open gate.

He had the pit laying on its side and strapped to the industrial size dolly. Within minutes, he was rolling the dolly onto her concrete patio.

"I'll stand where I'd like it to go." She rushed to a vacant area along the length of the patio. "Here would be great."

He moved it to that spot, carefully untied the straps, and stood it upright.

"It looks huge!" Ella blurted. "I love it!"

"You've got a great investment. Just cover it with a small tarp when not in use. Should last for many years."

"Thank you so much! "

"You are quite welcome. Enjoy it!"

"I will."

He nodded and waved to her as he walked to the truck pushing the empty dolly. After loading it, he waved again as he drove off.

Ella stood in her doorway smiling, and waved bye to him.

"He is such a gentleman, and I was so nervous around him! Now I can relax and get out of these clothes! What a day!"

Ella went to bed early and kept remembering the scene of the injured people she'd helped at the wreck. Her mind drifted over each detail until she prayed for peace.

And she thought again of looking at Sam Baldwin like a young teenager drooling over her first crush and slowly smiled to herself.

She prayed: this time for others, and she fell asleep saying her nightly prayers…

Chapter Eight

The 'Do Drop-In Diner' was packed with an early morning breakfast rush.

Standing room only.

A few potential diners boldly stared at those eating… prompting them to hurry and leave …emptying a table for someone else to occupy…

And in absolutely no hurry, Jack Rogan ignored them, savoring each bite.

Half of his plate held soft scrambled eggs with chives and melted cheese; the other half had crispy fried hash-brown potatoes, lightly salted. And served with a side plate of thick slices of beef bacon, and two rolls. He enjoyed it all with a cup of robust black coffee and a chilled glass of milk, truly delicious!

Mounted to a wall, a large TV screen displayed a solemn newscaster with the words Breaking News.

"And in Texas, authorities are searching for the woman who medically treated those injured in a wreck. According to eyewitnesses, she left the scene before police arrived. Who is the heroine...and is she a doctor like she told the EMS workers?"

Jack casually glanced at the screen and swallowed a bite.

"It's Ella!" He sputtered out loud as a piece of pancake flew in lodging in the back of his throat.

A waitress rushed over, her voice rising, "Sir, are you alright?"

His face instantly turned beet red. Wide-eyed, he stared at her, clutching his throat, and she promptly struck him on the back.

Jack gasped and caught his breath, "I…I am now, thank you."

Other diners glanced at him and kept on eating.

But he didn't care about them.

He focused on the TV screen and watched as a blond-headed Ella was unknowingly videoed.

The announcer continued.

"…anyone with information on the woman's identity are asked to contact the Longview Police Department.

You can also call the Anonymous Tip number at the bottom of this screen. With KJYK, this is Duke Lassiter reporting."

His phone rang immediately. Glancing at the caller I.D., relief flooded his mind as he answered it.

"Hey, Ted! Good morning!"

"Same to you. Guess why I'm calling?"

"Oh, you've been watching TV again." Jack laughed.

Laughter boomed as Ted agreed, "yeah, you got that right. Can we talk about it?"

"Sure."

"Was that her at that wreck? Ella Reed in Longview?"

"You saw it too?"

"National news picked it up here in Dallas. It's not just local news anymore."

"Reporters will be swarming. I don't know if it was her, I haven't talked to her yet."

"I'd like to be with you when you talk to her. I'll be in Longview all week anyway."

"I was about to call her when you phoned. It's okay with me, in fact, I'd value your opinion. She may not have her license to practice medicine in Texas, if that was her."

"Oh, brother!"

"Exactly. Listen, I'll call her and find out. If she says it was her, I'll meet you in Longview and we'll talk to her together."

"Good. I'm on the docket in Gilmer for a child custody case. I'll be staying at Mom's all week in Longview. Where are you?"

"I'm in Uncertain, Texas."

"Where?"

"Uncertain, it's about twenty miles from Marshall in one direction, and fifteen miles from Jefferson in the other. Right on Caddo Lake."

"Never been there."

"You need to go; Caddo Lake is fantastic. The scenery in and around the lake is breathtaking. At night you can hear the chorus of tree frogs chirping in synchronized rhythm. It's especially enjoyable against a dark star-studded night sky."

He took another bite of pancake and continued. "And a day on the lake is just as spectacular…moss covered cypress trees in the water, great fishing…"

"Easy now, sounds like relaxing…I don't know if I remember how to do that." Ted laughed.

"Force yourself…hey, I'll call Ella and get right back with you."

"Deal."

Jack rubbed his chin and considered the situation. He glanced at his remaining breakfast and finished eating. After a warmup of hot coffee, he phoned Ella.

"Well, hello, Jack."

"Good morning, Ella. You sound happy!"

"I am happy! Getting settled in here. How are things going with you?"

"Okay…"

"You don't seem too sure of that…what's going on with my lawyer friend?"

"Well, you might be able to answer that question…"

"Oh? How can I do that, Jack?"

"Have you watched TV this morning?"

He heard her sharp intake of breath. "Uh…don't tell me I'm on it…"

"You tell me."

"Now, why would I be on TV?"

"Doctoring those injured at a wreck? Looks like you on the aired video. Authorities are investigating. Want the identity of the woman…"

"Oh no…no…" Ella whimpered and began sobbing.

"Ella, I'm sorry…but we need to talk."

Her breath jerked as she tried to stop crying, and finally moaned, "I…yes, we do."

"I'll be there this afternoon and I'm arranging for an attorney friend of mine to join me. Stay inside and don't talk to anyone."

"Okay..." Sobbing again, she ended the call.

Jack immediately phoned Ted.

"Hey, it's a go. Can we meet at 4:00 in Longview today?"

"I'll be there. Do you remember where my mom lives?"

"Yes, I'll pick you up there, four o'clock sharp."

"Great, and Jack?"

"Yeah?"

"This could turn ugly."

"I know."

Ted Davis got a full tank of gas in his car and drove out of Dallas. Concern for Ella remained heavy on his mind. Four hours later, lost in thought, he almost missed his exit off I-20.

Horns blasted him as he swerved into the exit lane at the last minute.

"Sorry guys! Welcome to Longview to you too." He muttered.

He drove to his mom's house and parked in her circle driveway. Grabbing his suitcase and covered bag of hang-up dress suits, he approached her front door and poked a finger on the doorbell.

Minutes later, Lucille Davis flung the door open.

"I was out back," she gushed while giving her son a hug. "So glad to see you!"

"You too, Mom." He smiled at her. "You look great!"

"Well, thank you! I'm going to a fundraiser tonight with Frank. It's for the Gregg County Woman's Shelter; dinner and games and a silent auction."

"I know how you love a silent auction!" He swung his arm out towards a painting on the foyer wall entrance.

"Yes," she grinned. "That artist is incredible! Captured Caddo Lake at daybreak with spectacular detail!"

He nodded, setting his suitcase down. "It is beautiful! My friend Jack was just talking about Caddo Lake."

"Well, bring your stuff on in. Same room as before. Make yourself at home."

"Will do. Oh, I have a business appointment at four today. We'll chat later, okay?"

"Yes, I'll look forward to it! And I'll get you a key to the front door, I don't know how long I'll be out."

"Sounds good to me." He sauntered down the hallway to the bedroom and unpacked.

The doorbell rang again as Lucille entered Ted's room.

"Here," she handed him the housekey and frowned. "Who could that be?"

"It might be Jack Rogan. He's meeting me here before our appointment with a client."

Lucille hurried to the foyer and opened the door to see Frank standing in the doorway with a pleasant grin.

"And hello to the lady of the house!" His arms surrounded her as they quickly embraced.

"And I'm glad you're early!" She beamed.

He winked at her. "I thought we'd go early to look over the silent auction. You know something there is…calling your name." He teased.

"Ha-ha-ha! You know it!"

Ted heard the commotion and joined them.

"Frank, good to see you!"

They shook hands.

"You too, Ted. I hear you'll be here in court all week."

"Yes sir. Busy days."

"Well, my treat to dinner sometime. When it's convenient for you."

"I'd like that! Thank you!"

"Good!" Frank glanced at Lucille. "Ready?"

"Of course!" She grabbed her purse and they sailed out the door.

Ted sat on the veranda after they drove off.

Jack arrived.

The atmosphere thickened as Jack drove his car in the driveway, and locked eyes with a solemn-looking Ted as he exited the car.

"This is a tough one, Jack." Ted frowned. "I've sat here considering Ella's situation… options revolving in my mind…" His voice wavered.

"The effect of her being represented by us as a team will appear strong, Ted. Just govern your mind."

"Good point. Let's get this ball rolling."

Chapter Nine

Ella paced in front of the expansive picture window in her living room. The slight tint removed the glare of the last rays from the setting sun, but she didn't notice.

Worse case scenarios flashed across her mind as she stared at the carpeted floor…and her walk continued…until Jack Rogan and Ted Davis knocked at her door.

Stopping mid-stride, Ella suddenly stiffened her posture.

She opened the door with a darting glance at the two men.

"Come in." She shuffled back a step or two as they entered.

Jack frowned. "Are we still friends?"

"Yes, of course."

Jack hugged her quickly and she whimpered a sob.

"Okay, friend, chin up." He patted her back and stepped away.

Jack addressed her in a steady, lower-pitched voice. "You're going to make it through this. Ella Reed, this is Ted Davis. He's an attorney friend of mine who will be helping with your case…that is if you want us to represent you…"

"Yes, that's smart! I pray you can untangle this mess I'm in."

"Ted and I will coordinate. And you know not to discuss anything that happened?"

"I understand. Come on in," she waved them inside.

Ted sprawled his lanky frame out on the love seat. His shoulders were lowered and loose.

Comfortable.

Directly across the room, Jack and Ella sat apart on the couch.

Ella couldn't sit still.

She crossed her legs and moments later uncrossed them. And fiddled with her bracelet until Jack reached over and patted the top of her hand.

She smiled and let go of the bracelet. She quickly clasped her fingers onto the armrest of the couch, and her stiff posture remained.

Leaning forward, Ted smiled, making strong eye-contact. "Ms. Reed, relax. We are here to help you, and I can assure you, we will."

Jack nodded. "Tell us exactly what happened when you were being videoed."

"I was leaving the store, and I heard a horrific crash. Loud metal scraping against metal, and it sounded like an explosion at the same time. I looked in that direction and saw a horrible wreck in the parking lot; twisted vehicles, exposed framework from under them, broken glass scattered about, and…bodies laying in the midst of it."

Ella leaned her head back, closed and opened her eyes.

She whispered, "it's something you cannot forget."

"No, that had to be shocking to witness." Ted replied softly. "But we need to know…then what happened?" Ted prompted.

Ella sat upright and seemed to regain her composure.

She continued.

"The wreck was in the parking lot, and someone yelled, 'Call 9-1-1.' Another shouted, 'Is there a doctor here?'

Her face crumpled as she suddenly started sobbing. "I can still hear them…"

"Ella…" Jack squeezed her hand. "I know this is difficult to relive but we have to know everything that happened."

She nodded and continued again.

I yelled, "I'm a doctor!"

"And I instantly took off running to the wreck. Three people were injured."

"Excuse me." She stopped and blew her nose.

"I got the medical bag from the ambulance and went to each of the injured, helping them. I focused on them and never thought about being videoed."

She paused and looked at the two attorneys with pleading eyes. "No one asked me if they could video me. The crowd grew, and I heard sirens approaching… I immediately cringed. I kept thinking the police will find out I may not have a license to practice anymore, and I could go back to jail." Her voice trailed off in a sob.

Taking a deep breath, she wiped her eyes. "So, I finished treating them and stayed until the EMS arrived in another ambulance. I told them I was a doctor, and they said I did a good job. They took over and I quickly slipped out behind everyone. I made it to my car and drove out of the parking lot as a police car entered from the opposite direction. I thought no one would know it was me," she added, in a defeated tone, "until I saw the video on T.V."

"Under the circumstances, you didn't do anything wrong." Jack stated.

"It's not like you opened an illegal business practicing medicine without a license. And if it does go to court, we can clear you of all wrongdoing." Ted added.

Ella attempted a smile. "Thank you, I needed that."

Jack crossed his arms and frowned. "Only one problem. The blond wig. Authorities may want to know if that was to conceal your identity, and we three know that it was. You were protecting yourself from being the brown-haired woman on TV who the public thought robbed a bank in Dallas. And, if that goes public, you will not have any privacy here at all."

Ted stood and shoved his hands into his pants pockets. "So…where is this blond wig?"

"It's under the recliner." Ella mumbled.

Jack glanced first at Ted, then Ella. "Well, it's got to go. Let me have it."

Ella pulled it from under the recliner and handed it to Jack.

"I will get rid of it tonight. And you know if I am caught with this, or if the authorities find out what I did, I could go to jail and lose my license! This is never to be mentioned…ever!"

Ella's face paled and she stared at him wide-eyed. "I…I won't…ever!"

Ted stood in front of the window. "I had my back to both of you. I never saw a blond wig, but someone is pulling in the driveway."

Jack glanced at Ella. "Where is your bathroom?"

"At the end of the hallway."

Jack took off and came back before anyone knocked at the door. He returned having a small belly at his waistline. The wig was hidden well inside the bottom of his shirt.

A forceful knock pounded against the front door. Ella flipped on the porch light exposing a police car parked in her driveway.

Jack whispered to Ella.

"Stay calm."

She opened the door.

"Ms. Reed? Ms. Ella Reed?'

"Yes, officer."

"We'd like a word with you, ma'am."

Ella blinked at the two police officers.

"Certainly, come in. What is this all about?"

"Well, that's what we want to know."

"Please, sit down."

They looked at Ted and Jack on the couch and remained standing.

"It won't take that long. I understand you recently moved here from Dallas."

"Yes, sir, I did."

"And aren't you the one who knew the bank robber, Sybil Ponder?"

"Yes, that's correct."

"And all charges against you were dropped?"

"Yes."

The officer narrowed his eyes. "Ms. Reed, Ms. Ponder is in prison for robbery, but it is strange the doctor who treated injured people in a wreck in Longview…looks exactly like her. Do you have any information about that?"

"Oh no, officer. She is in prison. I haven't talked to her. I don't even know which prison she's in."

"Well, we do. And you know nothing about this?"

"No sir, I do not."

"Well, if you happen to hear from her, contact us immediately."

"Yes, sir, I will."

"Well, thank you, Ms. Reed."

"You're welcome."

They walked to the door and left quietly.

No one spoke until the patrol car drove away.

Jack sucked in his breath. "They know it couldn't possibly be Sybil..."

Ted grimaced. "They connected the dots. They are not dumb…let me assure you…they think Ella knows something about it or they wouldn't have come here."

Ella frowned. "But how do they know I moved here?"

"Detectives scroll through all kinds of records. New applications for electricity, new accounts for water, gas…easy way to locate someone new to the area. They figured that woman could have been Sybil because she was the surgeon from Dallas with blond hair…Dallas is only a few hours away…but even though she is in prison…maybe her friend who happens to live near Longview …knows something …and a smart detective searched records for her friend, Ella Reed. Bingo! They found you here." Ted blew out a loud breath. He shook his head and looked at Jack. "Wow!"

Ella sat on the couch and squeezed her eyes shut. "They would have taken me to jail." She moaned. "And poor Sybil isn't here to defend herself. Forgive me Lord!"

"But they didn't take you to jail. And you didn't lie. You have not seen Sybil." Jack ran his hand through his hair. "Oh man. I need to get rid of something. Ted, stay here with Ella. It's best you two don't know what I'm going to do…" he paused, "my mind is flooded with ideas."

Ted nodded, and Jack pivoted walking out the door.

He stood still for a moment and glanced around the area.

Not one neighbor was outside, and no one was driving in or out of Ella's driveway.

He walked to his car and climbed inside.

Scanning the area, he carefully backed out the driveway and left the neighborhood.

"Burger Land, that's it!" He grinned to himself as a plan developed.

Minutes later, he pulled into the drive through lane, ordering thirty-five hamburgers. Inside, employees scrambled to fill the order. He paid and drove to the outskirts of town.

And there they were.

The homeless.

He was just helping the community.

Fixing to give them a meal.

He drove near their tented area into the woods.

And walked among them passing each a bag of Burger Land's finest.

As he neared the ones huddled together, he handed each of them a bag, and in one swift movement, he jerked the wig out of his shirt, pitched it into the burning barrel they used to keep their hands warm…and no one noticed it.

They were opening their own bag of food from Burger Land.

Jack heard the crackle and hiss as the wig caught on fire.

It stunk.

But so did piles of discarded clothes and garbage scattered about the ground.

The rustling sound of paper bags continued among the homeless as Jack handed out the rest of the bags.

He waited for the wig to completely burn beyond recognition.

A fast glance into the barrel showed flames but no trace of the wig.

The homeless group thanked him and began throwing their empty Burger Land's paper bags into the fire.

Jack nodded at them and whistled a tune as he drove back to get Ted.

Chapter Ten

Lucille and Frank arrived right at dusk. A chill was in the air, and they walked briskly through the parking lot.

"Looks like everyone had the same idea." Frank laughed as they meandered past many parked vehicles.

"Yes, it does. Let's check out what's available inside."

Frank nodded as they soon strolled in.

An attendant stood by a cash register and Frank paid for two tickets. The attendant promptly rubber-stamped a smiley face in black ink on their right hands.

"Goodness, I haven't been stamped since attending the State Fair." Lucille marveled.

"Well, we don't have to stand in line." Frank laughed, glancing at everything.

Round dining tables were scattered about the main room. The smell of fresh flower arrangements… the centerpiece of each table, lingered in the air. Signs pointed to attached rooms with information on what to find where. Chatter drifted as people mingled with each other.

"Do you know anyone here?" Lucille asked.

"No, I don't. That's strange. I was born and raised here. You'd think I'd know somebody."

"Odd." She nodded and motioned to the area with the silent auction. "Let's go before it gets too packed."

One long row of tables placed side by side ran along the entire wall. Each item had a clipboard with numbered paper on it. Rules were displayed across the top of each page.

People wandered in front of the tables, stopping to write a bid on the page of something they wanted. Several women were gathered in the middle obviously discussing a certain item.

"I can't stand it. Let's see if that's something I want to bid on." She whispered to Frank.

They eased toward the women as the group dispersed. Many had placed their names, phone numbers, and amount of money they bid for the item.

Frank got closer.

"Looks like a book."

"All of that activity for one book? Not a set, or a series?" She inquired.

"No, just one book."

Lucille scooted toward the book, and gasped. "Well, my goodness! It's a book with homemade recipes for Herbal Medicine. I've heard of them, but I don't trust them. In fact, I'd never use them. It certainly got a lot of attention though. Look, there are over fifteen bids for it."

"Some people claim good results with Herbal Medicine, not exactly what I thought we'd find here, though…" Frank whispered.

He scanned the tables and noticed several candles to bid on, a few paintings of cats in dark landscapes, many gift certificates from various local restaurants, a free car wash for a month, and a free spa day in

Longview. Also many trips were offered; Branson, Missouri, Las Vegas, New Orleans, Galveston, and in Vicksburg, Mississippi. A total of thirty items to bid on.

Frank lightly nudged Lucille. "Let's bid on the trip to Branson."

"Yeah! Let's do it! Well, the silent auction is more interesting now."

They walked to the end of the long tables and spotted a gigantic TV with a splash of color behind it on a sign that read 55 inch, 4K resolution.

Frank raised his eyebrows at Lucille. "What do you think about this?"

"Oh, that's got to be expensive!"

"Well, what do you think about us getting it for," he paused, "maybe for us in the future?"

Her eyes widened and a coy smile brightened her face.

She took his hand. "That sounds good."

They bid on the 55-inch 4K TV and glanced at each other.

"Done?"

"Done."

"Let's get a table." Frank led them back to the main room, squeezing through the attendees still milling around.

They selected a table near the side wall of the dining room, away from the traffic of the kitchen employees. And simple chatter rose to a noise level… the room had filled to capacity with excited people.

"Wow! I'm glad we got a table when we did!" Lucille blurted.

"Yeah, looks like it could be two hundred people in here…" Frank scanned the room.

A waiter hurried to hand out menus as an announcer suddenly took the microphone.

"Welcome, ladies and gentlemen. This is our fourth annual fundraiser for the Gregg County Women's Shelter. Our host tonight is our own local gal, Betty Baldwin! Take it away, Betty!"

Out from behind the velvet curtain sauntered a beautiful woman with bright blonde hair and a perfect hour-glass figure draped in glittering scarfs and twinkling bells.

Lucille's mouth fell open as Betty made her entrance. She quickly looked at Frank who glanced up from the menu.

Frank shook his head in disbelief as Betty sailed around the room with every eye on her.

"At a fund raiser?" Lucille thought.

Her scarf fluttered, as she passed by leaving wide eyes, gasps, and smiles in her wake.

Betty snatched the microphone from the announcer and gyrated to the middle of the room.

"Tonight, we are determined to raise more money than we did last year. And …for $10.00…I will do a belly dance at your own individual table. Also, for $20.00, I give you a personal reading with my tarot cards…for those interested in what your future holds! Ready to have fun? Who wants to go first?"

Someone on the other side of the room raised their hand and Betty sashayed toward them.

"…Did I hear that right? Tarot card readings?" Frank sounded shocked.

"Yes, I couldn't believe it either. Isn't that witchcraft?"

Frank gave Lucille an incredulous stare. "It is. We'll wait for the next speaker and order our food. And we'll pray for her when we pray for our food."

"I agree."

Ignoring the host as she paraded around the room, they studied their menus.

"This is easy…I want the beef fajitas with a side order of guacamole, and corn tortillas." Lucille smiled.

"What no sopaipillas?" Frank teased.

"I'm trying to work on my girlish figure." She smiled again.

"Lady, if I wanted to be with someone who had a girlish figure, I'd be with a girl. And I'm not a boy…I'm a man dating a woman! Eat your sopaipillas, I know you love them!"

Lucille laughed. "Okay, sopaipillas it is."

Frank grinned.

He glanced at the waiter and ordered with a solemn voice. "I'll have the same thing she's having."

Lucille laughed and hit him with her menu.

"That's why you had me order sopaipillas, you sly dog!"

"It worked!" He beamed.

A waitress brought chips to their table with each a small bowl of salsa.

They were soon enjoying their meal when someone made the sound of a growling cat.

And made it loud.

And did it again.

Heads turned to the table it came from.

A group of young men obviously taunting Betty.

Most ignored them.

Except for one older gentleman.

"You're making a fool of yourself, young man. Behave yourself!"

The young man instantly stood facing him.

"Are you talking to me?" He demanded.

"If you are the one at that table acting lawless, then yes, I am."

"Lawless? Shut up old man! We're just enjoying the show."

"And you're acting like a yowling tomcat, and you need to settle down. This is a fund raiser not a strip club."

The young man stuttered.

His friends pulled on his shirt. "Sit down. That's enough. This isn't a bar fight."

He sat down with folded arms.

Turning to again look at the older gentleman, he huffed in anger but remained silent.

Frank raised his eyebrows at Lucille.

"Best show in the house." He nodded at the table of young men, while buttering his stack of hot corn tortillas in their covered bowl. "What do you think?

I'd say they were about twenty-three, maybe twenty-five?"

Lucille shook her head. "Yes, that seems about right. And Betty?"

"Oh, I'd say Betty was about thirty years old."

"Old enough to know what kind of results her actions will bring." Lucille pointed out.

"Exactly."

They focused on their meal, refusing to give Betty the attention she was after. She laughed and twirled around the tables until she spotted Frank.

"Look out, Frank. Here she comes." Lucille mumbled.

"Well, hello-o," Betty drawled out the last word slowly.

Bent over Frank, she stood with her wispy scarf top exposing most of what was under it.

"And what can I do for you?" She bubbled.

"No thank you, I'm a Christian."

Her bubbly smile dropped and in its place was a sneer. She rolled her eyes and turned away and put on her zestful face again.

"Well, if you change your mind, I'll be around." She purred.

Frank and Lucille exchanged concerned looks, and he put down his fork.

"Ready to go, my dear?"

Lucille nodded eagerly. "Yes, more than ready."

Chapter Eleven

Ella stared at the almost empty greenhouse.

"Vegetable plants…that's it. Surely, I can find some that grow in the fall…"

She drove to a well-stocked private nursery on Hwy. 80 outside of Longview; Bountiful Gardens. Besides their employees being knowledgeable about plants, they were extremely helpful and friendly. Just the kind of place that made you want to return.

She parked, careful not to block their driveway. Scanning the area, she burst into a wide smile, *"Great! Fall plants have arrived!..."*

A large assortment of fruit trees caught her eye, but today she was after vegetable plants. Several 6 packs of various vegetable plants were on tables directly to her left past the office. She made a bee line straight to them and felt someone tap her on her back. Turning, she squinted into the smiling face of Sam Baldwin.

"Ms. Reed…nice to see you again!"

"And you too!" Ella beamed at Sam.

"How's the barbeque pit holding up?"

"It's waiting on me to grill! Just a lot of interruptions lately…" She gave him half a smile.

"I know too well how that can happen!" He raised his eyebrows and nodded.

"I was hoping to grow vegetables this winter in the greenhouse. I've never had a greenhouse before!"

"Good for you! I always grow a few tomato plants in the spring, but that's all I have time for."

They ambled towards the tables loaded with small plants, both stopping to examine each variety with instruction markers.

"You sound busy!"

Sam nodded. "A lot of my work takes me out of town. Limits me on what I can grow…or when."

"Sometimes you just have to stop and make time." Ella grinned.

He turned his head quickly toward her, making eye contact, and smiled. "Thanks, I need to remember that...sounds like you don't let your work interfere, that's inspiring!"

"Thanks, but uh…I'm not working right now." Ella shrugged her shoulders. "Long story."

"Well, I'd like to hear it sometime."

"Uh…maybe later." She gently bit her lip and grabbed a 6-pack of broccoli.

"I'll look forward to it; hey, that's what neighbors are for!" He laughed.

"Oh, really? That's nice to know!" She chuckled.

"Well, there you go! And now these plants are calling your name!" Sam tried to be serious and not smile, but they both burst out laughing.

He reached for a 6-pack of brussel sprouts. "Now this is what I would grow if I had a greenhouse."

"Brussel sprouts are delicious roasted!"

"Oh, yes!" He agreed.

"You know, you'd make a great farmer." She announced mischievously.

"How ironic! I get told that every day!" He exclaimed, as his phone rang. "Just a second." He nodded to her.

"Sam here…"

His face wrinkled with a frown.

"Okay. Okay. I'll take care of it. And thanks…"

He ended the call and drew his mouth into a tight line.

"I have to run…but I'll get back to you about those brussel sprouts!"

"You do that." She beamed.

Sam Baldwin hurried to his truck and Ella was still smiling as he drove away.

… *"now that was nice…I like him…"*

Picking through the table of vegetable plants, she'd recall Sam and glance down the road in case he happened to return.

But he didn't.

She sighed and selected brussel sprouts along with kale, collards, beets, broccoli and cauliflower. One lone tomato plant remained in a five-gallon container. It had managed to survive and looked healthy. And it was huge. She grabbed it, more soil, fertilizer specifically for vegetables, and pots to grow them in. And as an experiment, she grabbed a 6 pack of cucumbers.

Finally, she gathered her items and with help from an employee, had them at the desk inside the small office.

And it was so pleasant!

House plants were displayed in the office for sale; as where local produce, fertilizer, rocks, and a variety of other items including pots.

Ella chose a beautiful blue and white African Violet plant to place in her kitchen and paid for all of her items.

Placing them in the back of her Toyota, she admired the variety and drove home. With a burst of energy, she organized them in the greenhouse, re-potted each one, and cleaned up the area. After placing supplies onto shelves, she stood back and admired her work.

"… I've done everything I can to help them grow! Hopefully, I'll enjoy fresh vegetables this winter…"

Leaning against the doorway, a wave of fatigue overcame her, and her stomach growled. Glancing at her watch, she stared wide-eyed at it.

"5:30 pm? I've worked all day. No wonder I'm tired," she chuckled to herself, *"and I've loved every minute of it!"*

She hurried to clean up and changed clothes.

Taking her smartphone, she googled 'Restaurants in Longview' and scrolled through the list.

And stopped scrolling when she came across a certain Chinese Restaurant.

"…Golden Star Restaurant on 2nd Street…5-star reviews…hmm…here I come!..."

She treated herself to a bowl of Kung Pao Chicken, and the food was not disappointing!

The blend of flavors and spices stirred her senses in a way that helped her troubles disappear.

Service was also exceptional! Ella finished the last bites of the meal when she heard someone clear their throat loudly.

She turned and gazed wide-eyed at Ted.

"Of all people! What are you up to?"

"I'm having lunch with my mom, and I recognized you."

He gestured toward his mother from a few tables away. Ella followed his hand to meet the eyes of the familiar woman and she gasped.

Lucille's face lit up with a wide smile, and she stood up quickly making her way over.

Ella stood to greet her. "Well, hello lady!"

"Ella, it's so nice to see you again." Lucille continued smiling. "Ted told me you were wrongfully charged with being part of that robbery …and all charges were dropped! Thank the Lord!"

Ted looked surprised, and blurted, "I thought you were just asking about someone on the news. You mean you two know each other?"

Lucille nodded. “I met her in Dallas when I went shopping there.”

Lucille gave Ella a hug. “About the bank robberies…I was at the wrong place at the wrong time. Thanks for believing in me! And what are you up to in Longview?”

“I moved to East Mountain, and I’m here enjoying my day out.”

Lucille laughed. “Oh, how the tables have turned!”

They all laughed.

“Small world.” Ted replied.

The two women sat at Ella’s table.

Lucille leaned onto her elbows. “So, what have you been up to today, lady?”

“I ordered some plants, came to grab a bite, and fixing to go to the She Shed Emporium for some new plants.”

Lucille’s face lit up. “I love plants. I’ve been meaning to go. Would you like some company?”

“Oh yes, I certainly would.” Ella assured her.

"Well, I have a bunch of e-mails I need to get caught up on. You two ladies go have some fun." With a half-smile Ted waved to them and he started towards the exit.

Lucille and Ella waved back.

"I'll see you later." Lucille called out.

Ella paid for her meal and the two women walked through the parking lot to Ella's car.

Climbing in, they talked like long- lost friends.

Ella set her GPS to the She Shed Emporium and drove off talking.

"I don't have any indoor houseplants, yet." Ella announced.

"And I can always find a spot for one more." Lucille remarked. "So, how long have you lived here?"

"A few weeks."

"Well, welcome to Longview. I'm glad you're here."

"Me too, thanks."

The two women arrived at the She Shed Emporium, and focused on purchasing plants while not realizing it, but their budding friendship was growing naturally.

After scanning the area, they located the plant section and hurried to it.

Careful examination of different varieties and sizes had over eight plants pulled from tall racks and standing apart on the aisle walkway.

"Stick your finger in the dirt and see if it's too wet. That will rot the plant and cause the leaves to turn yellow and fall off." Lucille advised.

"Okay, and I always look for brown spots on the leaves…could be a diseased plant…" Ella stuck her finger into the dirt of one potted plant and quickly returned it to the stand.

"Yuck! Too mushy!" Fetching a tissue from her purse, she wiped the mess from her finger.

"Hey, I think this is a good one, and here's another like it. Both are in great shape."

Ella turned to gaze at two gorgeous fiddle leaf fig trees. Both were over four feet tall, and covered in massive, green leaves.

"Oh, I have to have one of those!" Ella exclaimed. "What are they called? Fiddle leaf fica trees?"

"Some say fig trees, some say fica trees; either way the fiddle leaf variety is number one in my book! You pick one and I'll take the other."

"Done!" Ella scooted the two away from the others. "And only $25.99 each! They sell elsewhere for over $100.00 each! I can't get over this!"

"The Emporium has healthy plants and great sale prices!" Lucille nodded. She glanced at Ella as excitement beamed from her face. "Let's check out the bird of paradise plants."

Ella scrutinized the green leaves of several tall plants. "Excellent," she commented and did the dirt test with her finger. The soil was perfect; not too wet and not too dry.

"What color will their flowers be?" Lucille asked.

"Uh, the tag says white, they are selling the ones that bloom white."

They quietly removed two of the taller ones to the others they were planning on purchasing.

"And they are $25.99 each and four feet tall also…" Ella muttered.

Next came the philodendron. They both selected a multi-colored one with each having a solid yellow, solid green, and solid rusk colored long leaf.

Same price.

Same happy glances exchanged with each other.

Checking out was a breeze, and loading plants into the back of the Toyota Rav4 was no problem at all.

Ella followed Lucille's instructions to her home and helped her place them at the front door on the sidewalk.

"Ted will bring them inside for me." Lucille said as she reached over and hugged Ella bye. "I've enjoyed our shopping trip together! Let's not be strangers, call me sometime!"

"I'd like that." Ella assured her, and they exchanged phone numbers.

Ella smiled contentedly as she left Lucille's home, reminiscing about their time together.

"Thank You, Lord! I think I've found a friend…and I pray we're spiritually like-minded! That's the only way she can be my friend of mine…"

Stars twinkled overhead as she drove through the cool darkness of the night.

In order to reach her residence, she had to drive by Sam Baldwin's house and observed that several lights were illuminated in the downstairs windows.

…*"Hmm,"* Ella pondered, *"wouldn't it be nice if Sam could help me unload my plants...and I could help him grow his…"*

Her heart fluttered at the thought of a rosy future with Sam, and she parked her car at her house with the same big smile she'd had earlier.

Chapter Twelve

Ella took her well highlighted study Bible, a large mug of coffee, and her phone outside to the patio. She lounged on the chaise, extending her legs, while she admired the pink and purple streaks painting the early morning's blue sky.

She said her personal prayers audibly, then added to them by opening her Bible to Psalms 91 and Psalms 51; not just reading them but praying each one out loud.

Earnestly.

She leaned her head back and watched as oak leaves drifted down from trees scattered across the property. Wind whistling through the trees brought an unexpected chill to an early fall season.

She briefly shivered.

"…but I'm not going in…this is too peaceful…"

Her phone rang, abruptly breaking the silence. Frowning, she glanced at the caller I.D.

"Jack Rogan…must be important…"

"Hello?"

"Ella? I hope I didn't call you too early, did I?"

"No, I'm outside relaxing on the patio."

"Well, I hate to interrupt but I'll be in court all day. I need to give you an update on your license to practice medicine."

"Please do!"

"The Board of Directors are meeting with me at 9 AM. Since you aren't here in Dallas, they want me…as your attorney… to sign off on the case. They are not removing that you were charged with robbery but the charges were dropped. They intend for this to stay on your record, so whenever someone checks your employment history, you'll need to clarify that you were wrongfully charged with assessor to a robbery and charges were dropped."

"No! I will fight them! I had a perfect record, and I will sue them for defamation of character and anything else you can think of. Do not sign off on it!"

"I agree! I'll file the lawsuit paperwork and give it to them at 9 AM today."

"Oh, thank you, Jack. This is so unfair. I can't figure why they are doing this to me. They aren't getting anything out of it."

"They claim that only the best can work for their hospital. The Board of Directors are all about their own self and their own arrogant, elite position in the community." He remarked angrily.

"And don't forget their fundraisers…can't interfere with that." He continued loudly. "Ella, you are a scrape goat they're displaying even though acquitted."

He paused and calmed down. "Now, I can talk all day about who qualifies for their group, but I've got to run. It's not about you, it's all about them. Self and pride. I'll call you later."

"Okay, and thanks again."

She ended the call fuming.

"…and they don't care how difficult they make it… for me to get another job…"

Slipping her phone into her pocket, she grabbed her cup and Bible and rambled back to the house. A final glance of the patio…her relaxing, happy place…as she entered her home had her sighing with slumped shoulders.

Dressing for the day, she went through the motions with a wave of gloom engulfing her.

She poured another cup of coffee and noticed her CD player on the kitchen counter.

"That's it! I can't let the Board of Directors ruin my mood…I have to get my joy back…God is in control…and He is with me every step I take and everything I go through…"

She turned on the music and smiled. Randy Travis performed country-gospel and classic hymns so movingly that listeners couldn't help but join in.

Uplifting.

She sang along with the CD belting out the hymns with passion…and throwing in several 'Amens' to the lyrics as she renewed her faith and trust to her Heavenly Father.

Her stomach growled and she noticed the time.

"8:30…no wonder I'm hungry..."

Pulling ingredients from the pantry, she mixed a bowl of pancake batter and continued singing along merrily. Frying a short stack of pancakes, she added pats of butter between each one on the plate. Then for the masterpiece: she fried one egg…over-easy… and set it on top of the pancakes. Drenching all of it with maple syrup, she lightly salted the egg and had a dash of fresh ground black pepper to the top.

Next, she put two strips of beef bacon in the air fryer: placing them on a separate plate when done.

And she poured a cold glass of milk before sitting down at the kitchen table.

"Heavenly Father, thank You for this day, please forgive me of my sins, I pray for Your continued Guidance and Your Will in my life, that I may be a light to others, and thank You for this food for the nourishment of my body, and my body for Your service. In the Holy name of Jesus Christ I pray, Amen…"

Savoring each bite, she lazily cut into the stack and enjoyed the music.

"Yum…I probably won't eat anything else all day…"

Later, she washed the dishes and straightened the kitchen, placing her cast iron skillet inside the stove. Sauntering to the laundry room, she sorted two loads of clothes to wash.

And opened the container of homemade laundry detergent to discover only a fourth of it was left.

A quick scroll on her phone and she found her list of items with instructions for making her homemade laundry detergent.

---

1. 1 box Borax 4 lb. 12 oz. size.
2. 1 box pure Baking Soda 4 lbs.
3. 1 box super Washing Soda 3.7 lb.
4. 1 box of Zote(www.zote.com) Laundry Flakes 17.6 oz. (not recommended for high-efficiency machines) or three, 5.5 oz. bars of Fels-Naptha and finely grated.
5. 1 box Oxy-Clean 1.3 lb.
6. 1 container of Downy Un-Stoppables or Purex Crystals for scent.
Mix all items together and use only 1-2

Tablespoons per wash load
....love it...and it lasts a long time...

A quick trip to the bustling town of Longview for supplies and her day would be well on the way.

Slowing as she drove past Sam Baldwin's home; she squinted to see if he was home yet.

He wasn't.

Nor was he home all week.

"But I saw lights on... from a downstairs room two nights ago...maybe he came home for fresh clothes and is working on a trial case out of town..." She hummed along to her playlist and dismissed Sam. *"None of my business anyway...he's just busy..."*

Arriving back home later, she mixed a new batch of laundry detergent and filled her large plastic tote container.

As she threw a load of clothes into the machine and set it for a regular cycle, her phone rang again.

Viewing the caller I D, she frowned.

"Hello?"

"Ella, this is Lucille. I hope I'm not calling at a bad time."

"No, of course not. I didn't recognize the initials with the name Davis on the caller I D."

"That's my late husband's initials."

"Oh! Well, it's good to hear from you, Lucille, and feel free to call anytime. How are you?"

"Not well. That's why I'm calling."

"Can I help?"

"Yes, thank you! I fell and broke my hip day before yesterday. I'm in Dallas. They did surgery yesterday, and I'll be here for a while with re-hab."

"Oh, I hate that for you! I'll be praying for a fast recovery, and I hope you aren't in a lot of pain!"

"Not like it was! And I need all the prayers I can get, thanks. I was wondering, though, if you happened into Longview could you check on my plants? Ted is home, but I'm afraid he'll over water them and they'll rot." She laughed. "I told him I was going to ask you to take care of my plants. It would be such a relief to me, I barely had time to enjoy the new ones I got with you..." Her voice drifted off.

"Sure! Just concentrate on getting better."

"Oh, that is a big relief. I knew I could count on you!"

"I'm glad to do it. I'll need to call Ted before I drive over there, just to make sure he's home to let me in. What's his phone number?"

Lucille gave her the number when Ella suddenly heard a nurse in the background greeting Lucille.

"Did you get the number, Ella?"

"Yes, I did."

"Well, a nurse is here now to take my vital signs, so I must go. Call Ted and tell him I want you to be warned about Betty. He'll know what I'm talking about."

"Betty? Oh! Okay, I'll tell him."

"Thank you so much, and we'll talk later."

Lucille ended the call before Ella could answer.

"Warn me about Betty? Who is Betty?" Ella grimaced and gazed at her phone.

She rubbed the back of her neck and started phoning Ted.

"Hello, Ted? This is Ella Reed. Remember me?"

"Yes. Mom said she was going to call you. How are you?"

"I am blessed and marching right along." She bubbled.

Ted laughed. "Great to hear!"

"Yes! Listen, I'll only come over once a week to check on her plants, and I'll call first to make sure you are home; but she also wants you to warn me about someone named Betty."

"I take it you don't know her…"

"No, Ted, I do not. Who is she?"

"She is your lawyer neighbor, Sam Baldwins' sister. Recently she got divorced, and moved in with Sam. He made her move out; said he discovered her spiritual beliefs were not the same as his."

"Huh! He seems nice…I bought my barbeque pit from him. If he made her leave… it had to be a good reason for it."

"Yup. And she's upset many in the town of Longview with her actions."

"Hmm…Sam hasn't been home in days, otherwise I'd ask him about her now. I guess he's out of town working on a case."

"I don't know. Schedules have to be checked often; court dockets change at the last minute. I am only here for two more weeks. My case is being held in Gilmer, and my client was granted an extension, or I'd be back in Dallas now."

"It's a wonder you're here!"

"Yes. And I'm off all afternoon, would this evening work for you to water the plants?"

"It would. What time should I come over?"

"Well…how about me picking you up, you check out the plants, and we go out to dinner?"

"I'd love it!"

"I'll pick you up at 6:30 this evening. Will that work?"

"Yes, and thanks. I'll see you then."

Ella completed her laundry.

She peeled and cored a Honey Crisp apple, sliced it and placed the slices in a bowl; lightly salting across the top. Walking back outside, she sat on the front porch with her 'light lunch' and decided she had time to blow the leaves off the patio and porch before Ted arrived.

But first, she enjoyed the crunchy bites of apple.

Slowly.

The chill was gone in the air, and the noon-day sun felt good on her face and arms. She stretched out her legs and thought about the new people she'd met since moving to East Mountain.

"Everyone seems pleasant and friendly, but…like Sam and his sister Betty, you don't know what they are going through…"

Lost in thought, she finished her apple.

And blew leaves off the patio and porch for an hour; only to have a breeze arrive cascading a new supply of leaves falling from the trees.

She smiled and sat on the front porch.

A truck pulling a long trailer went by loaded with lawn care equipment. Someone in the truck waved at her.

She waved back.

"Either they're friendly, or think I could be a possible new customer…"

Her stomach growled.

"I am not eating anything else until dinner…I refuse!"

She sat outside a while longer, finally going inside for a glass of cool water.

Satisfied she was really thirsty and not hungry, she got out of the kitchen while she still had willpower.

And strolled to the bathroom. Sprinkling the tub with bath salts, she filled it with warm water and soaked for almost an hour.

The smell was a combination of fresh spring flowers and a sweet, delicate soap.

Relaxing and soothing.

Afterwards, she got ready for dinner, her thoughts lingering on Sam and Betty.

"Since Ted won't arrive for another hour, I have enough time to swing by Sam's place once more—just in case he has come back home."

And with that thought, she grabbed her car keys and took off.

Sam only lived a few houses up the road from her, and it didn't take long for her to arrive. She slowed her vehicle and noticed the same lawn maintenance crew at work in his yard that had driven past her house earlier.

She pulled into the driveway and exited her car.

A worker instantly approached her. "No one is home lady."

"Oh. Okay. Thank you!" Ella smiled and turned towards her car.

The worker followed her. "Here," he said handing her his card. "If you need any lawn work done, we'll be glad to give you an estimate."

She nodded and took the card. "Thank you, I may have to call sometime."

Walking back to her car, she wrinkled her brow deep in thought.

"Strange…he stopped me before I could knock on the door…oh, well…probably doesn't mean anything…probably…"

Still frowning, she drove back to her home and waited for Ted.

He arrived early.

And drove straight to his mother's house.

Once inside, Ella checked on the houseplants Lucille had scattered about the home, and the larger ones in the sunroom. Most didn't need watering, and within thirty minutes, she had completed her task.

"Ella?"

"Yes?"

"Let me give you a spare key in case I'm ever gone and you need to water plants. Mom would come unglued if all of her plants died!" He assured her.

"Well, we can't let that happen, thanks!" Ella grinned as she took the house key from him.

"Ready?" Ted asked.

"Yes, we're good to go." She replied.

Ted escorted her outside, locking the front door.

"How does barbeque sound for dinner?'

"Sounds great to me." Ella smiled, and they drove off again.

Big Tex Barbeque was a popular restaurant in both Longview and Marshall, Tx. They weren't far from the one located in Longview and could smell the aroma of the smoked meat as soon as they drove into the parking lot.

"Oh my gosh, Ted! That smells delicious!"

"Yes ma'am, delicious and tender! Try the brisket—it's outstanding."

"Brisket it is." Ella grinned as they entered the restaurant.

They ordered and Ted paid for their food. He selected a table; and they were finally sitting and enjoying their drinks. They each had unsweetened tea and immediately began talking at the same time.

And laughed.

"So, I'm curious, tell me all about Sam's sister, Betty." Ella began.

"She was raised in Dallas. While her brother left for college and later began his career as a trial lawyer, she toured Europe. Never worked…never had to work. And yes, their parents were wealthy. She ended up in New Orleans, and Sam told me that's where she became friends with some shady characters."

He quickly stopped and took a sip of iced tea, then looked directly at Ella. "She later married a guy from Dallas who became Captain of the Dallas Police Department. Based on what I heard, she decided to prioritize her questionable friends instead of her husband. They divorced, and she moved in with her brother Sam."

"Excuse me, would you like a refill on your tea?" A waitress politely asked.

"Yes, thank you." They both held their tea glasses towards her.

She quickly filled them and hurried to the next table.

Ted continued. "So, that didn't last long. Sam made her move out, told me he had to insist she move out, and was she ever angry! He said she was uncontrollable. He had a time trying to calm her down." Ted took another sip of tea.

"I asked him why he insisted she move out of his house, and he said Betty's spiritual beliefs were not the same as his."

"Huh, makes you wonder what in the world her beliefs are."

"I'll get to that." He assured her.

"Well, have you ever met Betty?"

"No, and what I told you isn't gossip. It's fact. Proven fact."

"Where does she live now?" Ella questioned.

"I don't know."

"What was her spiritual belief?"

"I'm pretty sure that's what Mom wanted me to warn you about." Ted stated.

At that moment, the waitress served their food. Ted and Ella bent their heads as Ted said the prayer.

As soon as the prayer ended, they both took a bite of the sliced brisket, and all talk ceased immediately.

Between nods and raised eyebrows they enjoyed the meal. Both had potato salad, and because the restaurant was temporarily out of pinto beans, they both enjoyed deviled eggs as a substitute. Between bites, and gulps of tea, Ted leaned forward and resumed their discussion.

"Mom and her friend, Frank went to a fundraiser for the Gregg County Women's Shelter, and Betty was the host. She came out prancing around as a belly dancer wearing nothing but scarfs. Mom said it was disgusting…and she'd approach each table saying she'd do a belly dance for $10.00 at their table, or she'd give a personalized tarot card reading for $20.00."

"Tarot cards? That's witchcraft!"

"Yes ma'am, it is. And that is what she practices. That is her belief."

Ella frowned, shaking her head as she took a bite of potato salad.

Ted raised his fork at her as he continued talking. "A lot of Mom's friends are still talking about it. Shocked."

He took another bite and raised his eyebrows.

"Our town is right in the middle of the Southern Bible Belt and witchcraft is not accepted here. The townspeople are furious."

Ted paused, and grimaced. "Reading tarot cards isn't just fun and games. It invites demonic spirits into their life, their families, and the same for whoever they are giving a reading to. Curses follow and nothing good ever happens to them."

Ella shuttered involuntarily.

"It's evil," Ella continued, "and unless you call on the power of Jesus Christ to rebuke it, it grows and so do the evil spirits."

"You are right on all counts, Ella. Stay away from her, if you encounter her."

"Oh, I will and pray daily for God's protection for us. God is in control!"

"Amen again!" Ted grinned.

Ella sat her napkin across her plate.

"This was scrumptious! Thank you!"

"Glad you enjoyed it. Ready to go?"

"Yes."

They left the restaurant and drove away in his car.

Both contented.

Both enjoying the peaceful evening.

Relaxed, Ella began talking first.

"Ted, did I tell you I noticed lights on at Sam's house when he was supposed to be off working?"

"No, but we can check it out as we drive by tonight."

"Good." Ella nodded. "And I hope your mom improves soon. Seeing Betty couldn't have been fun for her either."

"Nope. Remember how you felt when Jack brought me over to meet you? It appeared you needed two lawyers…a team to defend you…and you had no idea what those policemen wanted at your door that night…that's how Mom felt that night with Betty prancing around…especially with what she was saying."

"Her world came crashing down…like mine almost did. That reminds me, Jack called this morning. The Board of Directors won't remove probation from my work record. They want it to remain on my work history as to why I don't work for their hospital…so I'd have to explain I did not rob a bank, or have anything to do with it. And I'm not doing that. They wanted Jack to sign off on it, and I told him not to. I am suing them for everything we can think of."

"That's what I recommend doing. Want me to work with Jack on it?"

"Sure! I do like Jack, but he is fresh out of law school…and my court appointed attorney. I'm glad you two are friends and especially glad about your years of experience. My having a team of lawyers is better than my having one lawyer facing their five or six. Jack filed the paperwork this morning, but you can still work with him. Thanks!"

"Glad to help!" Ted nodded as they neared Sam's house.

"Well, would you look at that… lights are coming out of a side window." Ted uttered.

"And no car parked out front…" Ella blurted.

"I got an idea. Feel like playing detective?" Ted questioned.

"Why not?"

"Let's park my car at your house and go for a walk tonight. A long walk."

"Okay."

"We'll walk to the back of Sam's house from the woods where we can't be seen. Then ease up to that side window and see who is inside. If it's Sam, we'll knock on the window and probably scare the socks off of him, but if it's someone else…we'll quietly leave and walk back to your house."

"Alright, let's do it. I'd love to know who's in there."

He soon parked his car in Ella's driveway. She entered her house and turned on the living room light to make it appear they were inside.

And they struck out for an evening stroll.

At 10 PM there is usually little traffic in the rural neighborhood.

There was absolutely no traffic while they walked.

And they walked side by side on the shoulder of the road until they were nearing Sam's home.

"Follow close behind me." Ted whispered as they rambled into the woods.

Not a full moon, but they could see enough to not stumble on fallen oak branches. A pine thicket scratched at their sleeves, resin thick in the air. A few scratches later, and they immerged into an area not as dense.

Carefully, slowly… they made their way closer to Sam's house.

And both instantly stopped at the sight they discovered.

A car was parked directly behind the house, and the faint sound of distant voices filled the air.

Exchanging a glance at each other, they quietly proceeded closer.

"It can't be Sam in there." Ted whispered.

"I know." Ella's low voice quivered.

Even closer now, they were about twenty feet from the side of the house where light was shown from a single window.

Ella gasped suddenly as the rustle of a mouse skittered through a clump of weeds directly in front of her.

They stopped…obviously hoping no one heard her. Ted put his finger to his lips and faced her. She nodded instantly.

As they stood silently, they heard the sound of a motor advance towards them. Ted studied the area around them and saw no headlights from a vehicle, nor one on the road.

Lifting his head, he gazed at the sky and noticed the tiny speck of light blinking as an airplane went by. One more glance around them showed no signs of any movement…except for the black birds…crows or buzzards…roosting in the tops of the trees.

"Creepy." He muttered to Ella.

Her eyes widened and she nodded.

They continued…this time they tip-toed non-stop to the window.

And heard it before they saw it.

A low chant crept through the glass, barely louder than breath.

It did not rise or fall. It did not rush. Each word pressed forward at the same dull pace, steady and wrong, as if time itself had been flattened inside the room.

Ted leaned closer to the window.

The woman stood with her back to them, unmoving. Candlelight flickered around her, casting warped shadows that stretched and shrank across the walls. The air inside looked thick, heavy, like heat above pavement.

White lines covered the floor beneath her feet.

Salt.

Poured carefully, deliberately, forming a perfect circle that enclosed her completely. She did not sway. She did not hesitate. Her lips moved without pause, the chant flowing through her as if it were not her own voice at all.

Ted's chest tightened. His heart hammered so loudly he was sure it would give them away.

He glanced at Ella and saw her frozen beside him, eyes wide, face pale, breath shallow. She stared at the circle, at the woman standing inside it, as if something unseen might step out at any moment.

The candles flickered harder.

The chanting stopped.

Silence pressed against the window, sudden and complete.

Ted barely had time to react before the sound came.

"Get out."

The voice was deep.

Too deep.

It scraped through the room like stone dragged across bone.

It did not echo.

It did not come from the woman. She never turned.

Ted jerked back and slammed his elbow into Ella's side. She gasped softly, eyes never leaving the window.

He motioned urgently toward the woods, his hand shaking.

The candles flared. The air inside the room seemed to bend inward, pulling tight around the circle.

Whatever had spoken was not trapped by the salt.

It was aware.

And it was angry.

Ella tripped over Ted's feet trying to leave and Ted grabbed her arm…pulling her with him.

They ran through the woods, crushing twigs and hurrying as tree branches slapped them in the face. Ted fell across a fallen limb…bringing Ella down with him, but it was softly decayed so neither got injured.

They rose from the ground and rushed on.

Out of breath, they limped to the road and tried to straighten their posture as if it were merely a nightly stroll …if a car happened by.

They finally shuffled into Ella's front yard…both visibly shaken.

"Are you okay?" Ted panted.

"I am now…" Ella groaned. "I think we're done playing detective."

"You got that right! And I'm calling Sam's law firm in the morning. I must talk to him…and only him!"

"I sure won't talk about it!"

"Try to get some sleep. I'll call you after I talk to Sam. That had to be his sister we saw."

"I agree. Goodnight." She spoke in a shaky voice and turned to go inside her house.

"Goodnight." He waited until she was safely inside and locked the door before entering his vehicle.

He started his car and backed out of her driveway.

Turning on his bright lights, he narrowed his eyes watching both sides of the road and muttered to himself…

"I hate to even drive by that house now…it was evil whatever it was…"

Chapter Thirteen

Ted could not locate Sam.

No one could.

His law firm was baffled.

And clients weren't happy settling with another attorney…each holding the law firm accountable for monetary damages to their cases.

Meetings were held, conferences were cancelled, clients shuffled around like a game of tic-tac-toe.

Still no Sam.

And no one wanted to report him missing.

No one wanted to answer to Sam…for reporting him missing…if he wasn't.

And so… the questions began.

Who spoke to him last?

How did he act?

What was the last thing he talked about?

And once again, Ella Reed was in the spotlight.

She overheard him talk to someone on his phone and then he left abruptly.

"Okay. Okay, I'll take care of it," I heard him say. "And he said 'thanks' then ended the call and told me he had to run. But he said he'd get back with me."

Ella repeated her story to his associates of the law firm. Each time she felt her stomach knot up…over and over again.

As a doctor, she knew she should eat, but she simply could not. She thought about Sam day and night. And yes, she was making herself sick.

Jack had called.

He needed her signature on a document and was driving in from Dallas to get it. And no…an electronic signature wasn't considered authentic…not for this legal document. Too much at stake imposters might hack…

Ella's voice was muffled as she talked to him. Still in bed, she simply said she wasn't feeling well… not mentioning Sam's disappearance. She didn't think Jack knew Sam anyway.

Ella propped herself up in bed against her king size pillows.

Weak.

And waited.

And waited.

Finally rising and getting dressed for the day.

Combed her hair.

Brushed her teeth.

Spritzed a pleasant-smelling mist of a tiny amount each of essential oils in an 8 oz bottle of jojoba oil… over herself. A combination of grapefruit, orange, and lemon…instantly refreshing!

And great for dry skin…

And she felt like making coffee…

Ate a light breakfast…

And waited on Jack to arrive…

Walking outside she glanced down her road and no Jack.

The merry sound of wind chimes filled the air, and she smiled.

She sat on a bench and …taking in the sights and sounds of the day…she said her morning prayers.

Wind blew her hair in all directions, but it felt invigorating!

Birds darted in and out of evergreen bushes loaded with small red berries…and brilliant white clouds rolled by against a baby blue sky.

She sighed and looked down her road again.

"Come on Jack…where are you?"

Jack's vehicle was the only one on the road, and it was a long stretch of road with no houses.

This was cattle country, and the picturesque scenery was as multi-colored as a kids paint brush set.

Cows grazed in green pastures with an occasional round bale of beige hay where a few cows munched contentedly. Black cows with splotches of white on their sides or face, some weighing over 800 lbs., some were 40 lb. young calf's… leaping and running after their mother…brown, tan, white, black, or black and white. And yes, the traditional barn painted bright red was always nearby. A bright green John Deere tractor was a staple for the farms also. An occasional longhorn, splattered white and light brown, roamed majestically with his ten-foot spread of horns balanced on his head and slightly curved on the ends.

"So colorful and peaceful…I never get tired of seeing this…" Jack scanned the horizon and slowed his speed enjoying it all.

Glancing at the time on his car's dashboard, he nodded insentiently.

"Less than an hour to Ella's…not bad…"

Further down the long stretch of road, he spotted a car parked off the pavement with its hood raised.

"Someone's having trouble…not a good place to get help…"

Security training kicked in from his Army days, and he recalled how three men could be hidden laying down in the back seat with a gun…waiting to rob and/or kill you…with a decoy outside the car with the hood raised. Decoy was usually a senior citizen, or an attractive woman.

"And yes, this is a woman…"

He frowned as she stood on the shoulder of the road waving her arms in the air trying to flag him down.

"*My security training tells me no…and my gut instinct IS* YELLING NO..."

"But she looks so pitiful standing alone…and the wind's blowing her hair like crazy…"

Jack slowed down anyway.

He raised an eyebrow as he looked at her for the second time.

"High heels, short length dress…yeah…that's pitiful…" He chuckled to himself.

He pulled off the road and parked a few feet in front of her vehicle.

"Oh, thank you!" She bellowed, running towards him.

Jack nodded as he exited his vehicle. "Having car trouble?"

"Yes. I have a flat tire. Must have run over something, they were fine this morning when I had them checked."

"Got a spare tire?"

"I think so."

She ran back and opened the trunk before Jack had time to protect himself… if it was a hold-up.

"Thank God no one climbed out of the trunk…" Jack thought as he sighed in relief.

He gazed into the trunk and retrieved a spare tire and found the jack.

"Oh! You're wearing a three-piece suit! It will be ruined! I am so sorry!"

"I'll be careful, ma'am."

He glanced at her again and suddenly felt drawn to her. For some reason, he wanted to get to know her better. She seemed like she needed a friend.

And he hadn't made many friends since he arrived in Texas. Always working. Maybe it was time for a change.

His pulse quickened as he became drawn to her again.

"Those innocent looking eyes…" He stared into her face that began to appear so sweet.

"…Guess I'm just lonely…and have been for too long…"

"You must be a professional businessman." She challenged.

"Kind of." He smiled and hurried to jack the car up off the ground.

"Are you from around here?"

"No ma'am. Are you?"

'Uh, no. I'm here visiting."

"Well, that's nice. I'll have you on your way soon."

He removed the lug nuts and changed out the tire; smudging grease on the knees of his dress pants during the process. He glanced down at his pants and grimaced.

She immediately saw his reaction.

"Oh, I hate that, shug-ah." She never blinked at calling him sugar with a deep southern accent. It was simply the natural way she talked.

He smiled.

"A real southern damsel in distress…who would have thought?"

She leaned over to watch him work, when a strong wind blew her hair across his face.

"Oh!" She gasped and slid her hand over his face removing her hair.

He instantly blushed.

She appeared not to notice.

"You didn't tell me where you are from?"

"Originally from Ohio, but I work in Dallas now."

"Oh. Many professionals work in Dallas. Lots of corporations."

He tightened the last of the lug nuts onto the wheel, and grinned at her.

"I'm a lawyer, ma'am."

"Well, if you're ever in the area again, while I'm here visiting…I'd enjoy treating you to dinner sometime. Do you have a card?"

"Uh, yes." He reached into his vest pocket and handed her a card.

"Well thanks for your help…" she glanced at the card, "Jack."

"You're welcome. The car should be safe to drive now."

He put the flat tire and the jack into the trunk and turned towards his car.

"Oh, wait." She pulled a card out of her purse and gave it to him. "Gentlemen are hard to find. I'd really like that dinner sometime." Her face lit up with a warm smile.

"Thank you, ma'am." He nodded, placing her card directly into his pants pocket, and returned to his car.

"If I had worn a hat, I'd have tipped my hat at her…" He smiled. *"And I may take her up on that dinner sometime…after I check her out…"*

Driving off in the opposite direction from the woman: his eyes darted to the clock again.

"Oh man! I'm almost an hour late…"

He grabbed his cell phone and pulled off the road.

"Ella?"

"Jack! Where are you?"

"I'm running late. I changed a flat tire for a lady."

"Oh, was it someone from around here? I might know her."

"No, she was just passing through, but I'm on my way now."

"Well, no hurry. I'm not going anywhere."

"Thanks, I should be there within thirty minutes."

"Sounds good." Ella replied.

He slipped the phone into his pocket and pulled out the woman's card.

"Betty Baldwin…hmm."

Chapter Fourteen

Jack drove straight to Ella's house.

Didn't stop to clean up.

And decided to keep his new friend to himself.

No one's business anyway.

He grabbed his briefcase, strolled to Ella's front door, and rang the doorbell.

"Jack, come in!" Ella flung the door open, smiling from ear to ear, and ushered him into the living room. "Can I get you anything?"

"I would love some water, if you don't mind."

"Certainly, have a seat, I'll go get it."

"How nice to spend time with my friend!" She thought, stepping towards the kitchen. Grabbing a cold bottle of water from the fridge, she hurried back to Jack and handed it to him.

He was still standing near the front door. He unscrewed the lid and took a long gulp of water.

"Oh, thank you, Ella! I needed that!" He opened his briefcase and pulled out a document. "Sign where I placed an x. I have a copy for you. Quick summation: you are suing the hospital for all damages listed here, and Ted Davis and I are legally representing you."

A crushed expression passed over her face as she tried to be professional. She leaned over and signed the document.

Jack ripped off the copy and gave it to her.

She took it and frowned at him. "Hey, why the hurry? I thought we might have dinner after your long trip…"

Jack shook his head. "Thanks, but I have to get back to Dallas this evening."

"Well, as a friend…and I think we're still friends…I can say you have to eat somewhere, so why not here? I can call Door Dash to deliver, and no one will see your greasy knees!" She grinned.

"Oh, no, that's not it. I really must go on back now; I have an early meeting in the morning."

"I understand."

He opened the door, glancing back at her as he left.

"I'll be calling you when I hear from them." He emphasized.

"Thanks, Jack. Have a safe trip."

He nodded and continued to his car and drove off.

She stared as his car disappeared down the road. Closing the door, she plopped onto the recliner.

"He wasn't even here for five minutes..."

A thickness formed in her throat, signaling the onset of tears.

"And I thought we were friends...but...my goodness, did he ever brush me off! Poor Jack...I guess he felt I was pushing him to have dinner with me..."

She sighed deeply.

"Maybe I was too friendly...maybe I came across as desperate...but he's the one who claimed he didn't have friends that cared about him...and he wanted us to be friends...and it was only words ...not spoken from the heart...

Squirming in the recliner, she suddenly couldn't get comfortable. Phrases he'd spoken to her before kept racing through her mind.

And she had to face the truth… *"that hurts…caring for someone who doesn't really like you back…"*

Overwhelmed by a sense of betrayal that rocked her mind to the very core, she felt wounded, and with a slow, disbelieving head shake, she let go of their friendship.

"Professional and courteous…that's how I will be with Jack…like I've been all the years of being a surgeon…throwing myself into my work…no time for friends…well, that is stopping now…I refuse to become lonely…"

Reexamining herself, she decided to do volunteer work locally.

And with that conclusion, she prayed and turned it all over to God.

Her phone instantly rang, and she managed to answer it, brushing off the negativeness with Jack from the morning.

Caller I.D. only displayed a number, not a name.

"Hello?"

"Ella! Praise God you're there!" Ted bellowed.

"Ted, what's wrong?"

"It's mom. She's the same but insists on traveling to be with her Aunt Tilda in Houston…Aunt Tilda fell and broke her hip yesterday. Mom wants both of them to have the same doctors and do therapy together…so here we are at the airport…Mom's on a stretcher with her private nurse in attendance."

"Wow! Tell her they are both in my prayers. Is there anything I can do to help?"

"Yes, I won't be back until this weekend. Could you keep an eye on Mom's home?"

"Of course! No problem!"

"Thanks, Ella. Oh, and Ella?"

"Yes?"

"You haven't seen Betty, have you?"

"No, and I hope I don't."

"Just stay away from her if you do see her somewhere…go the opposite direction…and fast! I can't seem to shake the thought of her being in East Mountain…East Mountain, of all places! That's like a snake curling up for the night amongst innocent rabbits in a wobbly wire cage!"

"Exactly! East Mountain is no place for her…ever!"

"Right! Hey, they are starting to board our flight, I must run. I'll call you later, bye."

"Bye, Ted."

Ella absentmindedly fiddled with her necklace as the horror of Betty returned to her mind.

"Nope, no problem, Ted, I'll always stay well away from her…"

Ella spent the next day leisurely working in her greenhouse. She carefully pruned a matching pair of symmetrical gardenia bushes in pots. Next, she tenderly placed vines from all six cucumber plants onto a clothed wire she'd nailed onto a board of lattice, hanging down much like a light fixture.

Standing back, scrutinizing it, she nodded to herself.

"Great experiment, o' girl…" She hummed a happy tune and finished watering plants in the greenhouse.

Glancing at the time, she hurried inside the house.

A quick shower and fresh clothes had her ready to go.

Driving into Longview, she stopped for lunch at a pizza buffet, then continued to Lucille's house to water her plants.

The house was quiet when she unlocked the door, except for the steady ticking of the tall, Grandfather 's clock in the foyer.

The fresh smell of lemon oil filled the air as everything wooden had a glistening shine to it.

Clean.

House uncluttered.

Ella got the watering can from the kitchen pantry, filled it with water, and took off. Merrily humming a song, she wandered from each room lightly watering each plant. Stopping to refill the can, she instantly froze.

"What was that? I know I heard something…"

Setting the can on the counter, she tiptoed to a window facing the front door. Just as she raised her head to look out the window, a car drove off.

"Huh…who could that have been? Whoever it was, didn't see my car. Mine's parked by the back door…unless they had time to walk around and check out the back of the house…"

She involuntarily shivered and hurried to finish watering.

Locking the house up, she drove off in her own car.

"That could have been anyone Lucille knew…no need to add drama to someone stopping by…my goodness!... enough drama in my life..."

Later, about a mile from Ella's house in East Mountain, she noticed a car leaving from her driveway.

Slowing her vehicle, she stared at the approaching car. As it neared, she honked her horn and waved her arm out the window.

It was Sam!

He turned round and followed her back to her house.

Filled with excitement, they got out of their cars and shared a quick hug.

"Ted told me you were at his mother's watering her plants. That sounds just like you." He beamed.

"I didn't know you knew Ted." Ella blurted.

"We went to law school together…years ago." He laughed.

As he gazed into her face, his smile disappeared. "Ted also told me about Betty."

"It was horrible! Sam…there's something wrong with her. It's hard to explain, but she doesn't think like the rest of us."

"I need to tell you the rest about her." He paused as if remembering. "When we grew up, my parents put all the attention on me, and Betty was left on the sidelines. I went to law school, and she resented how our parents made over me. She tried to find people who cared about her, but in the wrong crowd. She didn't find the peace with those people, so she went to drugs." He took a deep breath.

"And when drugs didn't do it, she turned to witchcraft. After that she married…we were never close."

"Sounds like some strong sibling rivalry, there…" Ella observed.

Sam nodded. "Completely! When she got her divorce and came to my house, I tried to talk to her; but she wouldn't listen. Even though she was hurting…she had resented me for so long she would not accept anything I said. I kept trying to talk to her and we got into an argument…and haven't spoken to each other since." He shook his head.

"So now, I'll have to take legal steps to get Betty out of my home. Until then, Ted gave me a spare key to his mom's home. I'll be staying there for a while…and visiting you!" He grinned.

Ella stood in front of him with a huge smile… as the corners of her eyes crinkled in merriment…

"I'd like that, Sam…"

"And I like that you like that." He winked at her.

Chapter Fifteen

The stillness surrounded Ella.

Birds had not begun to chirp or sing.

It was her early morning coffee time outside on the patio. Looking up at the sky to admire God's creation, there was nothing but an unbroken stretch of darkness—a color somewhere between deep, dark blue and midnight black.

Stars were not visible.

A tiny glow on the horizon slowly crept upward against the black silhouettes of treetops.

She scanned her small patio area illuminated by a security light on a tall, electric utility pole.

No critters.

Not even a nosy raccoon.

She began saying her prayers…out loud and private.

With both hands clutching the hot coffee cup, she took another sip.

"Such a time to treasure...I pray others are able to start their day in prayer as I do...

"Heavenly Father, I pray for Your Guidance, and Your Will in my life, and please forgive me of my sins...I thank You for all the blessings You have given me and my family ...I stand on Your Word in Psalm 23, and I pray for safety and protection for all my family and friends."

..."and for anyone caught up in the world's material gain and trying to be someone elite...I pray they surrender to Our Heavenly Father...to be humble, repent, and ask for forgiveness...to have Jesus Christ as their Lord and Savior...not some club, organization, or other idol, and serve Him and not be for only ourselves...in the powerful, Holy name of Jesus Christ I pray, Amen."

A soft rain fell as clouds began gathering.

Ella tipped her head back for a moment, closing her eyes as if experiencing rain on her face for the first time.

..." always refreshing..." Momentarily forgetting all else, she suddenly felt the rain intensify and hurried inside.

A noisy clap of thunder filled the air as it approached with a persistent clamor.

She flinched and heard a knock on the front door as she wiped her face with paper towels.

Hair wet, and still wiping her face, she flung the door open.

"Sam!" She gasped.

"Good morning!" He responded. "I didn't have your phone number…"

She interrupted him. "Come in, you're getting wet!"

"Thanks." He stepped in from the rain.

"I'll get you some paper towels." She dashed off to the kitchen.

Sam waited at the front door as she hurried back, handing him several paper towels.

"Here you go."

He quickly dried off and looked wide-eyed at her. "Where do I put these now?"

"You don't, I do." She smiled and put them into a waste basket in the living room.

"You are so organized, lady. I hope it's okay I dropped in unannounced."

"You are welcome anytime, but I will give you my phone number for the next time."

"I'd like that, and I'd feel better with you expecting me to come over."

"And I'd like to expect that."

"And I like you expecting that." He laughed.

She smiled and grabbed her phone. "Just a second, I'll add it here." She scrolled and scrolled until finally at the right location.

She glanced at him with a wide smile. "Okay, I'm ready."

He handed her his phone. "Mine is ready too. Just put your number here and I'll enter mine in yours."

"Well, that will work." She handed him her phone, and they quickly entered their numbers.

"Here you go." He took his phone from her and gave her phone back to her.

"Organized…" She grinned. "I like that."

"Not often enough." He gave her a half smile.

"Would you like a cup of coffee?"

"Thanks, Ella, but I'm done. I would like to talk to you though."

"Sure. Come in and sit down." She motioned to the couch.

She noticed his size as if seeing him for the first time. Broad shouldered, medium-built, with sandy brown hair and brown eyes.

And tall. The top of her head came to the top of his shoulders.

…*" He must be about 33-34 years old to my 30 years…"* She considered.

He eased down on the couch and leaned back while a solemn expression erased his smile.

"Most people don't know you here in East Mountain. They know me. And they know the Christian values, and principles I have. I'd like them to know we are friends."

"Fine. That's fine."

"I don't think you fully understand. I want them to know we are like-minded. I want them to know you are the opposite of my sister Betty."

"Oh, I agree! Yes!"

"With all of that in mind, I want you to go with me this morning. I'm going to the local courthouse to file an eviction notice to remove Betty from my house and property. I've got to get it started."

"Good. I'd be glad to go with you. Let me change clothes, and I'll be right back."

Ella took off in a rush. Within minutes, she had her teeth brushed, long hair pulled into a ponytail, and she was wearing a pullover sweater with jeans and boots.

Sam's face brightened the moment Ella entered the living room.

"Ella! You look stunning"" His pulse raced as his cheeks flushed.

"Thanks, Sam. You do too, by the way. And I'm all ready to go." She smiled.

"Wait. I still need to talk to you, though. We have time."

Nodding, she looked concerned and sat next to him.

"What is it?"

"Ted told me what you have been through; wrongfully placed in connection with the robbery, jail, the news media, the hospital…and all charges against you were dropped…but the most important part is that you are a Christian." He paused and looked directly into her eyes. "I may have just met you, but I want you to know…I don't ever want anyone to hurt you again…you or your feelings."

He reached over and squeezed her hand.

Ella's eyes teared up, and she bit her bottom lip.

She squeezed his hand back, and they sat on the couch still holding each other's hand. The pendulum clock on her living room wall struck ten o'clock and it methodically chimed ten times.

Neither heard it.

They continued talking in a low, confidential manner as it chimed.

"I'm glad Ted told you. I was going to, but this way I didn't have to relive it."

Sam spoke in a warm, caring voice. "And you don't have to relive it. It should never have happened."

Her posture relaxed, and she gave him a shy, radiant smile.

"And Sam…I want to know all about you." She heard him inhale deeply.

He beamed at her. "Oh, you will." He exhaled easily. "Are we good?"

"We're good." She grinned.

"Okay, lady, let's go."

They left.

Forgetting it was raining, they opened the front door and ran laughing to his truck.

With no thought of an umbrella.

And it was fun running in the rain…

Inside the truck, another bone-chilling clap of thunder rolled as they shook rain from their hair and settled in for the ride.

Windshield wipers slouched at water as they remained happily silent.

Sam turned to her briefly and winked at her.

"Hey lady, let me prepare you for our courthouse visit."

"Oh?"

He nodded.

"I fill out the paperwork, pay the fee…I think it is $200., then they file it, and Betty has 60 days to leave. I must also document 5 different things as to why she must leave my home and property. I can come up with ten different things so that's not a problem, or the fee either. Then we are both scheduled to appear in front of the Judge."

He faced her quickly, raising his eyebrows. "But there is a problem."

"Should I be concerned?"

"No, prepared is a better word."

"So, what's going on at the courthouse?" Ella narrowed her eyes, frowning.

"The main clerk is annoying. I tolerate her because I need my legal documents filed. If someone else takes the information, she runs to take over. Pushy. Acts like we're long-lost friends or something. I can't stand her."

Ella shrugged her shoulders. "Maybe she has a crush on you."

"She's wasting her time on me if that's it!"

"A woman can read another woman's motives. I'll be watching her…" Ella announced.

Sam grinned at her. "You do that!"

Ella continued in a serious tone, "She probably just can't control herself around you…" Trying to remain serious, Ella hid her hand over her mouth to hide her smile and burst out laughing.

"Now, stop it!" Sam laughed with her.

He parked the truck shaking his head at her.

Exiting the truck, he walked around to Ella's passenger door and opened it.

"Thank you, I'm glad you are a gentleman."

"I'm glad you're glad." He winked at her.

She grinned. " and I'm glad it quit raining."

"So am I."

He took her hand and motioned towards the entrance. "Shall we?"

"Yes, we shall."

Both gave each other a mischievous grin and entered the courthouse.

Sauntering down a long hallway proved uneventful. They turned the corner and faced a long room with people standing in line at a wide counter. Several clerks were helping others, and suddenly a woman comes sashaying to the counter in an absolute hurry.

"Sam! Good to see you! What can I do to help you?" She beamed.

"Oh, I need to file an eviction on someone."

"Well, let me get the form, and that will be $250.00 paid in advance."

"No problem."

She took off and momentarily returned with the document.

"Here it is." He paid her and began filing in the information. She hummed a tune as she made out his receipt.

Then she spotted Ella.

"Excuse me, ma' am? You'll have to come back later. We are about to close for lunch."

Pivoting toward Sam, the clerk gushed, "Have you had lunch yet, Sam?"

"Uh, no." He turned and put his arm around Ella. "And she's with me. We haven't decided where we'll eat yet."

He smiled cordially at the clerk, and she smiled back.

She handed him a copy of the document and held her head high.

"You can bring the evidence of wrongdoing this week, if possible. The Judge should have the case scheduled by then."

"Will do." Sam nodded as he and Ella turned to leave.

Her voice floated over the counter towards him…cheery and determined.

"And I'll see you again…then." She stated.

"Us. You'll see us." Ella turned, smiling at her, as she and Sam walked away.

They strolled around the corner into the long hallway and Sam moved to get closer to her.

"Lady! You amaze me!" He whispered excitedly.

"Well, it ought to stop her…and she was after you."

"She can forget that!"

He reached for her hand again, and they walked pleasantly out of the building, and across the parking lot. He helped her into the truck, then quickly got in on the driver's side.

"So how about it? How about having lunch with me?"

"I'd love to have lunch with you!"

"Do you like buffets?"

"Yes."

"Great! I know just the right place; I think you'll enjoy it."

He winked at her again, and she blushed as they drove off.

The buffet turned out to be Chinese and the best in Longview, Texas.

Eight long tables offered the most extensive variety Ella had seen.

And it was good.

After desert, they had their fill and left moaning.

"That was delicious! Thanks for bringing us here!" Ella remarked as they entered his truck.

"Hey, I couldn't stop eating! Those flavors are blended to perfection!"

He started the truck and began backing it up.

"I agree, that was perfect." Ella replied.

Sam put the truck in park and turned to her.

"Yes, and you know what else is perfect?"

"What?"

"You." He leaned over and gently placed his hand under her chin and kissed her.

She carefully kissed him back.

"Our first kiss." She smiled.

And someone honked their car horn at them.

Sam's emotion filled voice firmly stated, "but not our last!"

He swung the truck around and headed back to Ella's.

And the moment was enjoyed by simply holding hands.

Chapter Sixteen

The next morning, Ella fluffed her pillow trying to get comfortable.

Moaning, she shifted her position in bed and gently caressed her hand across her forehead.

"Sinus headache...it's that time of year again…puffy eyes, sinus drainage, and sore throat…"

Glancing at the alarm clock on her dresser, she gasped. *"Eight o'clock in the morning! I have got to get up! I'm making my homemade blast of vitamin C…to stop this sinus mess!"*

Throwing the covers back, she stumbled to the kitchen and turned on the coffee pot. As it made coffee, she opened the file on her computer for her recipes.

"Hmm…here it is…My Lemon Concoction for Sinus/Cold/Sore Throat. It always works for me…"

She opened her pantry and grabbed 6-pint, Bell glass jars, and her water bath canning pot with rack.

Pouring her cup of coffee, she drank half of it as she dressed for the day. Quickly refreshing herself in the bathroom, she retrieved her car keys and drove to Stevens Grocery in Longview.

…"Let's see…I need a large bag of the largest lemons they have, and a medium size fresh ginger root, and 2 bottles of raw & unfiltered Texas Honey, and it is 100% real. Glad I did the honey test…pour 2 tablespoons of honey in a bowl and add about 3 tablespoons of water. Stir. If the honey maneuvers itself to form hexagonal prismatic cells making a honeycomb shape; it's real. If not, it is a mixture of who knows what…or where it came from. And Desert Creek Texas honey forms a honeycomb shape with water poured on it!"

She shuffled past customers in the store, selected her items, and bolted to the check-out area.

A wave of fatigue came over her just as she paid and left the store.

Returning home, she washed and boiled the glass jars to sterilize them.

And then got her wooden cutting board out and placed it on the table. After washing the lemons, she began cutting them into round, thin slices and removed all the seeds. The slices went into one bowl, and the seeds were thrown away. Next, she washed and cut the ginger root into round thin slices and placed them in a smaller bowl.

Setting a hand towel on the counter, she set each hot jar onto the towel and began boiling the jar lids and screw-on metal tops to sterilize. Using a long handled wooden spoon, she put a one-inch layer of lemon slices, then two slices of ginger on top of that. Each were then filled with honey. And layered the same way until reaching the top of the jar…stopping $1/4^{th}$ inch from the top of jar. Then, she used a sterilized plastic knife inserted into the inside of each jar to remove any bubbles. A paper towel dipped in sterile water to clean and dry off the top of the glass jar, and she was ready to place the dry lid on and screw the top over it.

Placing all 6 jars onto the wire rack in the canner, she boiled them for 10-15 minutes. Removing them with a canning lifter and going to another clean hand towel on the counter to cool off…was the last step.

Later, jars made a popping sound to prove they were completely sealed.

Ella cleaned her kitchen, ate two slices of lemon…peel and all…and had a tablespoon of honey … a wooden or plastic spoon must be used…as a metal spoon kills all the goody of the honey.

Task completed, Ella went back to bed.

Now, when she felt bad, all she had to do was retrieve a jar of lemons from her pantry, open it, eat 2 slices and drink two tablespoons of the juice and put the opened jar in the refrigerator. The jars can last for several months.

Ella woke to her phone ringing.

Stretching her arms, she lay on her back and focused on the wall clock again.

"…Four-thirty! In the afternoon! Man, I must have needed that nap!"

Revived, she cleared her throat and answered the phone.

"Hello?"

"Ella, it's Jack. How are you doing?"

"Just fine, Jack. And you?"

"Couldn't be better!" His voice was filled with excitement.

"I have great news! You won your case! The hospital is paying you off!"

"What? What? They did? That is such a blessing! Thank You Lord Jesus!" Ella yelled into the phone; stood and yelled "Thank You Lord Jesus" throughout the room!

Heart racing, she stared at the phone in shock.

"Jack…it's all over? For good?"

"Yes ma'am. You never lost your license to practice medicine, and they removed the charges from your work record. The transfer of money is going to your bank account as we speak. You can then disperse it into funds, shares, or whatever you decide on. I would advise you to obtain an accountant for those decisions, and I will also advise you to remain quiet about your settlement. You certainly don't need to be robbed or scammed out of it."

"Thanks, Jack. I agree. Wow! I can't believe the hospital board of directors realized they were wrong to do me that way."

"Ella, their attorneys are the ones who realized that." Jack chuckled. "I just wanted to give you the good news, so enjoy!"

"Oh, I will! And thanks for all your help."

"Oh, it was great experience for me, I loved it! But, hey, I've got to run, got a dinner date tonight to get ready for."

"Well, I'm happy for you, Jack. I'm glad you are dating."

He seemed both a bit embarrassed and amused. "Me too, bye."

"Bye, Jack."

Overwhelmed she'd won all of her lawsuit; her medical license no longer in question, a very nice settlement of money …in case she didn't want to return to work, and her renewed reputation would hopefully follow.

She prayed and gave God the Glory. A moment of reflection had her in awe of the Heavenly Father and how He'd always fought her battles for her. She thanked Him again and felt ready to face the day…or anything!

Her stomach growled as she finished her prayer.

"I can't believe I haven't eaten all day…man…I'm hungry! Think I'll pick up a pizza and take it to Sam's …" She grinned and texted him.

"Hey, are you hungry? Want a pizza? I'd like to bring one over to Lucille's house if you're going to be there this afternoon…"

"Yes ma'am. What time?"

'In an hour?"

"See you then!"

Ella called her order in to the local pizza restaurant, locked the house and drove towards Longview.

Two stops on Gilmer Road had her ready for Sam's: she ran into Powell's Grocery for a gallon of unsweetened tea and pulled into Lewegee's for the pizza. It was an extra-large, Philly Cheese Steak Pizza and was loaded with mushrooms, green banana peppers, black olives, and green bell peppers. The aroma instantly filled her car, tempting her tastebuds, and her stomach growled again.

She made it to Lucille's house a few minutes early and Sam was sitting outside on the veranda.

True to form, he helped her out of the Toyota Rave4, as he greeted her.

"Welcome, pizza lady!" He grinned.

"Hey, I hope you're hungry!"

"I am. Can I help you carry anything?"

"Yes, there's a gallon of tea with the pizza in the back seat. Grab the tea, and I'll get the pizza."

He nodded, opened the door and handed her the pizza. The smell assaulted his nostrils as he passed it to her.

"Oh, that smells so good!" He removed the tea and shut the door.

"Yes, it does! I haven't had pizza in a while."

"Me either. Great idea, lady!"

They ambled to the house, and Sam held the door open for her.

"I've got everything ready for us in the dining room." He motioned down the hallway to the first room on the left.

Ella entered first, noticing again how clean and uncluttered Luculle's house was…and the beautiful crown molding surrounding the elaborate mural on the ceiling.

"How nice!"

"It is." Sam nodded, pouring tea in the glasses he'd set on the table.

Ella placed the pizza near both table settings and put her purse down.

She smiled as Sam pulled the carved wooden, high-back chair out for her to sit in and then sat next to her.

And the aroma wafted between them tantalizingly as he blessed the food.

Sam flipped the lid open on the box…no words were spoken between either of them; they eyed the gooey slices piled high with many additional toppings, and both dove into the pizza. Neither were bashful eating together for the first time. Sam grinned and wiped cheese from Ella's chin and she laughed.

"Oh, this is a treat, Ella. With this combination of toppings, it is my favorite pizza!" He crammed another bite into his mouth and reached for a napkin.

"With extra cheese and garlic sauce..." Ella commented.

"Oh, I love it!" Sam took another bite as Ella reached for her second slice.

They devoured it.

All of it.

Sam refilled their iced tea glasses.

"Bring your glass, let's go into the living room."

She followed him down the hallway and into a huge living room with a theatre screen, wall to wall sound, and reclining theatre chairs.

"You just lost me if the movie is right!" She grinned.

He tilted his head at her and raised his eyebrows.

"Then the movie can wait…I need to talk to you."

"I need to talk to you too." She beamed making direct eye contact.

"Oh? Okay, you go first. Please take a chair and relax." He pointed to a soft leather recliner.

She eased into it and placed her drink into the attached holder.

Sam sat next to her and reached for her hand.

She took it and immediately squeezed it.

"Sam," she bubbled in a light, happy voice, "I won my lawsuit today!"

"What! And you sat through dinner without saying a word about it!"

"It was tough, believe me! But I wanted to wait for a special moment to share it with you." She glanced at him shyly, and his face flushed.

"Ella, I pray we have many special moments together."

She briefly closed her eyes to capture the feeling they shared and felt him squeeze her hand.

"So do I, Sam, many special moments."

"And it's time you know all about me." He took his forefinger and gently rubbed it across the top of her hand.

She gazed at him, perfectly relaxed, and totally comfortable being with him.

She nodded and smiled.

Sam hesitated at first, then leaned forward looking directly at Ella.

"I…uh…I was married before. It didn't last. We were unequally yoked, if you know what that means…"

"Yes, I am completely aware of it. That's when a believer is married to an unbeliever. They each go in their own separate journeys instead of them going on a life journey together, putting the other first, and putting God before each other."

"Yes…I was unequally yoked with my first wife. She was a social butterfly, and I didn't know it. Prior to our marriage, she consistently supported my beliefs and preferences. I discovered that she just wanted the prestige of being an attorney's wife. Not that I think it's a flashy job, it isn't, but she thought it was. She put on a show everywhere we went. She's strictly superficial. Still is. I divorced her after one year. That was four years ago. And I've been leery to date since."

He paused, struggling to speak and find the right words, and slumped back in the chair.

"I thank God we didn't have a child! She's now married to some poor guy in London who thinks all American woman act that way. He calls her his Princess…it was in a London news tabloid. Anyway, we don't have anything to do with each other, but I was married before. And I'm so thankful it's over."

Ella nodded. "And I've never been married. It was close once, but I was so naïve then. He was strictly for himself, and thankfully I discovered the real him in time to end the relationship. My family was so supportive. I am the oldest of three siblings. I have a younger sister and brother. We do keep up with each other, but we are scattered all over the United States. My parents still live in Minden, Louisiana, where I was raised. I went to law school and moved to Dallas…and now…here I am!" She beamed.

He gave Ella a shy, radiant smile.

"And now, I have to admit, all I can think about is you."

"Sam, I do feel the same way. You are on my mind day and night!" She admitted.

"Then we're an us?"

She beamed, "Yes! We're an us!"

He got up and helped her out of her chair.

She looked at him tenderly, as he pulled her to himself and gently brushed his lips to hers.

And kissed her again.

With arms wrapped around each other; he sighed and stepped back.

"One more thing I have to tell you."

"Tell me." She breathed.

"When I was gone recently, and no one knew where I was..."

"Yes…"

"It was strictly business. Strictly confidential. I cannot reveal what it was about, but as long as I am an attorney, it will happen again. Safety matter for a client…happens to all attorneys. You will have to trust me. I can't even tell you about it."

She felt the solidness of his arms still around her, and the seriousness of the moment prevailed heavily.

"I trust you, Sam, or I wouldn't be here."

He reached down and kissed her, rubbing his hand across the back of her hair.

Pulling apart, he lightly kissed her on her forehead.

He grinned at her.

"Either pick out a movie from that box," he pointed to it, "or you'll have to go home."

"I'll pick out a movie!"

"Good!" He kept grinning. "I'll go make the popcorn."

She drew her mouth into a stifled smile and went to pick out a movie.

For these Ella secured her settlement into various funds advised by her accountant. Her portfolio was diverse.

She wanted something meaningful to do though and then considered opening a medical clinic in East Mountain.

Discussion with her accountant [illegible] was feasible, and she could easily afford it. She told Sam and he thought it was a smart and progressive move on her part. Fulfilling for her and validating for the community.

Excitement [illegible].

The director then advertised a town hall meeting on Monday night at 7 PM to inform the community and get their opinion. It was on the radio stations, in the newspaper and on the local cable television station.

And it was nearly 7 PM with standing room only in the hall of the new center located in East Mountain.

Chapter Seventeen

For days, Ella secured her settlement into various funds advised by her accountant. Her portfolio was diverse.

She wanted something meaningful to do though and kept considering opening a medical clinic in East Mountain.

Discussing it with her accountant, he told her it was feasible, and she could easily afford it. She told Sam, and he thought it was a smart and progressive move on her part. Fulfilling for her and fulfilling for the community.

Ted even liked it.

The three of them advertised a Town Hall meeting on Monday night at 7 PM to inform the community and get their opinion. It was on the radio stations, in the newspaper, and on the local television station.

And it was nearly 7 PM…with standing room only in the conference room of the civic center located in East Mountain.

Ted, Ella, and Sam sat together in tall chairs behind the podium facing a crowd of over two hundred people.

Many milled about, greeting neighbors, and waving at others across the room.

Chatter exploded into louder conversation as 7 PM approached.

Ted began the meeting.

"Ladies and Gentlemen, please have a seat. We'd like to start. Silence please."

Everyone hurried to their seats where purses and hats held their places on empty chairs.

Quite prevailed as expectations rose.

Ted, Ella, and Sam scanned the faces of the townspeople, and were obviously relieved; they all seemed filled with excitement.

And Betty wasn't there.

Ted sat and nodded to Ella.

Ella smiled at the crowd as she stood facing them.

"Let me introduce myself. My name is Ella Reed. I am a doctor, and I would like to open a clinic in your town."

A murmur went through the crowd as they whispered to one another.

Ella continued.

"I specialize in Internal Medicine. I can set your broken arm, I can remove your ruptured appendix, and I am the one who helped the injured victims at the wreck in Longview."

Heads ducked down as people huddled together talking as loud remarks spoken rudely surfaced.

Smiles disappeared.

"I didn't say anything …at that time…that I was the doctor who administered aid to them, because …at that time, I wasn't sure if I had my Medical License or not."

She paused and glanced into their shocked faces.

"I certainly didn't want to go to jail for helping those injured at the wreck."

They continued mumbling to each other and would occasionally stare at her wide-eyed.

"And yes, I have been in jail. I have nothing to hide. I was accused of being connected to the two bank robberies at the same bank in Dallas, and I was cleared of all charges. There was no evidence against me, but I was in jail at first, and believe me, I didn't want to ever go back to jail…there or anywhere."

Ella took a drink of water and briefly glanced at Sam before continuing.

"I want to turn what was bad into something good for everyone, and I like the East Mountain community. Good people live here and deserve their own clinic without having to drive to Longview for medical treatment."

"We go to Longview like everyone in the surrounding towns do." A man bellowed from the back of the room.

"I am aware that people in Marshall, Tx. cannot have their babies delivered at the hospital in Marshall anymore. They have to drive over an hour to the Longview hospital. Same thing with a heart attack.

Marshall does not have a cardiologist department anymore. Those patients also have to drive to Longview. The Longview hospital can get overwhelmed with patients often."

Other people stood at random and all talked at the same time.

"So, who are the two men with you? Are they doctors also?" Someone else asked.

"No, they are not doctors, they are attorneys." She pointed at Ted. "This is Ted Davis, born and raised in Longview."

Ted nodded at the people.

She turned her back to the crowd and smiled at Sam. Pivoting around, she addressed the townspeople. "And this is Sam Baldwin local attorney. I'm sure you must know of him, he lives here in East Mountain."

Sam smiled at the group.

One woman stood with her hands on her hips and shouted in anger.
"Are you related to that Betty Baldwin?"

Sam studied her body language and answered calmly. "Yes ma'am, she is my sister, and I am having her evicted from my home and property."

"She's into witchcraft!" Another yelled.

"She reads tarot cards." A man shouted.

"We don't want her kind in our town!" Someone else blurted.

"I have filed legal documents to have her evicted. We don't want her here either." Sam declared.

People started getting up from their seats and walking out.

All were upset and shoving others out of their way to leave.

Someone then exclaimed, "she's a witch! We want nothing to do with your clinic!"

The room emptied as fast as it had filled.

"You don't understand." Ella pleaded as the last of the people hurried out.

Sam was stone faced.

"I'm so sorry, Ella. I still think being upfront and telling them the truth about everything is always best."

"So, do I. And we have nothing to do with Betty." She swallowed hard. "We'll be praying for all of these people…and Betty."

Sam nodded. "Yes ma'am! And we don't want any association with witchcraft, either."

Ted drew his mouth together in a tight line.

"We'll all be praying…"

Chapter Eighteen

Drying off from the shower, Jack dropped the towel and splashed cologne across his neck and arms.

He'd carefully laid out his clothes in the bedroom and began dressing.

Thoughts of Betty surfaced repeatedly as he marveled at getting a date with her at all.

"Maybe this will last…I've never had an attractive woman be this excited about me…"

He slipped into his clothes and sat on the side of the bed putting on his socks and shoes, smiling.

"She keeps me on my toes…extremely intelligent…and humorous too… got to be careful…don't want to mess this up!"

He'd had his car cleaned and detailed as well.

Every inch of it…vacuumed, polished, and scrubbed to perfection.

It shined.

Spotless, the crisp smell of cleanliness was impressive.

"A woman would notice…" He smiled again.

He glanced at himself in the full-length mirror; soft pull-over sweater, casual pants, brown hair combed to the side…muscular physique, medium build.

"And I caught her eye." He grinned. "Nice…and only 27 years old…got a long way to go o' boy!"

Locking his house, he strolled to the car.

At first, he whistled.

Then the closer he was to her house, the more he noticed his heart began to pound.

And suddenly, he arrived.

He parked his car and approached the front door.

Knocking firmly, he waited for Betty to open the door.

And waited.

And waited.

"Betty?" He called.

Instantly, the door was violently opened and Betty stood; hair disheveled with burning hot eyes greeting him.

"What!" She demanded.

"I... I..." Jack hesitated, struggling to find his words.

"Oh, Jack! Come in! I'm furious." She rambled.

He gazed wide-eyed at her as her brown eyes took on a blackness that grew in depth.

"Betty, is everything okay?"

"No! I've been evicted."

She marched to a corner table in the foyer. Snatching a letter lying haphazardly on the table, she opened it and flung it at Jack.

"Here it is! I found this in the mail while ago. And I'm not going to comply! Not like he wants, anyway!"

"Who?"

"My brother, Sam Baldwin…I may leave, but I'll leave fighting!" She huffed.

"Calm down, Betty. Let me see what I can do to help. I am an attorney."

He opened the letter and examined it.

With a deep sigh, he folded it and shoved it back into the envelope.

"It's perfectly legal. Sorry, I thought I could help." He grimaced.

Her eyes suddenly sparkled.

"Perhaps you can…" She said slowly.

"I want to leave today. I'll be packing my clothes immediately." She approached him with a twisted smile. "You can help me get a quicker start by getting me a gas can and filling it with gas. That way, I won't have to worry about running short on gas…and not finding gas stations when I need one."

"Is that safe to drive with extra fuel in your car?"

"Safer than someone trying to rob me. I could stop at a gas station during the night only to discover it's closed. And there I'd be…" Her voice trailed off.

She sounded pitiful then…all of her rage had vanished.

“I don’t know Betty. You could turn a curve too fast, and the container of gas could tilt onto its side, gas spilling out inside your car…dangerous situation…for anyone…”

“I am not a careless driver, Jack. And I trust you not to repeat this, but I am driving south to the border. I’m going to Mexico. I have my Passport.”

“Mexico! Now I am concerned! No woman should go to Mexico alone!”

“Jack, I’ve made several trips there. I know where to go and where not to go. That’s why I need to take the gas with me!”

“I realize that’s a long journey but…it doesn’t seem practical enough to dismiss the risk of an accident happening.”

“Oh, you attorneys. Always reasoning too deeply. And that is so sweet of you to be concerned about my well-being.”

He gazed at her with his frown unmoving.

"Betty…"

She smiled and interrupted him.

"I want to get away from here, and I want to leave now. I refuse to see my brother in court. I'll be gone and there won't be anyone to evict!" Her voice changed to a softer tone. "And I am sorry about our date. I have no control over my brother or his actions."

"I know you don't. Alright, alright. I'll go get the gas and gas can."

"Oh, shug-ah, thank you! Thank you! Thank you!" She gushed.

Still frowning, he shook his head in disbelief.

"I'll get a five-gallon plastic can and only fill it up to hold four gallons. It will be easier for you to handle. But this is against my better judgement."

"It will be okay, Jack. I'll be upstairs packing my clothes. Hurry back, okay?"

"I will. Don't worry." He sighed.

Jack plodded outside angrily and drove off fast.

The deep sound of Betty's chuckle would have unnerved him.

Her eyes glistened as her plan developed in real time.

She stomped up the stairs and pulled clothes off their hangers from her bedroom closet.

Dresser drawers were opened with more clothes scattered on the floor and piled onto the bed.

Stuffing her suitcase to capacity, she filled a large tote with shoes and purses, another one with make-up and toiletry supplies, and scanned the closet again.

"I'll take an armload of hang-up clothes to the car and lay them on the back seat…" she muttered to herself. She grabbed nearly half a section of clothes from the closet and draped them across her arm. The unexpected weight made her stagger into the doorway. She caught hold of the door frame and steadied herself.

She almost stumbled again bolting down the stairs and emitted a loud gasp as she caught hold of the railing.

Finally outside, she laid the clothes flat on the back seat and returned to get the rest of her belongings.

And she was huffing.

Out of breath.

She surveyed the inside of the house within her view as she climbed the stairs again; the

furniture in the foyer, the paintings on the wall, and a quick glimpse into the living room.

She smiled.

"I'll show you, Sam Baldwin. I certainly won't be here for you to evict." She made her threat audibly, tossing her head back as she let out a hearty, full-bodied laugh.

She stopped midway up the stairs and gazed at the stained wooden panels of the Cathedral ceiling above her.

"Now why did he want a ceiling that high?" She muttered. "Because he can? He's an attorney and can show off …" She huffed climbing the stairs.

"For once he won't be on top of the world" She laughed. "It's about time things didn't go his way!" Filled with energy again, she bounced up the remaining stairs.

After several trips, she had her suitcase and the totes out of the house and on the floorboard of her car.

And started humming to herself.

She retrieved some snacks and two bottles of water from the kitchen and put them in the passenger seat of her car.

"And I want something of Sam's…" She glanced around with raised eyebrows.

"That's it!" She eased toward the fireplace, grinning.

"The first thing he made welding…his five-piece, fireplace tool set."

Heavy; it took both of her hands to clutch it and carry it to her car.

"Done!" She smiled to herself and hummed the tune again; stopping when she saw Jack return, pulling into the driveway.

With a pitiful pout pasted on her face, she turned to squint at him.

"I'm ready to go. If you don't mind, I'd like a few minutes alone…"

"No, I understand. This is a traumatic moment for you, leaving is so final…"

She cut him off.

"Yes. Could you please bring the gas can, now?"

"Of course. I'll set it in the trunk for you."

He sprinted to his vehicle and brought the can to her.

"See if it's too heavy for you to lift."

She picked it up by the handle. "It's just right, Jack. Thanks again."

He nodded. "I want us to keep in touch." He spoke firmly.

Betty stepped forward and lightly hugged him.

"We will, and I've got an idea. When I arrive in Mexico, safely across the border, I'll make a collect call to you, so you'll know I made it. And it won't cost anything. I'll say I'm Kassie Leigh. You tell the operator that you don't know Kassie Leigh and the operator hangs up. And bingo! You know that was me, and I'm okay!"

"I could pay for the call, Betty."

"But neither of us has to. I 'll call you in a few days after I've settled in. We can talk then."

He gave an impatient huff.

"Okay, you win." He smiled and swung his arms around her in a bear hug. "And I'll be waiting to hear from that operator calling for Kassie Leigh!"

She smiled politely.

He walked to his car and turned towards her.

"Take care. I'm going back to Dallas." He yelled and waved goodbye.

Betty returned the wave as he drove off.

And sang the tune out loud she'd been humming, "Hit the road, Jack, and don't you come back no more…no more…" She burst out laughing until she could no longer see his departing car.

Alone now, the quiet of the place seemed to press in around her.

She looked across the property at Sam's shop on the other side, and at the well-manicured lawn she was standing on.

Her breathing increased noisily. "You are not in charge of me, Sam…I am!"

A cool breeze rushed by her, and she absentmindedly slapped at it.

Taking a deep breath, she took the gas can from the trunk of her car and silently stood focusing on it. Widening her eyes, she lazily shuffled around the area splashing the liquid out as she walked.

A huge smile grew across her face as she then weaved in and out of the house and the shop with a trail of gasoline following her steps. Laughing, she skipped like a child playing a game, continuing to spill gas as she skipped.

As soon as the can was empty, she set it on the ground clapping her hands together in excitement.

She drove her car to the entrance of the road, and parked.

Exiting the car, she stumbled a few feet back down the driveway. Narrowing her eyes, she glanced about the area, and seeing no one, she struck a match to the trail of gasoline.

Bolting to her car, she climbed in and stared into her rear-view mirror. Adrenalin pulsed. Energy intensified uncontrollably throughout her body as she positioned her arms in the air, slamming both fists into the car's ceiling.

"Yes, oh yes!" She screamed with a blood curdling cry while the trail of fire spread across the property.

Wildly gawking from the house to the shop, she briefly became strangely quiet.

Her eyes took on a sunken appearance.

Evil darkness overcame her.

Her face became slack and emotionless.

A choked growl, eerily wicked, came from Betty… as she drove away with a sweet smile.

Chapter Nineteen

Ella reached into the bowl and filled her mouth with a handful of hot, buttered popcorn while not taking her eyes off the theatre screen on the opposite wall.

Sam watched her out of the corner of his eye and had to stifle a smile.

She was obviously relaxed and comfortable with him.

And that made his day.

His ex-wife wouldn't watch a movie with him, much less eat popcorn.

She only did something if it were seen publicly; and then only to promote her own self.

Sam eased out of his chair and slipped into the kitchen. Returning with two fresh glasses of iced tea, he sat his down and bent to hand one to Ella.

"Oh, I didn't see you leave."

"And you won't either." He winked at her, taking her empty glass along with his to the kitchen.

"Thank you." She called out.

She swirled ice cubes around in the glass and took a sip of the tea as he returned.

"This evening is full of treats! Places of The Heart staring Sally Fields is one of my favorite movies, and here I am watching it, and you have fixed us hull-less Amish popcorn…perfection that nothing can compare to, and I get to spend time with you!" She grinned at him and gave him a thumbs up sign with her hand.

He grinned instantly.

"Well, hey! Same time, same place tomorrow?"

"I'd love it."

"Me too. Only, I'll surprise you with dinner."

"Fair enough."

He settled back in his chair, and they watched the rest of the movie.

The ending showed the cast sitting in pews in a church singing, "Blessed Assurance" and Ella sang along with it.

"This is my story; this is my song, praising my Savior all the day long…"

Sam joined in with her.

"You knew the lyrics to that hymn." Sam remarked excitedly as the song faded.

"Used to sing it in church often, before my work schedule took over."

"Same here. Work has a way of interfering with life!"

"But so needed!" She suddenly yawned placing her hand over her mouth.

"Guess it's time I drove home, Sam. Thanks for such a special evening."

"I enjoyed it too."

They both rose from their chairs, and he walked her to the foyer.

"That's an hour drive back to your house. Why don't I come to your place tomorrow and bring dinner?" He raised his eyebrows at her.

"I'd like that…and we could sit out on the patio, if you'd like."

"I'd like." He walked her to her car and hugged her bye.

"Call me when you get home so I'll know you made it alright."

She smiled. "Okay, I will."

She drove off and he stood there smiling to himself.

He went inside and retrieved the popcorn bowls, setting them in the dishwasher along with their glasses, still thinking about Ella.

And still smiling to himself.

And somewhere on the road, Ella smiled to herself.

Traffic was light leaving Longview, and she kept remembering her evening with Sam.

The crinkle around his eyes when he smiled.

Him winking at her.

And just him.

She yawned again and focused on her driving.

She met an occasional car heading to Longview as she neared East Mountain and noticed a faint glow on the horizon.

"Hmm, maybe a ball game at the school." She pondered.

As she approached her neighborhood, police cars blocked her lane halting all traffic. A barricade stood on her lane behind their vehicles.

She could see the glow was larger and wondered what it was … as she had to drive right by it to get home.

She lowered her car window. "Officer, what is going on?"

"A house fire, ma'am. Fire trucks are on the scene now. We don't need locals driving by to see it… and getting in the way. We're asking everyone to turn around."

"But I live down this road, my home is a few blocks away."

"As long as you drive straight to your house and not interfere with the firemen doing their job…"

"I 'll go straight home. You have my promise."

"Okay. And your name?"

"Ella Reed."

"Okay, Ms. Reed, I'll take you at your word. Go on, just drive slowly."

"Thank you, officer."

He proceeded to turn other cars around and sent them off in the opposite direction.

Ella drove carefully around the barricade and soon saw the flashing lights of several fire trucks. She was the only vehicle on the road.

She drove in silence as she peered through the darkness trying to figure out which house it was.

She neared the still burning structure, suddenly slamming on her brakes.

Bursting into tears, she sobbed, "it's Sam's. Oh, dear Lord, it's Sam's house…"

Shaking, she managed to drive past it without running off the road.

She couldn't take her eyes off of it.

Pulling into her driveway, she parked her car and locked it. Crying so hard, her hand shook as she unlocked her front door.

Running inside, she collapsed into her recliner and phoned Sam.

Sam finished unloading the dishwasher when he heard his phone ring.

"That's my girl! Sounds like Ella made it home okay…" He smiled warmly picturing her.

"Hello lady!"

Ella screamed, "Sam! Sam!..." She choked and couldn't speak.

He instantly bellowed, "Ella! What's wrong?"

"Your house is on fire!" She yelled, sobbing again.

"What?" The feeling of ice-cold water suddenly thrown at him had him shaking in disbelief.

"My house? Are you sure it's my house?" He asked incredibly.

Ella answered between sobs. "Yes…yes Sam, it is…the police and fire trucks are there now…"

"I'm on my way." He bellowed, and the phone went dead.

He dropped it on the kitchen counter and rushed outside, stopping only to lock the front door.

Mind awhirl, he raced to East Mountain in record time.

"How in the world did it happen? Faulty wiring? A burglary gone wrong? Oh, dear Lord, thank you I wasn't there…thank you I didn't die in the fire…I just met Ella…"

He sailed through the darkness of the night and turned on his high beams. Light flooded the empty road, and he tried to clear his mind.

But it kept returning to the burning house as he shuttered.

"So thankful I wasn't there…or Ella! My precious Ella! Thank God she wasn't there…I couldn't stand it if something happened to her…the house can be replaced…she can't…"

He choked back a sob as he neared the fiery glow on the horizon.

Flashing lights instantly slowed his progress, and he stopped for the officer standing in the road.

He briefly noticed that barricades were up and the road was closed.

He lowered his window. "Officer, that's my house on fire!" He exclaimed. "I have to get through!"

"I'm sorry sir, but you can't go there. The fire chief just called in detectives…it's now a crime scene."

"A crime scene? My house?" Sam groaned as a burnt smell of something like singed hair created a bad taste in his throat.

"Yes sir. There will be a full investigation." The officer held a mask over his mouth.

"Why a crime scene?" Sam choked as the smoke rolled in closer.

"Arson. The fire chief heavily suspects arson."

"Arson! Who'd do that?" Sam cried. And the realization of what his sister was capable of flooded his senses…the thick air of burning carpet, lumber, synthetics; the burning material of his home…made him gag.

"That's what we intend to find out." The officer assured him walking back to his patrol car.

Sam nodded, quickly turning his car around.

He blinked his eyes staring at the still burning property and felt his gut cramp.

"Betty…how could you?"

He took a deep breath to calm himself.

One last, long look at his house and his shop crackling with flames over forty feet high, and he drove straight to Ella's house.

He parked and rang the doorbell.

Ella opened the door and ran into Sam's arms.

He held her tightly with neither speaking before pulling apart.

She brushed a falling tear from his cheek as he beheld her tear-drenched face with love.

"It will be okay." He tried to smile and his face quivered.

"I know." She whispered.

The stench of the burning house drifted over the neighborhood quickly surrounding them. It was nasty to breathe, and it started stinging their eyes.

He grabbed her hand and they hurried inside her house.

She fixed hot chocolate hoping it would soothe and calm them both. They sat side by side on the couch, his legs brushing against her legs, each lost in their own thoughts.

He finally stood, placed his cup on the coffee table, and paced the living room.

"Ella, I do think Betty did it, but until we find out for sure, everyone in the neighborhood needs to be on alert. It could be some crazy lunatic running around laughing and enjoying the disaster he started. He may want more chaos."

"It's too horrific to imagine." She shuttered. "I'll keep my outside lights on all night…just as a precaution."

She finished her hot chocolate and set the cup on the coffee table beside his.

He nodded. "I think I need to stay here tonight, if you don't object?"

"Object? No, I feel safer with you here! I've got a spare bedroom."

"The couch will be fine. I'll try to sleep. A bed won't help." He smiled at her.

"Well, alright then, I'll bring you a pillow and some cover."

She dashed off and returned with a pillow, throwing the cover onto a nearby chair.

"Make yourself comfortable." She yawned. "I'll get these cups out of the way."

He nodded as she grabbed them and headed toward the kitchen.

Placing them in the sink, she frowned at a sudden noise.

It came from the living room.

She quietly tiptoed there.

Sam was stretched out on the couch and lightly snoring.

"He has to be mentally exhausted…" She thought with concern.

Ella covered him with a quilt, and he slept all night.

Ella remained in her recliner, praying, and dozed off and on.

They both woke up the next morning startled by the sound of Ella's automatic coffee pot perking loudly from the kitchen.

Stumbling out of the living room, their day began.

"We need to eat, I'm afraid it's going to be a long day." Ella told him.

"And I want to find a place near here to move to…maybe an apartment…before they attack you for letting to sleep on your couch last night."

Ella grinned, "I've been attacked for worse."

"Not on my watch," he replied with a sly smile.

"I want to get my things from Ted's mothers house, and then go see what's left of my house, work in apartment hunting, and call my insurance company to file a claim…and not in that order…just thinking out loud…"

She nodded as they entered the kitchen and got busy.

Sam worked on air frying the beef bacon and Ella fixed the soft scrambled eggs with cheese and chives…

They set the table, and Sam said the blessing.

Breakfast was a huge success regardless of the underlying disaster they still had to face…

Chapter Twenty

"Arson…" Ted paused.

"The fire chief gave his official report, and the investigation is ongoing." Ted folded The East Mountain News and handed his mother the newspaper.

"Well, who do they think did it? Who burnt down Sam Baldwin's house?" Lucille demanded.

He drew his mouth into a tight line and shook his head. "They don't know for sure, Mother, and we can second guess all day."

"Poor Sam. He lost everything. It's so unfair."

"Yep, it is. But there is a bright side to it…at least he did have insurance. He was completely covered."

"Thank God for that, but I sure wouldn't want to rebuild on the same spot where someone torched my house…"

"Mom…they may capture the one who did it. They've just begun to investigate."

"I hope they do. Time will tell." She sighed.

Lucille jumped when her phone suddenly rang.

"Hello?"

"Lucille? Ella. I didn't know you were home, but…welcome home!"

"How nice and thank you. Yes, it's good to be home!" Lucille eased back in her chair and got comfortable.

"Ella, let me catch you up on what's going on here. Ted was surprised when I called him last night that I was released. The doctor had a late start on making rounds to patients and I happened to get released at the last minute." She rushed on breathlessly. "My Aunt Tilda is also returning home. She lives in Houston; we received the best of care!"

"You were both blessed."

"Amen! I agree! And Ted and I got here in Longview early this morning. I'm so sorry about Sam's house. Is he okay?"

"Yes, that's why I'm calling. He's upset, but doing better. He needs to come over to your house and get his clothes and stuff."

"Tell him he can stay here. Just because I'm back home doesn't mean he has to leave."

"Thanks, Lucille, but he wants to be close by here in East Mountain. He wants to look at apartments this morning."

"Oh. Has he got a chance to sort through the rubble at his place yet?"

"No, it's still considered a crime scene. He wants to hire a contractor to bulldoze it all down and get rid of it."

"I don't blame him." Lucille sighed again. "Tell him he can come get his belongings anytime…and why don't you come with him? I'd like to see you too."

"Are you sure you're up to it? That was a long drive you had coming home…"

"Oh, I'm fine, dear, and Ella; you did a great job looking after my plants. Thank you!" Her voice rose merrily.

"You're welcome. It was my pleasure. I'll tell Sam. He left his phone on your kitchen counter…that's why he couldn't call you."

"Well, I'll go plug it in and charge it for him!"

"How thoughtful! We'll see you soon, Lucille. Bye!"

"Bye."

As soon as the call ended Lucille exhaled deeply. She ran her hand behind her neck and frowned at her son.

"Ted, I didn't want to alarm Ella, but whoever torched Sam's house could do the same to another house…hers included."

"Yes, they could, and you're right; don't alarm her. I'm sure law enforcement will be patrolling the area. That's standard procedure when arson is involved."

"She'll be here soon with Sam to get his things…he's going apartment hunting in East Mountain…so, he'll be near her anyway."

"Mom, there's something I need to tell you…" He averted looking in her face.

"Okay."

"I have a client in trouble. I need to return to the office, and don't know how long I'll be gone." He glanced at her frowning.

"Dallas, again?"

"Yes, Dallas."

She flashed a pleasant smile at him with raised eyebrows.

"Don't worry about me. Frank will be in and out of here, and I won't miss you…for a while, anyway!"

He grinned. "I'm glad you've got Frank."

"And I guess Frank and I'll have to fix you up on a blind date…"

"Mother! You wouldn't dare!" He exclaimed with a gleam in his eye.

"Well, the thought just flashed across my mind…but it is a good idea!"

"No, no it's not." He drew his mouth together attempting to stifle a smile. "I'm going to pack my suitcase now…I have to leave right after lunch."

"Alrighty. I'll be in the study; I have a lot of mail to sort through."

He gave her a crisp nod and sauntered towards his bedroom.

Lucille smiled watching him leave.

"I'll discuss the blind date idea with Frank…"

She kept running that thought through her mind as she ambled down the hallway to her study.

And smiled to herself again.

She shoved a waste basket close to her desk and began opening stacks of mail.

One large, yellow envelope stood out from the others in the stack.

It was addressed to "Davis" in beautiful handwriting.

"Huh, came from someone in Marietta, Ohio…" She pondered.

Lucille ripped it open… prepared to quickly throw it in the trash.

And pulled out a typed letter addressed to Ted Davis…with newspaper clippings attached.

She scanned through the information and liked what she saw.

A naturally beautiful young woman promoting herself for a job.

And not wearing tons of make-up. And backing up her accomplishments with sections of newspaper clippings.

"Hmm…upcoming attorney wins fight against foster care couple in Little Rock, Arkansas…"

Lucille sorted through the other clippings briefly reading the headlines.

"Sure beats a cold impersonal resume listed with a job placement company…"

She quickly resumed sorting the rest of the mail; made one stack to read later and threw the rest away.

Except for the yellow envelope.

Scooting her chair back from her desk, she grabbed it and pranced towards Ted's room.

"Hey, you need to take this with you. Looks promising. You could use an assistant with your work. Check this out…and the qualifications."

She handed him the envelope.

Ted stopped midway from stuffing socks inside the corners of his suitcase, and emptied the contents from the envelope onto his bed.

Taking more time than usual, he didn't speed read…he spent some time with each article, and the letter.

"Interesting. Sounds like someone who isn't just in it for the money…apparently, she has a heart for mankind…"

He placed everything back into the envelope and slipped it under his folded shirts.

"I'll check this out in Dallas."

"Good. She certainly went the extra mile to get a new job. Wonder why she wants to come to Texas?"

Ted raised his eyebrows. "Winters are cold in Ohio!"

"True."

The doorbell rang and Lucille's face beamed.

"That must be Sam and Ella." She rushed off, still talking to Ted. "They've had enough time to get here."

Approaching the foyer, she paused and looked through the peep hole in the top center of the door.

And yes, there stood Sam and Ella.

Lucille opened the door wide. "Welcome! Come on in!"

They both had shy smiles entering quietly and briefly hugged her.

Lucille frowned at Sam. "I'm so sorry about your house."

"Thank you."

"And Sam, I understand about you moving out of my house. Ted is moving out too!" She laughed.

Sam and Ella gave her a look of shock…Ella even gasped out loud.

Lucille waved her hand in the air. "I didn't mean it like that. He's going to Dallas for work."

They all laughed, and the couple seemed more at ease.

"I'll get my stuff together and say hi to Ted." He smiled and left the foyer.

Ella, scrutinizing Lucille, nodded at her. "And you like great, lady! Can't tell you broke anything!"

"Thank you, and I'm so glad it's over…no more physical therapy!"

They walked into the living room clearly happy to see each other.

"Can I get you anything?" Lucille offered.

"I appreciate it, but no, I'm fine. We can't stay anyway."

"I'm sure you two have a lot to take care of!"

"Yes, it will be a busy day, and probably a long one." Ella sighed. "Sam wants to file his claim with his insurance in person. That office isn't far from here. So, we'll knock that off the list quick!"

Sam hurried by with his suitcase and an oversized carry-on bag heading outside.

Ella smiled. "He has been through so much, but God is in control. It will all work out for the best."

"Amen to that." Lucille agreed.

Sam returned making long strides toward the bedroom he used when the doorbell rang again.

Lucille raised her eyebrows at Ella. "Now who could that be…" she mumbled, easing towards the front door.

Another look into the peep hole and she hollered with excitement opening the door.

"Frank!"

He grabbed her in a bear hug and kissed her on her forehead.

"You look great, Lucille!"

"I feel great! What a nice surprise! I wasn't expecting you!"

"I know! I'm fixing to take you out for breakfast…at your favorite breakfast buffet!"

"Oh Frank! How nice! Come on in." She walked with him into the living room.

Ella turned towards them with a smile.

"Frank, this is my friend, Ella. She took care of my plants while I was gone. And she's with Sam Baldwin, he's moving out. And Ted is fixing to leave for Dallas."

Frank approached Ella and shook her hand. "Nice to meet you, Ella. My goodness, this is sure a busy place here." He laughed.

"Good to meet you too, Frank! We are about to leave, so that was perfect timing!"

Sam entered the room with another load of clothes, and a pair of boots.

Frank rushed over to him. "Here, let me help with some of that."

And before Lucille could introduce them, Sam nodded at him.

"Thanks! I'm Sam Baldwin."

"Frank Haden." He grabbed half of the clothes and followed Sam outside.

"Well, Sam; I'm sure you know it's all over town. I'm so sorry to hear about your house."

"Thank you, Frank. And I am thankful it was all insured!"

"Amen to that!"

They placed the clothes in the car when Frank opened his mouth to say something and frowned…his mouth still open.

Sam looked at him quickly.

"I…uh…hope I'm not speaking out of line, Sam, but Lucille and I met your sister…at a fundraiser in town…a while back…and she is my first guess on who torched your place."

Sam gazed at Frank. "How did you know about the eviction?"

"What eviction? I'm going on her actions at the fundraiser…"

"Wow…I'd like to hear about that. It must have been something else for you to get that kind of negative opinion of her."

"Oh, believe me, it was." Frank replied.

Ted came out of the house at that exact moment, bringing his suitcase to his car.

"Ted, what's your opinion of Betty Baldwin? Sam needs to know…"

Ted hung his head. "Sam, I hate to say it, but I saw it with my own eyes…she is a genuine, evil witch…and that's putting it mildly."

"Huh! I just evicted her from my house. She'd moved in after her divorce, and I could tell her spiritual beliefs and mine were not the same…of course, even then, I wasn't around her much…but enough to know something wasn't right..."

"We'll have to sit down one day and clue you in." Frank added.

Sam nodded. "I'd appreciate it." He grimaced.

The men returned inside the house where Frank grabbed Lucille by her arm. "Let's go lady! Breakfast is waiting!"

"Now? I've got a houseful of company!" She laughed.

"They can lock up, they're about to leave anyway." He insisted.

Sam grinned. "I'm packed and ready to leave now."

"Me too." Ted chimed in.

"Well, okay…all of you…we'll talk later." Lucille held onto Frank's arm.

Frank muttered something to her, and she grinned as they climbed into his car and left.

Sam, Ella, and Ted walked outside as Ted locked the door.

They watched Frank's car turn onto the main road.

Ted shook Sam's hand and patted him on the back. "I'm praying for you man."

Sam got choked up. "Thanks! I need all the prayers I can get!"

Ted climbed into his car, waving at Sam and Ella as they got into Sam's truck.

He slowly drove out of the driveway, as Sam and Ella followed.

Sam turned to face Ella. "Big day. Are you ready?"

"I'm ready!"

"We don't," Ted chimed in.

"Well, okay. Talk to you... we'll talk later," Lucille giggled and took Frank's arm.

Frank muttered something to her, and she grinned as they climbed into his car and left.

Sam, Ella, and Ted walked outside as Ted locked the door.

They watched as Frank's car turned onto the main road.

Ted shook Sam's hand and patted him on the back. "I'm praying for you, man."

Sam grinned wryly. "Thanks. I'll need all the prayers I can get!"

Ted climbed into his car, waiting for Sam and Ella as they got into Sam's truck.

He slowly drove out of the driveway as Sam and Ella followed.

Sam turned to face Ella. "Okay. Are you ready for this?"

"I'm ready."

Chapter Twenty-One

"I made it!" Betty parked beside the cantina and was instantly approached by Pedro and his buddies.

"I watch car for twenty dollars. You shop."

Betty paid him and three of his friends sat on her car daring anyone to touch it.

She smiled at them and strolled towards the border crossing, stopping to buy two tacos and a bottle of water. She paid the vendor and took a bite.

"Delicious!"

Another quick bite and she nonchalantly walked the remaining four blocks to the Mexican border.

Both tourists and locals were chattering with each other as she quickly stood in line.

And the weather was nice.

No rain.

Betty had her Passport and Texas driver's license together inside her purse.

The long line she was in had stopped.

Still munching on a taco she'd just bought, she stood patiently waiting.

"This could take a while…"

She gulped from her water bottle and took another bite of taco.

"So… they'll never find me…I can get away with the arson…I'll trick all of them…enter Mexico at Eagle Pass by walking in…place the operator assisted phone call in Piedras Negras… hide in a truck to return to the U.S.…walk to where my car is parked….and take off to Colorado…"

Her eyes flashed with excitement while the sound of her heartbeat thrashed in her ears.

"And they can all be paid off…and if anyone checks on me…they'll think I'm still in Mexico…"

The line moved forward.

A group of women were in front of her excitedly discussing where they were going to shop. Betty picked up on key words and tried to remember them.

Then, it was their turn. They each displayed their credentials and I.D.

Mentioned where they would shop.

And they were sent on their way through the check point.

The two officials gazed at her.

"Shopping." Betty stated, showing her Passport and driver's license. Then Betty nodded towards the group of women walking across the border.

"Ah, yes, shopping trip." He nodded at Betty and waved her through.

She smiled and placed her driver's license and Passport back inside her purse.

Walking across was exhilarating and she tried to catch up and walk near the group of women ahead of her, for appearances sake…just in case. If questioned later, the officials wouldn't remember a woman walking across the border by herself.

But she'd remember being here…the traffic was insane!

Walking was even dangerous.

Motorcycles darted everywhere.

She ducked into a store and approached the counter.

"Telephone?" She asked.

An elderly man smiled at her.

"Si, senora." He pointed to a relic of a paid telephone on a wall behind her. Slots displayed on the front where coins were received…to pay for the call.

She nodded, walking to it.

Placing the receiver to her ear she heard a dial tone, then a woman spoke the fastest Spanish she'd ever heard.

"Memento, Senora…no hablo Espanol."

She was placed on hold until a different operator addressed her in English.

"I want to place a collect call to Jack Rogan in the United States."

"Your name?"

"Kassie Leigh."

She gave Jack's phone number to the operator and took a deep breath.

The phone began ringing.

She heard Jack's voice immediately.

"Hello?"

"International long distance collect call from Kassie Leigh."

Betty heard him suck his breath in.

"I'm sorry operator. I don't know anyone named Kassie Leigh."

"Thank you, sir." The operator ended the call with Jack.

"Ma' am? He said he didn't know a Kassie Leigh."

"I must have given you the wrong phone number. I'll try back later."

Once again, the operator ended the call.

Betty placed the receiver back on the phone smiling.

"And who's the sly dog now...?"

She stumbled back out on the sidewalk maneuvering through the crowd until she found the store she was after, Chico's Fresh Produce.

Upon entering, she glanced around for cameras and found none.

"Still safe…"

Several workers watched her from a distance as she roamed the aisles. Bananas, melons, lemons, grapes, apples; they were all quality produce.

But Betty wasn't after produce.

She walked towards one young man unloading a crate.

"Chico?"

He pointed upstairs.

Betty smiled and began climbing the stairs.

At the top, a man stood in front of a row of windows also watching her.

As she approached, he unlocked and pushed open the door.

"Chico?" she asked.

"Please have a seat. Tell me, what can Chico do for you?"

"I had a fight with my husband. He was mean. I want to return to the States without him."

"And why do you think Chico can do that for you?"

"I know you help senoritas hide. Senora Gomez told me."

"Ah, yes, Senora Gomez. But it will cost you."

"How much?"

"Two hundred dollars."

"Okay. If you get me across the border, can you drive me about four blocks from the border to let me out?"

"Certainly…for another hundred dollars." He looked directly into her eyes.

"That's a lot of money."

"And the risk is not?"

"Okay. How do we do this?"

"Pay me now. We leave right away. You will climb into the truck. I open the top of the passenger seat.

You hide in there. Three of my workers will then sit on the passenger seat. You are not to move, not to make any noise at all. Understood?"

"Yes. Understood."

She counted the money out to him and they walked back downstairs.

He motioned at three men to follow him.

No one said a word.

One man opened a door leading to a warehouse that housed several trucks.

They helped Betty into her hiding place. And put the seat back into place as the three men promptly sat on top of it.

Chico drove.

They soon approached the border. Chico prompted the men to chatter constantly.

Betty could hear them and moved slightly as her arm was pressed against a piece of wooden framework holding the seat together.

Then something tore at her arm. She felt blood ooze out and remained deathly silent.

The check point went well.

They soon crossed the border, and Chico began talking to Betty.

"You are back in the States again. Where do you want out at?"

"There is a cantina across from a grocery store near here…"

"I know it well."

He pulled up next to the cantina. The men hopped out and busied themselves around the door as Chico held the seat up.

"Hurry." He demanded.

Betty slipped out and the men helped her stand on the sidewalk.

She saw her car, and Pedro's buddies were still sitting on it.

Her arm stung and Betty glanced back inside at her hiding place noticing a rusty nail protruding from the wooden framework.

Chico looked around at the various people starting to wander about. "You have to go now."

"Thank you," she mumbled and hurried to her car.

The men climbed into the cab of the truck and took off instantly.

She paid Pedro a generous tip to share with his friends for protecting her car and drove away.

Blood continued to run down her arm.

"Okay…where is a drive-through hamburger place?" She uttered out loud scanning the area as she drove.

"Ah! Here we go! Wendy's!" She swung into the drive through lane and ordered a Dave's single hamburger, with fries and a bottle of water…with extra napkins.

Paying at the window, she picked up her order and found a place to park.

Pouring water on her cut, she wondered how long it had been since she'd had a tetanus shot.

Plastering a napkin over the wound, she rinsed her hands with some of the water and started eating.

"Yummy!"

It was almost sundown. She drove to a gas station and got a full tank on her way out of

town.

Chapter Twenty-Two

Ella leaned back in Sam's truck and didn't have to close her eyes to see a replay of Sam's house on fire.

It played on her mind constantly.

And she figured it had to play on his also.

Yet, neither mentioned it.

And the silence cut through the air.

"Babe?"

"Yeah?"

"Did you meet my sister while I was gone?"

Ella blurted. "I saw her."

"And your opinion?"

"She terrified me."

"Tell me about it…"

"Well, I was with Ted…"

"He told me…go ahead…"

"Ted is a friend, and I was concerned seeing lights on at your house when you were gone. So, the night Ted drove me home…he'd picked me up to water Lucille's plants and took me to dinner afterward… we both saw lights on at your house when he brought me home." She paused and involuntarily shook.

"Sam, we snuck up to your house that night and peeped into the window and saw …who I now know is your sister…doing chants and things happened that I didn't want any part of. She has to be a witch, Sam. No joke. I've never seen anything … like what happened there… that night." Ella involuntarily shuttered.

Sam reached over and brushed her cheek lightly with a kiss.

"I'm sorry that happened. And I know Ted is a friend. He told me a little about that night, and how it was creepy. Frank wants to tell me about her at the community fundraiser."

"We must stay away from her. And pray for her to get delivered from evil."

Sam nodded. "That's what Ted stressed." He raised his eyebrows. "There's no telling where she is now."

Ella let out a deep breath. "Exactly my point…"

He reached and squeezed her hand.

"We're in this together?"

"Together." She managed a smile.

He pulled his truck into the parking lot of the insurance company.

"Here we are."

"Sam, you go on in. I'll wait for you. I'm still too jittery thinking about that creepy night to sit pleasantly in some office and…"

"It's okay. You don't have to explain. I'll be right back."

He squeezed her hand again and left.

She watched him enter the building and took another deep breath.

"Lord, help us through this day…" she prayed.

Stretching her legs out, she relaxed and felt God's peace settle over her. Closing her eyes, she basked in it, and fell asleep.

Sam opened the door and she jumped, waking up wide-eyed.

"Hey, lady, someone loves you." Sam spoke softly.

"Oh, Sam…I love you too." She straightened her posture and sat upright.

He leaned over and kissed her lightly on the forehead.

"You looked so sweet sleeping in my truck." He grinned at her.

"And I feel so goofy…falling asleep here." Ella glanced at him shyly.

"No, that's not goofy. Tired? Yes. Goofy? No!"

"Thanks." She grinned at him.

"Ready to go apartment hunting?"

"Sure! Let's do it!"

He handed her his list of properties to check out and drove towards East Mountain. The first one wasn't an apartment after all. It was a three-bedroom house.

"Scratch that off the list." Sam sounded annoyed.

"And done!" Ella replied amusingly.

He turned and drove to the next address.

It was another house.

"I should contact a realtor. It would be quicker or look online." He rubbed his forehead. "But in a small town, I'd rather check out the neighborhood too."

"Most of this area is nice." Ella gently asserted.

"I guess I'm a hands-on type of guy…got to see for myself."

Sam continued driving and wasn't satisfied with any place they checked out.

He frowned. "I may end up at a motel…a room with a kitchen…until something else comes along. None of these I looked at felt right." He turned his head to face Ella.

"Know what I mean?"

She nodded. "I certainly do."

"Well, let's swing by… and see what's left of my place…"

Ella raised her head to face him and spoke in a low tone. "I'm here for you, Sam. Whatever you decide to do there, I'll help you. And remember, God is in control. I am a firm believer that everything happens for a reason."

Etched with worry, his face relaxed. He glanced at her with comforting ease that he grew to associate with simply being with Ella.

He reached for her hand and quietly squeezed it.

"It's like a puzzle." Sam commented. "We might spot two or three pieces that fit to each other, but God has the plan where all the pieces come together…and for a perfect picture."

He smiled at Ella.

"I like that, Sam. Thanks for sharing,"

Approaching Sam's property from the opposite direction, they arrived quicker, not having to pass in front of Ella's house.

The smell infiltrated the truck before they saw the charred remains.

Sam slowed down as they were nearing the property.

And then they saw it.

Black.

The entire area.

All black.

Fallen, caved in walls…like number two pencils standing in their yellow brightness…that someone pushed over, burnt to a crisp ...and completely destroyed. Standing at odd angles…forever ruined…and black…

They climbed out of the truck and the stench was sickening.

Crime scene tape stretched across the front lawn from the house to the shop. As if someone drew a long line and outlined the dismal area in an attempt to bring a happy, bright yellow color back into the landscape.

And the tape had fallen in several places, leaving an illusion of abandonment with no one returning to fix anything.

Perpetual ruin.

But appearances have a way of being misleading.

Sam took a picture with his cellphone.

"This is the before picture." He announced.

"My insurance agent said to hire a contractor to demolish this mess. I plan on bulldozing all of it down… completely removing everything. Scraping the ground clean."

They walked closer to the rubble and gagged.

The smell was thick in their throats.

Clung to their clothes.

Stung their eyes.

And seemed to seep into the pores of their skin…

"Come on, let's leave." Sam choked.

Ella blinked as her eyes watered and nodded.

They ran back to the truck and hopped inside.

The stench followed them.

Sam turned around in the driveway and headed towards Ella's house. Before entering the main road, he stopped and took one long, last look.

"Whoever did this is going to be responsible for their actions. I won't stop until that happens." His voice broke, and he wiped his eyes.

"This makes no sense. What reason would anyone have to do this?" Ella blurted.

Sam narrowed his eyes and looked directly at her. "Ella, people that do this do not reason like we do…"

"You are right, they don't. They chose a bad path to follow. And that's who? That's the devil; he comes to steal, to kill, and to destroy."

Sam nodded. "And they could have chosen our Heavenly Father; he brings life and He brings it more abundantly."

"We'll pray whoever did this repents and asks for forgiveness. If not, it isn't worth going to hell for."

"Amen on that." Sam agreed wholeheartedly.

He drove onto the main road, and slowed again to see his property as they passed by it.

Sam and Ella both stared in silence as they drove away.

Thankfully they were the only vehicle on the road.

As they approached Ella's house, a parked, police patrol car had it's red and blue strobe lights on…flashing across her front lawn.

An officer stood beside it obviously entering a report in his notebook.

While they drove up in the driveway, the officer stopped and took a picture of something in front of his vehicle.

Sam and Ella instantly looked at each other with a confused look on their faces.

"What in the world is going on now?" Ella bellowed.

"I don't know, but we're fixing to find out."

He parked the truck and they both jumped out rushing towards the police officer.

"What's going on here?" Ella demanded.

"Ma'am, exactly who are you, and what are you doing here?" He questioned.

"I live here! I am Ella Reed, and this is my friend, Sam Baldwin." She motioned to Sam who stood next to her in a wide stance, frowning.

Sam nodded at the officer.

"Sam Baldwin? The one who's house recently burnt?"

"Yes, sir. That's me."

"Well, that gives this incident a whole new perspective."

Sam raised his eyebrows and spoke to the officer, "What…"

Ella interrupted him.

"An incident? What incident are you talking about?" She gushed.

"It's in front of my car. Appears like someone decided to spray paint your white picket fence today. And spray painted it in red…guess they wanted to be sure you noticed it…and that it stood out enough for anyone driving by to see it, too."

Ella walked to the front of the patrol car.

And laughed out loud.

"Sam, come over here. You won't believe this!"

Sam took long strides and joined her.

He wore an astonished look on his face as he gazed at the picket fence.

And there, in large red letters was the message someone left: 'Yankee, Go Home!'

Sam and Ella both laughed and then became solemn.

"Officer, this isn't funny, and I will file charges against whoever did this." Ella explained, "but I'm not a Yankee. That shows whoever did this doesn't actually know me."

She shook her head in amazement. "The farthest north I've ever been is Dallas, Texas!"

Chapter Twenty-Three

Officer Griffith replayed the video again…this time in slow motion.

The grand jury members appeared fascinated.

"Ladies and gentlemen of the jury; I present solid evidence in our investigation of the arson committed at the home of Sam Baldwin." He paused.

"In this video, I am zooming in on the man clearly visible at the check-out counter in Walmart, showing him purchasing a large, red plastic gas container."

"Paid cash for it."

"Carried it outside with his purchase ticket."

"And then drove to the nearby gas pumps."

Officer Griffith then showed stilled pictures of his evidence.

"Again, caught on camera, he stepped out of his car."

"Opening the trunk, he removed the gas container, unscrewed and removed its nozzle, and filled it with gasoline. "

"And in no hurry."

"Placed the nozzle back on the top of the container, tightened it, and returned it to his trunk."

"Full facial recognition provided to the camera."

"No doubt on who the man was."

"He has a positive identification as being Jack Rogan…who happens to be an attorney."

The jury members murmured out loud in response to the complete viewing of the initial film, and pictures. Officer Griffith strolled in front of the jury box with his hands in his front pants pockets.

He continued. "I believe your only course of action is to find Jack Rogan guilty of committing arson. Our forensics department verified the melted plastic container found at the scene of the crime …is indeed the same one purchased moments before the fire was set."

Officer Griffith then addressed the Judge. "That is all Your Honor."

Officer Griffith then sat on a bench facing the court reporter.

The Judge rose and scanned the faces of each jury member.

"Ladies and Gentlemen of the Grand Jury, you may retire to your quarters for a vote. You are dismissed."

Each person carefully stood and walked in a straight line to the jury room.

Less than an hour passed until the Foreman of the Grand Jury sent a note to the Judge.

The Judge called the jury members back into the court room, where they returned to their chairs and were seated.

The Judge stood facing the jury box.

"Mr. Foreman, have you reached a verdict?"

"Yes, Your Honor, we have."

"And will you hand me your verdict?"

"Yes, Your Honor." He handed the slip of paper to the Bailiff, who passed it to the Judge.

The Judge cleared his throat and read the verdict out loud.

"We, the members of the Gregg County Grand Jury, find Jack Rogan guilty and have agreed to indict him for the crime of arson."

The Judge nodded at the jury members.

"Thank you for serving today. You are dismissed and may leave at this time."

As they quietly walked out of the courthouse, the Judge motioned Officer Grifith to approach the desk.

The Judge leaned forward and spoke in a low tone.

"You may inform Mr. Sam Baldwin of the Grand Jury's indictment of Jack Rogan, before it makes the six o'clock news."

"Yes sir, thank you sir. I'll call him right away."

Officer Griffith left the courthouse and noticed a news van driving into a parking space. The occupants began placing their camera and equipment on the grounds for live TV coverage.

He strolled to a bench under an oak tree pulling out his cellphone.

And retrieved Sam's private number from court records.

Quickly punching Sam's phone number, it started ringing.

"Hello?" Sam questioned.

"Mr. Baldwin, Mr. Sam Baldwin?"

"Yes…" Sam answered suspiciously.

"This is Officer Griffith at the Gregg County Courthouse. You may want to turn on the six o'clock news. They are setting up a remote here as I speak. The Grand Jury just reached a verdict in your home arson case. They found someone guilty and have indicted him."

Sam breathed a sigh of relief. "Thank you so much, Officer Griffith! Who was it, anyway?"

"An attorney…of all people! Goes by the name of Jack Rogan."

"Jack Rogan? I've heard that name somewhere before. Oh, well. Thanks again, Officer."

"You are welcome."

A warrant was instantly issued in Dallas County, Texas for the arrest of Jack Rogan.

He was there in court defending a client at the time.

And had just won his client's case.

The Judge had quickly dismissed everyone and returned to his chambers.

People were filling out of the courtroom, pushing to get out.

Some running down the hallway.

And two police officers waded through the crowd to enter the courtroom.

Recognizing Attorney Jack Rogan gathering his paperwork at a desk facing the Judge's bench, they silently approached him from behind.

One officer inquired, "Jack Rogan?"

Jack turned around startled by the officers.

"Yes, I'm Jack Rogan." Standing smartly in his three-piece suit, he raised his eyebrows at the two officers.

"Put your hands behind your back, and…"

"Get your hands off me…" Jack interrupted him.

"Sir, we have a warrant for your arrest. I suggest you comply."

Jack looked wide-eyed. "Do you know who I am? This is a mistake! This is absurd! Stop this nonsense!" Jack yelled as he pivoted and flung himself out of their way.

One officer grabbed Jack by the arm. "Sir, you are resisting arrest."

Jack went wild. He swung at both officers and attempted to run out of the courtroom.

They had no choice but to tackle Jack and hold him on the floor as one of the officers handcuffed him.

Inhaling and exhaling noisily, Jack's chest rose quickly.

Though now handcuffed, he still refused to be defeated.

"You are making a big mistake." He huffed. "And you will pay for damaging my professional reputation." His voice rose in anger. Drawing his leg back, he attacked one officer with a mighty kick.

The officers continued restraining Jack on the floor as he thrashed about.

"You have the right to remain silent. Anything you say can and will be used against you in a court of law. You have the right to an attorney. If you cannot afford an attorney, one will be provided for you. Do you understand the Miranda Rights I have just read to you?"

"Yes! I certainly do!" Jack bellowed, his frantic voice bouncing off the walls of the courtroom. "And I demand an attorney right now! Get me Ted Davis!"

One officer nodded at Jack.

Both officers grabbed him under his arms and stood him shakily between the two of them.

"We are escorting you out of here and into the patrol car. Now you can make a scene if you want to, but

TV cameras are still outside covering the last case." He spoke firmly and continued.

"It's not in your best interest to be on camera evading arrest…as an attorney you do know that is a correct statement. Let's go."

Jack closed his mouth in defeat.

The three walked quietly together out the door and into the hallway.

The crowd divided by opening a wide path for them.

People could be heard gasping loudly.

Some yelled," Isn't that the attorney who just won his case…"

Jack couldn't look at any of them.

Finally, after what felt like an eternity to Jack, they reached the doors to the outside of the courtroom.

The steps were agony.

The three men were not in step with each other.

That alone caused the crowd outside to stop and watch their progress.

"It's Jack Rogan! The Attorney!" One man shouted.

Stacy DuVall, a female news anchor from the local TV station, stared in disbelief as she noticed the three men. Sucking in her breath, she unknowingly opened her mouth in shock…and nodded vigorously at the cameraman.

He instantly began recording Jack and the police officers, then turned the camera on her.

"This is Stacy DuVall from KTAL-TV reporting live at the Dallas County, Texas courthouse. In a sudden move, police are physically removing Jack Rogan, local Attorney, from this very courthouse."

She motioned to the cameraman again, and he turned his camera back on Jack and the two officers…still recording.

And halfway down the set of eight steps, Jack stumbled. Both officers had to brace themselves against the railing to keep from falling too.

Silently, they pulled him upright and shuffled down the remaining concrete steps.

"What's going on?" Someone demanded.

"What did he do?" Another yelled.

"Step back!" One officer instructed the crowd as they approached the parked patrol car.

With one hand on top of Jack's head, the officer eased Jack into the back seat. Getting him secured, the officer ignored the crowd's questions and entered the front passenger seat of the vehicle. He nodded to the other officer in the driver's seat and they drove away.

The camera man turned to continue filming the news anchor.

"As you can see, the police have removed Jack Rogan from the courthouse. That is all we know at this time. Stay tuned for more information. With KTAL-TV reporting live, I'm Stacy DuVall."

"Let's go!" She yelled at the cameraman. "And get this back to the station fast!"

Within minutes they had their equipment back in the van and were sailing down the road.

Jack could not get comfortable.

His wrists hurt from the tight handcuffs.

Sitting normal was impossible with his hands tied behind his back.

And Jack sat fuming.

"What am I being arrested for anyway?" He grumbled. "You never finished telling me…"

"You decided to resist…and stopped all pertinent conversation…" One officer calmly answered.

"Well, I'm not resisting now. What am I being charged with?"

"Originally, arson…"

"Arson?" Jack's voice rose to a high pitch.

He stared at the back of both officers with an incredulous stare.

Instantly, his face paled.

"Arson…" The word grew louder and uglier in his mind.

"And disorderly conduct, resisting arrest, attempting to flee, assaulting a police officer…" The Officer continued.

Jack tuned him out.

Nothing else mattered after hearing arson…

Quickly, memories of buying a gas container and gas for Betty flooded his mind.

He gasped out loud.

He'd been set up…

He'd been used!

Realizing the severity of the situation, he felt his insides tremble.

He stared down at the floorboard.

"How could I have been so naïve? How could I have fallen for her?..." His stomach churned and he drew his mouth into a tight line.

"Men are visual…that's what I warn guys about…a superficial woman will draw attention to herself, either by her looks or her actions…buyer beware! Don't be pulled into her

web…said the fly about the spider…a Christian man has nothing in common with a non-Christian woman…"

Jack's shoulders slumped.

"And how often have I said those very words…"

His stomach contracted as pain shot through it.

"I need to pray…"

He did pray.

Earnestly.

Quietly.

Relaxing then, he tapped on the glass partition between himself in the back of the patrol car, and the two officers in the front seats. "I need to call Ted Davis to represent me as soon as I can."

Both officers briefly glanced at each other. And the one in the front passenger seat turned to face Jack and solemnly nodded at him.

By the time they arrived at the police station, Jack had accepted his fate, and was totally calm.

He knew the procedure. Mug shot, fingerprints, etc. Removing his clothing for the jail uniform.

On and on.

Routine.

Until a different officer brought in a belligerent drunk.

A major scuffle ensued.

Two officers tackled the man, and he still managed to escape the holding area.

And made his way running straight to Jack.

Breathing heavily, he collided into Jack's chest and held onto Jack's shirt.

"Get out of my face!" Jack yelled, shoving him away.

The guy towered over Jack and flung himself on Jack's back faster than a cowboy can rope a calf's legs together.

Three officers ran towards them as Jack's face turned beet red.

Jack twisted around from the man's grip, and instantly drew back his leg.

Ker-whap!

Jack kicked him directly in the knee, and the man yelled in agony.

And let Jack go.

But chaos erupted.

Others in the holding area yelled for the drunk to 'do the guy in' and they screamed remark after remark working themselves into a frenzy.

One officer grabbed Jack and walked him down a hallway.

Another officer removed the drunk.

And those men in the holding area… walked around cocky, bragging on what they would have done to the guy.

And so, it was decided to put Jack in solitary confinement …for his own protection.

Jack and the officer walked at a steady pace, both silent until they approached Jack's cell.

"Where did you learn to kick like that?" He questioned.

"In my High School years," Jack admitted, "I earned a Black Belt in Karate."

The officer nodded and unlocked the cell door.

Jack entered the room and the door was quickly locked behind him.

He laid down and stared at the ceiling.

And listened to each step made by the officer's shoes on the tiled floor… as he walked farther away.

And Jack continued fuming…

Chapter Twenty-Four

Ella stood several feet away from her white picket fence, taking pictures at different angles.

The police officer also took pictures to include in his report. He told her to call 911 right away if anything else occurred, then went back to his evening shift.

Sam grimaced shaking his head.

"Ella, I can't let you stay here where vandalism by someone… or by how ever many…could happen again…or worse." His face was etched with concern.

"Sam. It's okay. It was probably a one-time prank by some school age kids…"

He cut her off.

"I don't agree with that. You can never assume anything. And it's a good thing I didn't find an apartment." He spoke solemnly to Ella.

Ella frowned. "I don't understand."

He huffed. "I think you should stay in Longview with Lucille for a while, and I'll stay here at your house to protect it."

"Sam, I appreciate what you are offering to do but no."

"Ella it's for your safety." He insisted firmly.

"No, I'm not moving in with Lucille. This is my home. I'm staying right here."

"Just until things calm down here in East Mountain…with the fire and now this…"

"Nope, not going to happen, but ..."

"Ella! You are not thinking clearly…"

"Sam! I'm thinking logically—there must be a solution!"

He exhaled deeply and stared at her frowning.

"I've got an idea. Let's install some outside cameras for security. We can get them right now at Walmart."

"Now that will work. I'll go along with it."

They drove to Longview, purchased the cameras and returned to her home in East Mountain within an hour and a half.

The cameras were no problem installing.

And Ella now had four cameras to monitor: one on each side of her house.

Sam also installed solar powered flood lights on each side of her house as well.

He grinned. "Well, I'm satisfied with leaving you here now. It's lit up like a Friday night football field."

She grinned and spoke softly. "Thank you…"

He took a deep breath. "I'm going back to Longview and get a motel room with a kitchen. Call me no matter what time it is… if something happens, okay?"

"Okay, I will."

"And thank God they caught the arsonist!" Sam exclaimed.

"What? They did?"

"I'm sorry, so much has happened…I thought I told you. The police in Dallas called and told me the guy is in custody!"

"Well, hallelujah!"

"Amen to that! And …you know…it's strange, but I know I've heard the guy's name before. I just can't place it."

"A guy from Dallas?"

"I don't know where he is from…but he is in jail in Dallas."

"Huh. Maybe your paths crossed in court before…"

"Could be. Ever hear of a guy named Joe Rogan?"

Ella dropped her phone, choking frantically.

"Joe Rogan?" Ella clutched her throat gasping for air. "That's impossible!"

"Ella, are you okay?" Sam grabbed her as she went limp.

Ella blinked her eyes.

"Come on, I'm bringing you inside."

In one swift moment, he carried her in his arms and laid her inside the house on the couch.

Dizzy, she shook her head and took a deep breath.

"That came over me so fast! I suddenly got so weak…"

"You scared me. Are you okay now?"

"Yes." She nodded. "But Joe Rogan isn't. Sam, he couldn't have been the arsonist!"

"You know him then?"

"He was my court appointed attorney in Dallas when I was arrested."

"Oh my gosh! That's where I heard his name…from you!"

"Yes…that's why it was so shocking…hearing his name as the arsonist…"

Sam embraced her.

"The arsonist was your lawyer…who would have thought?" Sam muttered.

"Sam, he couldn't have done it. He's not the type. Ask Ted."

"Ted Davis? I stayed at his mom, Lucille's house. Remember?"

"That's right. And Ted helped Joe Rogan with my case. They ended up being great friends."

"Well, we'll have to check into this…what the evidence is…" Sam frowned.

"It doesn't make sense, Sam. He has no reason to do anything to you…much less burn your house down!"

"Ella…" Sam hesitated. "Are you okay with a trip to Dallas in the morning?"

"Yes! I'd love it!"

"Okay. I'll only get a motel room for one night in Longview, instead of for a week. We'll head out early for Dallas. I'll pick you up at six o'clock. We can stop for breakfast and still arrive in Dallas by noon."

"I'll be packed and ready."

"Alright, lady. We have a plan!" He winked at her.

She gave him a wide grin.

"I love you."

"I love you too, Sam."

He hopped into the cab of his truck and lowered his window.

"I'll wait to leave after you get inside and lock all the doors."

Ella nodded. "I'll flash the front porch lights when I'm done."

She waved to him as she entered the house.

And Sam prayed for their safety and protection as he waited.

The porch lights flashed.

And Sam cautiously drove off.

Chapter Twenty-Five

Betty's car made a sound she hadn't heard before.

A grinding noise.

Like metal rubbing against metal.

"And here I am in the middle of nowhere." She groaned out loud.

Her eyes viewed the miles of flat land with no houses, and no signs of civilization anywhere.

Only trees and brush…clumps of bushes struggling to grow in the drought stricken West Texas land.

"Nothing in any direction…" she raised her shoulders and exhaled deeply.

A loud knock, knock, knock clanged under her car suddenly. She couldn't control the steering and fought hard to maneuver the vehicle onto the shoulder of the road.

Sweat beaded her forehead as she jerked frantically to turn the steering wheel to the side of the road.

It only turned one inch at a time.

And Betty forgot to put her foot on the brake.

She saw the tree looming ahead and tried to avoid it.

Panicking, she pushed her foot on the wrong pedal…the gas pedal… and rammed the car into the tree.

The hard impact bounced the car off the side of the tree with Betty screaming.

And silence prevailed as the car rolled over.

Thrown from the car, she lay collapsed in the dirt.

Sprawled about in an unnatural position.

The crushed car lay upside down with one door hanging open…attached by a single hinge.

Unconscious.

Betty lay unmoving.

The sun was setting when she finally moaned and blinked her eyes.

And the rumble of an approaching old truck caught her attention…

Betty heard it clanging to a stop amongst male voices speaking excitedly in Spanish.

She lay still…quietly eavesdropping …laying yards away crumpled…the side of her face shoved into the dirt from the impact…

She kept thinking of what the Spanish words were that she knew.

Without moving, her mind raced,
"A..Ahme…Amigo…Amigo, that's it..amigo means friend…"

As three of the men removed the tires from her car, another one raised his eyebrows upon seeing Betty.

"Muchachos!" He yelled at them as he rushed straight to Betty.

"Hijole! Senora!"

His friends followed instantly upon hearing it was a woman.

Betty could hear them breathing heavily. She barely breathed and remained perfectly still.

One man pushed Betty over with the toe of his boot, saw the green matter oozing from her torn, blood encrusted arm…the red streaks shooting out of it…and the flies buzzing…

He flipped her back over.

And spoke to his friends, telling them she was very sick.

"Esta muy enferma."

Wide eyed they moved away from her.

Leaving her to her own demise, they finished stripping her car.

As soon as they removed everything salvageable; from entire seats to car wheels to anything technical, they threw it in the back of their truck.

With one disappointing glance at Betty, the leader shouted, "Va'monos de aqui!"

A flash crossed Betty's mind… "*that means…let's get out of here!*"

Betty breathed a sigh of relief as the left…

Weak, and in pain; her body ached like being attacked by a massive wrecking ball busting apart concrete.

"Help, I need help…" She moaned out loud. But she had grown weaker. Her urgent cry for help was slightly above a whisper.

"What's that?" She strained to listen.

"A car coming?" Her heart pounded in her ears, and she felt her chest rising quickly.

Closing her eyes, she listened again.

"No…it was only the wind picking up speed…must be a cold front approaching…"

And then she heard a lone coyote howl.

She sobbed.

"I can't give up! I can't lay here like a sitting duck for the coyote…"

With every ounce of strength she could gather, she held her head up and screamed.

It seemed to echo across the land.

Her mind raced again for the Spanish word for friend, and she managed to yell that word as loud as she could.

"AMIGO!!!...AMIGO!!!"

Exhausted, her head fell back to the ground, and she felt a bug crawl on the side of her face pressed into the dirt.

The cry of a predatory bird unnerved her entire being…it flew directly overhead.

This time she screamed bloody murder and could be heard for miles.

And this time she heard more than one coyote; it was now a pack of them and they howled frightfully close.

Tears streaked her face running in streams through caked on dirt.

And then she heard it.

A different sound in the dark night.

A twig broke apart nearby.

And soft leaves rustled nearby as someone shuffled through them.

Betty held her breath in fear and tried to close her eyes, feigning unconsciousness.

But it was impossible.

Instantly, a bright beam of light surrounded her, and she instinctively opened her eyes as someone held a flashlight on her.

She blinked gasping in terror.

The flashlight suddenly swung around to show a young Spanish girl about sixteen years old.

"You okay." She said in halting English. "I take you my casa."

"Casa…that's home…great! She's taking me to her home…"

Betty smiled for the first time since she'd left the Mexican border.

The girl grabbed Betty by her waist and tried to stand her up.

Betty screamed.

The girl shook her head and laid her back on the ground.

And that's when the pack of coyotes howled eerily close.

This time the girl grabbed Betty by her good arm and began dragging her.

Betty cried and whimpered as she was slid over debris from fallen tree branches.

The girl never said another word.

Her pace increased and Betty finally passed out.

Eventually, they approached a small shack made of dilapidated tin and old rotten boards nailed together helter-skelter.

She pushed the wooden door open, and it squeaked from its rusty hinges.

But it was warm inside.

The girl dropped Betty near the pot-bellied stove in the center of the room.

Betty lay deathly still and unconscious.

An older Mexican woman stood over her as she and the girl conversed in Spanish.

The woman reached down and snatched the rings off Betty's fingers, and slipped the watch, bracelets, and earrings from Betty's lifeless body.

Betty never moved.

Her breathing never increased.

The young girl stared at Betty curiously, then removed Betty's expensive tennis shoes.

She sat Indian style with her legs crossed and tried on Betty's shoes.

Her face beamed at the old woman; the shoes fit.

More conversation ensued between the two in Spanish.

The older woman nodded curtly at the young girl.

She argued but picked up the flashlight and headed back outside.

Betty never woke up.

The coyotes howled more often, and the young girl soon returned unharmed from finding Betty's purse.

She handed it over to her elder.

The woman held her hand in the air toward Betty.

"Mucho caliente!"

And the young girl backed away.

"Too hot…" She spoke the English words, and nodded climbing onto her cot to sleep for the night.

Betty wasn't aware of her raging fever.

And the elderly woman dumped everything out of the purse… onto the dirt floor…

Laughing… as she sorted through the cash and the credit cards.

Chapter Twenty-Six

Ella and Sam arrived in Dallas without making reservations at a hotel.

Both were too rattled about Jack to plan for a hotel. They simply packed their suitcases and drove off.

Of course, Sam had his belongings with him as he'd recently gathered them from Lucille's home.

There wasn't much for him to pack.

But they were both under a lot of emotional stress.

Indeed, it was shocking to learn Jack Rogan was arrested for arson for burning Sam Baldwin's home.

"Jack Rogan. Why would he want to destroy my house? It doesn't make sense." Sam exclaimed for the hundredth time.

"I don't see him doing it, Sam. That's not the Jack Rogan I know." Ella replied matter-of-factly.

They drove into the circle-driven entrance to a major hotel.

Sam hopped out of his vehicle and went inside to register. He'd settled the issue earlier that he'd pay for both of their rooms.

Ella sat compliantly in his truck.

Waiting.

And noticed the television news van from Longview, Texas in the adjacent parking lot.

She scooted down in the seat trying not to be recognized by the crew.

Sam came whistling back to the truck and the news team all turned in his direction and called out to him.

"Sam Baldwin! Can I have a word with you, sir?" One woman yelled.

Sam looked wide eyed, climbed in and drove out of the parking lot.

"Man! What are they doing here? And they spotted us!" He groaned.

"I guess they're here for the same reason we are; Jack Rogan."

"We just got here, and I'm already sick of hearing about Jack Rogan!" Sam uttered.

And so it began.

The race was on. The news van followed discreetly behind Sam's truck.

"Guess we'll be on television today…" Sam said with disgust.

Ella bit her bottom lip.

"I almost don't care anymore." She breathed, "but I'm glad we're going to see Jack."

"He ought to be glad he's got Ted representing him."

Ella wound a loose strand of hair around her finger.

Obviously lost in thought, she stared out the window as they passed by various buildings.

The blank expression on her face grew pale.

"Ella?"

"Hmm?"

"Where are you?" Sam teased.

"Oh, I keep trying to figure out how Jack got in this mess."

"Hopefully we'll know soon…if Ted lets him tell us…"

"Well, we both know they only let one person in at a time, and I intend to ask him when it's my turn..." She grimaced.

He zipped through the traffic and parked his truck near the courthouse steps.

"Ready?"

"Ready."

Ella walked hand in hand with Sam up the crowded steps of the Dallas County, Texas Courthouse.

And it was crowded.

The television crew wasted no time in setting up their equipment.

They were filming Sam and Ella as they continued walking up the steps.

Some in the crowd started making loud remarks to Sam.

"Hey, lawyer! Did you pay your lawyer friend to burn your house?"

Another yelled, "Getting some good insurance money, huh?" He laughed as did others in the crowd.

Sam kept his mouth closed, but his other hand drew into a fist.

Ella squeezed his hand that she was holding onto.

They didn't speak, simply stared straight ahead pushing forward.

Then someone else shouted rudely at Ella.

"Hey jailbird! They going to arrest you again?"

And Sam marched to the guy, grabbed him by the front of his shirt collar and told him something so low Ella couldn't even hear it.

Then he shoved the guy backwards, leaving him to stumble on the sidewalk.

Sam quietly took Ella's hand again as they calmly walked side by side entering the courthouse.

As soon as the automatic door closed behind them, Sam glanced at Ella.

"We just made the six o'clock news."

She gave a slight smile remaining silent.

They went through the security checkpoint in the hallway and after displaying their identifications immediately passed inspection.

An officer nodded at them that they could pass into the restricted area. They took the elevator to the fourth floor where prisoners were kept in jail.

They signed in at the desk and waited for their turn to visit Jack.

"Excuse me, officer?" Sam began. "Do you know if Ted Davis is here with Jack Rogan? If he is, we'd like to talk to Ted first. He's Jack's attorney."

The officer nodded at Sam. "I'll see what I can find out."

He went in a different direction and returned with another officer.

"You are wanting to speak to the attorney, Ted Davis?"

"Yes, sir. We both are. He's a friend of ours."

"Tell me your names and I'll see he gets the message."

"Thank you, I'm Sam Baldwin, and ..."

Ella interrupted, "And I'm Ella Reed."

Both officers left.

They sat and waited for over twenty minutes.

At first, Ella attempted to say something to Sam, but he put his finger in front of his mouth.

Cameras were everywhere for security purposes but neither wanted their conversations recorded.

So, they each looked around, looked at the ceiling, quietly counted tiles on the floor, etc. but did not talk to each other.

No privacy.

No conversation.

They did smile at each other.

And finally, they heard footsteps on the tile hallway coming closer to them.

It was Ted.

Sam stood and shook his hand.

Ella breathed a sigh of relief.

"Hope you didn't have to wait long. It's a mess up here." Ted blurted.

"Oh, it wasn't bad." Sam replied.

Ella smiled and looked tired.

"Is there somewhere we can talk?" Sam raised his head toward the cameras.

"Yes, follow me. We can talk in the hallway."

They plodded down the hallway for a good distance, when Ted stopped and leaned against the wall.

He searched their faces as he spoke.

"Jack desperately wants to talk to you, Sam, and let you know… contrary to evidence, he did not do it. And Ella, he wants time to explain to you how this came about in the first place."

They glanced at each other as Ted continued.

"As his attorney, I cannot say what my client has discussed with me, I mean…you both know that…but as your friend…I can tell you…after talking to Jack you will leave here with a different perspective."

He briefly smiled. "Who wants to go first?"

Sam frowned. "Well, I …I don't really know him. And he was Ella's attorney."

Raising his eyebrows, he gazed at Ella expectantly.

"I'll go first." She uttered.

"Follow me." Ted instructed.

They returned to the lobby as Ted arranged with a guard for Ella to visit Jack.

Sam found an empty chair in the room and plopped into it.

Ella left with the guard and Ted.

After walking through hallways, they had to wait to enter massive, locked doors made of steel bars. The clang of them opening echoed about, as they were allowed to enter…and promptly slammed closed behind them.

It made Ella shutter.

The realization of being locked behind these metal bars…totally confined… was mind-boggling…and brought back memories of her own time in jail.

Ella took a deep breath as they entered a room where Jack sat at a table behind a glass wall.

Sitting down across the glass partition from him, Ted and Ella grabbed headphones to talk to him.

Ella's face was etched with worry. Jack had aged the short time he'd been in jail. He looked pale and sickly.

And looking at him made Ella feel sick…at the situation he was stuck in.

Jack tried to smile at Ella, but his mouth just trembled. "Ella, thanks for coming. You don't know what this means to me! I have so much to explain to you…"

"Jack…you don't owe me anything. I want you to know that. Sam and I have been going together for a while. We make a great couple. I am here as your friend."

She let out a long breath and continued. "I can't believe you are even here, much less what you were arrested for."

"I did not do arson. You must believe me."

"Then what happened? It's all over the TV. You are shown on cameras buying the gas can and then buying the gas for it…all within thirty minutes before the fire started…"

He sucked in his breath. "It was Betty…Sam's sister…"

Ella's eyes widened as she gasped.

"Betty? How…how do you even know her?"

He ran his hand through his hair with a sound of defeat on his face.

"She was the one I fixed a flat tire for…remember I was late coming to your house…I told you I helped a lady…"

"Yes, I remember…but you didn't help a lady, Jack…you helped a witch!"

"I didn't know! I knew nothing about her. She was just stranded on the side of the road waving for help."

"And naturally you helped…but going to Sam's house with the gas can later…I don't understand…?" Ella's voice rose angrily.

Ted interrupted.

"Jack, be careful. If the prosecutor questions Ella, she cannot lie when answering."

Jack put both hands over his eyes and rubbed them over his whole face.

He exhaled noisily.

And looked at Ella completely drained and slumped in his chair.

"Yes, we exchanged phone numbers. She was…mesmerizing…I'd never had a woman come onto me like that…all sugar and spice…"

"And you fell for it…"

"Hook, line, and sinker."

He couldn't look Ella in the eye. Finally, he continued, raising his head in agony to look at her.

"Now, I know she was using me. I was the scrape goat…her scape goat. And I wouldn't have known what to do… had I known then… that she was a witch! It could have been so much worse!"

Ella bit her bottom lip frowning at Jack.

"Superficial…that's also what she is…" He shook his head. "I'll never get taken in by a pretty face and sweet talk again!" He blurted.

He slumped in his chair totally worn out.

"And she could put curses on me… or my family…and my future children! She may already have! She's still out there somewhere, Ella…I don't know how to stop her witchcraft against me…"

He appeared drained of energy.

No hope of any kind.

Defeated.

Ella's face etched with concern.

"Jack, you once told me you didn't have friends who cared about you…well…as a friend that does care…can I pray for you?"

He raised his head as a look of surprise flashed across his face.

"Yes." He spoke humbly.

Ella smiled at him and began praying.

"Heavenly Father, I lift up Jack Rogan to you for healing, protection, and comfort; and I stand on Your Word in Isaiah 54:17 'No weapon formed against you shall prosper; and every tongue that shall rise against you in judgement you shall condemn. This is the heritage of the servants of the LORD, and their righteousness is of ME, saith the LORD.' And Heavenly Father, I pray for spiritual warfare against all principalities Betty may have sent for evil to Jack or any curses, or generational curses to him or his family or friends, or future family. I pray Your Word in Psalm 91 over Jack for protection as man cannot fight evil alone. In the powerful, Holy name of Jesus Christ I pray; Satan get thee hence from Jack Rogan and all that is his. I pray to the God of Abraham, Issac, and Jacob to strengthen Jack's walk with You, to give him a hunger for Your Word, for him to want forgiveness of his sins, to want to repent, and chose You as his

Lord and Savior and to be a light to others for You. In Jesus Christ Holy name I pray, Amen."

"Amen." Jack and Ted both replied.

"Thank you." Jack exhaled in relief.

"Ella, could you bring me a Bible tomorrow? I'm going to need it!" He looked at her and smiled for the first time.

Ted interrupted.

"I'll bring you one when I return this evening. A study Bible that explains everything."

"Thanks, Ted!"

Ella leaned toward the glass partition. "Read Psalm 91, and all of Ephesians Chapter Six when you get it. And I'm very sorry for you, Jack. I honestly feel like you didn't deserve any of this. You just happened to stop to help someone on the road…maybe next time do not stop…simply call 911 and let the police help her."

"Oh, believe me I will. You can't trust anyone anymore…people are too crooked now-a-days.

Besides you could get robbed or hit in the head…it's not worth it…just not worth it…" He groaned.

Ella continued but spoke in a light tone. "I don't need to know any of the other details, Jack. Save that information for court. You have told me enough that I know she took advantage of you. It just happened you were the one who stopped to help her. The same thing could have happened to whoever stopped…not just you."

Jack hung his head.

Ted frowned at Ella.

"He can't share a lot with anyone right now. Sometimes you are better off not knowing all the details. An investigation is ongoing now, and there will be a trial."

Jack raised his head and stared at Ella with watered eyes. "Tell Sam I am sorry about him losing his house. Tell him I did not do it. Tell him Betty had to have done it…I supplied her with what she needed …supposedly to travel to Mexico with extra gas…that is what I was told…and then I drove off to Dallas."

"So, you weren't there at Sam's house when it was burning?"

"No, Ella, I was not."

A guard arrived and in a monotone voice addressed Ted and Ella. "Your time is up. You have to go."

Ted looked at Jack. "I'll be back this afternoon."

Jack nodded.

Ella blew him a kiss. "That's what a friend does in a situation like this…and I am still your friend." She smiled. "Hang in there and we'll all be praying this is over soon!"

She and Ted stood and removed the headphones.

They waved goodbye to Jack and silently returned to Sam.

Chapter Twenty-Seven

Betty moaned. She lay with her mouth wide open.

It was dry.

Slowly moving her tongue across the roof of her mouth, she felt the rough tiny bumps covering the inside of her entire dry mouth.

"*How long have I laid here?*" She managed to think coherently.

She tried to swallow.

And it hurt.

Everything hurt.

Her whole body throbbed in pain.

Even her eyes ached.

Struggling to open them, her eyelids felt weighed down with tremendous heaviness…and all she could manage was barely opening a tiny slit to see out of.

And everything was blurry.

She blinked excessively until her vision began to clear.

And the utter nastiness of the room she was in…made her gag.

Molded food lay abandoned on paper plates stacked high and placed on the dirt floor…roaches scurried amongst the plates as Betty gaged again.

It was a stench of rotted food mingled with the musty, damp dirt floor.

And something else she couldn't identify.

Nothing was kept in any kind of order.

No place to sit or sleep…except the floor.

And no one was with her.

She tried to raise onto her elbow…groaning out loud.

And forced herself to drag her legs toward the door.

A few feet at a time.

Painful progress…she continued as tears flowed down her face.

And she kept pushing her elbows forward, in more of a crawling effort now instead of dragging her legs.

Her knees were working…moving her along.

And she sobbed.

It hurt worse than anything she'd ever experienced.

She noticed the bruises on her legs and lacerations…many still bleeding…some scabbed over.

And no knowledge how her skin became so ripped open and bruised.

She made it to the door and collapsed in sheer exhaustion.

Taking a few breaths, she pulled herself off the floor, clutched the door handle, and shoved the door open.

And collapsed again.

But she was outside.

She made it.

This time she got on her knees and elbows, at first rocking back and forth, and then moaning in pain… she crawled on all fours and left the wooden shack behind her.

She fell often.

But she kept going.

Finally, she crawled into an area covered in brush and laid there to rest.

She sprawled out on her back and lay still.

And heard something.

Hard to distinguish.

She gazed up at the sky and saw where the sound came from.

Buzzards.

Over a hundred of them perched high in the treetops, scattered on the highest branches. Many were circling high above her.

When one of them would flap its wings to fly, still perched on a tree branch…it sounded like someone dropped a heavy, bushel basket of wet dirt onto the ground below the tree. Loud enough to notice.

And Betty noticed.

More buzzards took off in flight…only to join those circling above her.

Soaring higher and higher.. yet still above where she lay on the ground.

She struggled to crawl, and pain shot through her body like lightning.

Then a low train whistle sounded in the distance.

"It sounds so bleak and lonesome. Like someone hurrying to get away from this part of Texas and to a more populated place…"

She scanned the area and saw how frightening the land could be.

Total isolation.

She bit the inside of her cheek and rubbed her tongue over it.

"Think…try to think…"

She positioned herself to crawl again, and moaned as her knee scraped against a small, jagged rock.

But she advanced to a clearing before collapsing face first into the dirt.

And couldn't move.

"Plan…think of a plan…"

Her mind thrust out ideas in bits and pieces.

And exhaustion overcame her.

She closed her eyes and fell into a deep sleep.

And later still, a Kansas City Southern train went by close to where she lay.

But she didn't know it.

She couldn't even hear it.

The conductor happened to stare out across the flat country from his one window in the engine car, and frowned.

His train raced on by, but he gasped to himself in shock.

"I know I saw a body lying in the dirt!" He uttered to himself. "I know I did!"

He called in the exact location of the body and gave the report to the local authorities and to his supervisor.

And Betty slept.

Information was wired to the nearest Sherrif's department, and within an hour Deputy Hines arrived on the scene.

He smelt the shack before discovering it.

And it was putrid.

He secured the area before entering it and poked around with a stick into all the piles of debris cluttered about the floor.

And then he spotted it.

Betty's purse.

Empty, except for some tarot cards and a wicca card displaying a ten percent discount code for purchasing supplies for spells and curses.

He shuttered looking at it.

"So, what's going on here?" He asked himself out loud.

"No I.D., no credit cards, no cash…and no one to go with this purse…"

He snapped on his plastic gloves, placed the items in a sealed plastic bag, and left the shack.

And walked.

And noticed a trail that slithered through the dirt and brushes.

And found Betty.

Wide eyed, he knelt beside her placing his two forefingers against her throat.

And felt a pulse.

He radioed it in, asking for assistance, and for an ambulance.

Almost dead, Betty was immediately driven to a local hospital.

She remained drowsy and couldn't talk.

Besides the numerous cuts, and bruises, Betty also had sepsis.

Unfortunately, her right arm had to be amputated.

The doctor insisted a television be played in her room day and night to help wake her completely.

And to be played at a higher level than normal. He wanted it to catch her attention.

"She needs to hear people talking. There is no telling how long she was abused, or what trauma she endured."

They referred to her as Jane Doe.

Meanwhile, the investigation of Betty Baldwin quickly expanded with many organizations assisting.

East Mountain Fire Department, East Mountain Police Department, The Texas Rangers, and the Federal Bureau of Investigation pooled their resources, and worked as a well-oiled machine together.

Through their combined efforts it was discovered that Betty Baldwin did travel across the border into Mexico, and that she did so… hours after the fire was started.

In fact, the exact number of hours it would have taken her to drive to Mexico from when East

Mountain's reported arson fire began…is the exact time she legally entered a checkpoint to walk across.

No confirmation on her leaving Mexico though.

No documentation.

An APB (All Points Bulletin) and a BOLO (Be On the Look Out) were both issued with the description of Betty's car. She was also wanted as a Person of Interest.

The doctor made his morning rounds and entered Betty's room to check on her progress.

The television was still playing, and the sound level was still louder than normal.

He approached the side of her bed and addressed her.

"Good morning, ma'am!"

Betty slowly blinked her eyes and cautiously opened them.

"I'm glad you're waking up! You've been resting for a while." He happily announced.

Her eyes raised to the television set mounted on the wall over the doctor's head.

A news program was being aired, showing a man and a woman walking up the steps at a courthouse.

"…Ella Reed and Sam Baldwin arrived to visit the man arrested for the act of arson of Sam Baldwin's home…" The news anchor excitedly announced.

And Betty raised her finger at the television set.

"Bro…bro…"

"What is it, what are you trying to say?" The doctor asked her.

"Bro… bro…ther…" she managed to whisper.

The doctor stared at her with an incredible look of amazement.

"Is that your brother?"

She nodded in a yes motion and collapsed.

The doctor called for a nurse to stay with her.

He hurried to his office and made a private call to 911.

"911, What is your emergency?"

"This is Dr. Craighton. My Jane Doe patient just identified herself. I need the Sherrif at once. I'm at Hernandez Hospital, and I think this may be the woman you were all looking for."

"Yes sir. I'll relay the message right away and thank you for calling."

"Thank you."

His voice trembled, and he realized sweat had formed on his forehead.

He opened his small office refrigerator and grabbed an ice-cold bottle of water. He sank into his chair and took a long gulp of water and stared into space.

"That's her! I can't believe it! All the time I've spent alone with her in her room…and who knows what she was capable of doing…or if she was pretending to be asleep…" He spoke in amazement thinking out loud about his patient.

And flinched involuntarily.

Sam rolled over in bed and ignored the constant ringing of his phone.

He glanced at the time, 5 AM, and frowned grabbing his phone.

"Hello?" His rough voice bellowed.

"Mr. Baldwin? Sam Baldwin?"

"Ehh, who's calling?"

"This is Deputy Hines with the Val Verde County Sheriff's Department in Del Rio, Texas."

"Yes sir, what can I do for you?" Sam Baldwin.

"Well sir, this is an urgent call, but we have located your sister."

"What?" Sam shouted and sat up in bed.

"She's in the hospital and not doing well. I'd suggest you come as soon as possible. She is a person of interest in the arson case of your home. I assumed you'd want to be aware of that."

Chapter Twenty-Eight

Sam rolled over in bed and ignored the constant ringing of his phone.

He glanced at the time; 8 AM, and frowned grabbing his phone.

“Hello?” His rough voice bellowed.

“Mr. Baldwin? Sam Baldwin?”

“Uh…who’s calling?”

“This is Deputy Hines with the Val Verde County Sheriff’s Department in Del Rio, Texas.”

“Yes sir, what can I do for you? I am Sam Baldwin.”

“Well, sir this is an unusual call, but we have located your sister.”

“What?” Sam shouted and sat up in bed.

“She’s in the hospital and not doing well. I’d suggest you come as soon as possible. She is a person of interest in the arson case of your home. I wanted you to be aware of that.”

"Oh. I am aware. It's all over the news."

"I … uh…need to prepare you, sir. We don't know everything that's happened to her. She can hardly talk, and she's extremely weak…her arm has been amputated…"

Sam sat in silence. The words refused to settle.

"Thank you, officer. I'll leave right away."

He fell back across the bed.

"Wow!"

His mind whirled at the news and he immediately phoned Ella.

"Hey, good morning. I know it's early, but we need to talk."

"What's going on, Sam?" Ella sounded alarmed.

"They found Betty in a hospital in Del Rio. I'm fixing to drive there right now. Do you want to go? I hope you do. I don't think I can handle being civil to her by myself."

"Of course, I'll go. It won't take me long to pack."

"Thanks! I'll do the same. I'll knock on your door when I'm ready."

"Ok." She ended the call and hurried to dress for the day.

Packing didn't take long for either one of them.

Sam soon banged on her door, and they darted off to turn their keys in at the main desk in the lobby.

Sam paid for their rooms quietly.

Loading their belongings into the back seat, he seemed preoccupied.

He did turn and smile at Ella as they drove off in his truck.

A firm believer in preventive maintenance, Sam drove to a gas station, filled the tank, and checked the air pressure in the tires.

Again, he went through the motions almost mechanically. Cleaning his windshield, selecting Del Rio, Texas as his destination on the GPS, and finding a radio station there as well.

"Hungry?" He turned to Ella.

"No, but coffee would be wonderful." She yawned.

He nodded and drove through morning traffic in Dallas to a drive-through coffee shop. They loaded up with coffee, pastries, and egg and cheese croissants.

Both put their sunglasses on as the morning glare was intense.

Spanish music played merrily from the radio with a lively Mariachi band.

Sam tapped his fingers in time with the beat on the steering wheel.

Ella hummed along, and looked at Sam.

"It's still hard to realize why we're going to Del Rio, Texas. I can't help but wonder how Betty ended up there…" Ella muttered.

"I know…and with an arm amputated…" Sam's voice trailed off.

"That's so horrible! What caused that? And what about her car?"

"I don't know. I hope to get more information when we arrive…if it doesn't compromise their case in court…"

Ella's phone rang and she glanced at the caller I.D.

"It's Lucille. Can I tell her about Betty?"

"Sure. And tell her where we're going."

Ella nodded and answered the phone.

"Hi Lucille! I'm here with Sam, I'll put you on speaker phone."

"Oh, okay. Hi Sam!"

"Hi Lucille. How are you doing?" Sam inquired.

"Much better, now. Thank you!"

"Well, that is good news, Lucille. Glad you are getting back to normal." Ella assured her.

"Yes, I can even drive my car now. Frank is a big help, and I am so thankful for him, but it's so nice to just get up and go without asking someone to take you someplace."

"I can imagine!" Ella blurted.

"Frank calls every day to check on me; he is so thoughtful."

"That is a blessing." Ella replied. "And you are too. It's good to have friends to talk to…" Ella's voice choked up.

"Ella, it sounds like I called at the right time. Are you okay? Can I help with anything?"

Ella cleared her throat.

"I didn't mean to get emotional." Ella laughed. "I'm still waking up, still having morning coffee."

Lucille hesitated. "I'm sure seeing Jack in a Dallas jail was traumatic…Ted told me some of the details…what little he was allowed to discuss."

"It seemed surreal."

"It's so out of character for Jack…of all people…to be arrested for arson!"

"I agree, Lucille."

"Something else seems surreal, Lucille…" Sam interrupted.

"What?" She cautiously asked.

"I'll let Ella fill you in on the latest. Traffic is picking up and I'm driving."

"Sam, you're driving right now?"

Ella answered. "He is, Lucille. We're on our way to Del Rio, Texas and…"

"Del Rio, Texas!" She exclaimed.

"Yes. Betty has been located there."

"Betty? As in tarot reading, witchcraft Betty? And I'm sorry, Sam, but that was her decision to leave Jesus Christ and join the devil and his ways…"

"It's okay, Lucille. Ted and Ella told me what they witnessed, and what you and Frank saw at that fundraiser…" Sam stated.

"And when you stop following God's commandments…what exactly is left? I'll tell you what is left…lawlessness and chaos!" Ella chimed in. "And I intend to pray for her if I see her."

Sam jerked his head toward Ella. "You are?"

"Oh, yes, I am."

"Thank you… Ella." His voice broke.

"Oh, Sam…I don't intend to beat her up with a proverbial baseball bat in talking to her. I'll be gentle, but I will point out it's either Heaven or Hell. Her decision." Ella added.

"Please be careful around her!" Lucille cautioned.

"I'm praying about it." Ella sighed.

"And I'll be praying for all of you. I heard what happened to your white picket fence at your house…"

"Yeah, I didn't have time to paint over the graffiti before we left for Dallas."

"Local talk about it should stop any future vandalism. So many are watching your house…just wanting to catch someone trying to do that again!"

"It was kind of funny. 'Yankee Go Home 'spray painted red on my white wooden fence…and the farthest north I've ever been is Dallas!" Ella chuckled.

"The mayor of East Mountain is embarrassed about it. He said in an interview you have always been an asset to the community."

"How nice, I didn't know that!"

"Frank reads every word in the newspaper." Lucille confided. "And Ted tells me whatever it is that happened after it's all over with…just facts…no gossip. It's better that way. Keeps you safe and alert to any potential future crime."

"Yes, and I take it Ted is going to be in Dallas for a while."

"He is. Maybe finding Betty can shed some light on Jack's situation."

"Maybe so, time will tell." Ella replied.

"I'll let you go. You two have so much to talk about. Safe travels to you both!" Lucille added.

"Thanks, I'll call you later."

Ella ended the call and rubbed her hand across the back of her neck.

"I hope they let us go into Betty's room at the same time…"

"I'll insist." Sam smiled for the first time all day.

They later stopped at a local restaurant featuring home cooked lunch specials and ate their fill.

And continued driving.

Ella's phone rang again.

Caller Id displayed Lucille.

"Lucille?" Ella answered surprised.

"Hey, Ella. I told Frank you were gone, and he wants to paint your fence, it that's okay?"

"Okay? I'd love it! Tell him that will be so nice to see the graffiti gone!"

"Alright then, he said he'll start tomorrow."

"Tell him, I appreciate it! And thanks so much!"

"I will. Take care!"

"You too!" Ella ended the call and smiled at their thoughtfulness. She glanced at Sam.

"That was Lucille. Frank is going to paint my fence tomorrow."

"They are such good people! We'll have to take them out to dinner sometime."

"Yes, good idea."

Dusk fell with them still hours away from their destination.

Sam glanced at Ella. Softly snoring, she slumped against the seat and slept peacefully.

And it caught up with Sam…he was exhausted from the long drive.

Stopping to get out and walking around stretching helped some, but he needed sleep.

No motels in sight.

Nothing.

He slowly exited the highway and pulled into an eighteen-wheeler rest area.

It was well lit and had restrooms.

Parking directly under a security flood light, he locked the truck and eased into as comfortable position as he could manage.

And set his alarm on his phone for three in the morning.

Sleep came instantly.

No one bothered them.

And if anyone else pulled into the rest area, he certainly wouldn't know.

The 3 AM alarm was startling! Both Sam and Ella jerked awake and yawned.

Ella looked bug-eyed out the window, and Sam grinned.

"We're at a rest area. I got a few hours of sleep."

She nodded, trying to go back to sleep.

"Hey, we're fixing to leave. Come on and wake up. I'll walk you to the restroom and then we'll be on our way."

"Okay."

"Let me go in first to check it out. Don't want a homeless person in there sleeping and scaring the socks off of you!"

Her sleepy eyes grew bug-eyed again.

Sam walked into the restroom, found no one there, then stood outside while she entered it.

When she returned, he went into the men's restroom, and they soon left.

The night was cool and brisk. They strolled back to the parking lot, and Sam squeezed her hand.

"Thanks for coming with me."

"I wouldn't have missed it for anything." She smiled as they climbed into the truck.

Both remained quiet, obviously lost in their own thoughts, for the remainder of the trip.

Traffic increased the closer they approached Del Rio.

"Busy place." Ella mentioned.

"Indeed." Sam agreed as several vehicles raced past them at an excessive speed.

"We'll be at the hospital within thirty minutes."

"Maybe those people had an emergency…" Ella guessed.

"Could be… I sure can't picture someone being that anxious to get to work early!"

They both laughed and continued watching the traffic.

The exit for the hospital loomed ahead.

Sam eased the truck across an adjoining lane and took the exit.

It must have been a regular shift change at the hospital as many uniformed employees dashed across the parking lot.

Sam dodged them and parked close to the main entrance.

He and Ella exited the vehicle and nodded at the people hurrying towards the hospital doors.

He reached down interlacing his fingers with hers, and they walked in holding hands.

It was a massive hospital.

Sam and Ella both viewed its list of impressive physicians and physical therapists.

And it gleamed…shiny and clean!

They both looked tired as they approached the desk.

"May I help you?" A woman asked.

"I hope so. I'm Sam Baldwin, and we're here to see my sister, Betty Baldwin."

She scanned a clipboard and quickly entered something on her computer.

"Just a moment, sir. Someone will be here to assist you shortly." She smiled.

Antiseptic cleanser wafted through the air, and Ella recognized just a hint of orange mixed into the solution.

She'd encountered that smell at some of the best convalescent facilities in Marshall, Texas from years ago.

Back in her younger years.

As a student learning life…before Med School.

Before her family moved to Minden, Louisiana.

Ella and some of her church members would visit there and sing gospel hymns to the residents.

She smiled at the memories flashing across her mind and savored the smell of cleanliness.

Two police officers advanced towards Sam, and she felt uneasy for the first time.

Talking about Betty was one thing, about to be face to face with her was another.

Sam was reserved and polite.

"Mr. Baldwin?"

"Yes."

"I'm Nestor Santos, and this is my partner, Joe Wallace. We're Texas Rangers assigned to the arson case."

Sam extended his hand and shook theirs.

"My pleasure to meet you both."

"We will record all conversations with your sister. They will be used in court."

He turned to address Ella.

"And you are?"

"I'm Ella Reed, a friend of Sam's. I'd like to pray for her…" Ella left the idea hanging in midair.

"That can be arranged. If you two will follow us…"

He motioned down the long hallway, and Sam nodded.

The Texas Rangers walked side by side, and they spoke in low tones to each other.

Sam and Ella remained silent and were directly behind them.

The Rangers wore handsome cowboy boots that Ella recognized as some of the best handmade boots in Texas. Each step they took echoed on the tile floor, and Ella noticed how spotless the boots were.

Upon arriving at Betty's room, Ella sucked in her breath, obviously shocked by what she saw.

Another officer stood guard in front of the door.

A sign was displayed, "No Entry Allowed Unless accompanied by a Law Enforcement Officer."

Ella and Sam entered after the officers.

And stared at something lying on the bed.

Pale.

Ghostly white.

It should have been Betty.

They were expecting to see Betty.

But it was a multitude of bandages with Betty inside them.

Sam approached the side of her bed first.

And looked down at her.

She struggled to open her eyes and blinked at him.

Neither spoke.

With a restless stance, he stared directly at her.

"Are you playing the blame game again?"

She shifted her position in bed and turned to stare at the wall.

Sam continued.

"Those toxic people you chose to keep in your life…how's that working for you now?"

She whimpered.

"You are so deceived, Betty. I pray you choose Heaven and leave the Hell you're in."

He choked on his last words and quickly walked away.

Ella wiped tears from her eyes and leaned over the bed.

All she could see was the back of Betty's head.

Her hair was tangled.

Her small frame appeared so fragile and weak.

"Betty…" Ella whispered.

"Betty, you don't know me. I'm Ella Reed, and I'm going to pray for you."

Betty lay motionless.

Ella placed her hand lightly onto Betty's hair.

A low, guttural growl emitted from Betty's form.

Ella knew her spirit was battling with Betty's evil spirit and spoke firmly.

"Get thee hence, Satan; in the powerful, Holy name of Jesus Christ I pray! Amen!"

Betty's body seemed to sag deeper into the mattress as she took a slight breath.

Ella continued in a soothing voice.

"Betty…Betty, if you want to repent and ask for forgiveness, you can do that now."

Betty slowly turned to face Ella.

"Yes, please." She uttered, barely audible.

Ella bent closer to Betty and held both of her hands.

"Heavenly Father, I lift up Betty Baldwin in prayer for healing and comfort…and pray for her forgiveness."

"Yes, please forgive me…" Betty cried.

"I pray she wants to accept Jesus Christ as her Lord and Savior…"

"Yes, I do…"

"She repents and wants to follow Your ways…"

"Oh yes, I do…" She moaned.

"We pray to the God of Abraham, Issac, and Jacob in the powerful, precious, Holy name of Jesus Christ, Amen!"

"Amen…" she whispered.

Tears rolled down her face, and she scanned the room with weary eyes.

"Sam. Sam, come here." She managed to speak with shallow breaths.

He raised an eyebrow and stepped towards the head of the bed.

The Texas Rangers moved closer as they kept recording both audio and visual.

The air in the room seemed oppressive as the sounds of life saving machines intensified.

"I…I'm sorry…" Betty mumbled.

Everyone in the room strained to hear her.

Ella rubbed her hand over the top of Betty's.

"I… did it…I burnt your house…" Her body shook uncontrollably with sobs.

Sam gazed at her wide-eyed.

One of the Texas Rangers, Joe Wallace, instantly asked her, "And Jack Rogan, did he have anything to do with it?"

"No." She whimpered. "He never knew what I was doing."

Both Rangers exchanged a brief look at each other.

They had their confession.

Ella glanced at Sam.

The earnest prayer had saved Betty's soul.

His eyes watered as he swallowed hard.

"Betty, I…I forgive you." He told her.

She managed to smile and nod at her brother.

And Ella felt Betty's frail grasp of her hand release.

It lay at her side, and she became stark white.

Imperfections on her hand disappeared, even her blood veins could not be seen as blue or purple…all became completely white.

Betty had taken her last breath as a relaxed sigh.

Sam pressed the nurse's call button.

"Yes?" A curt monotone voice rang through the room.

"She has passed away. She's dead."

"I'm so sorry, sir. I'll send the doctor."

Within seconds, a doctor arrived and rushed to Betty. Immediately, he felt for a pulse.

Placing his stethoscope against her heart, he solemnly listened.

And instantly stared at the wall clock. "8:30 AM time of death."

No one spoke.

He pulled his glasses down and looked over his rims at the four people in the room.

"She had developed sepsis. Her arm was just the beginning of further amputations. I've never seen so many red streaks surrounding the awful rips and tears on her skin." He briefly paused and then continued.

"I understand she was found on a dirt floor…she must have been dragged across the dirt, and across rocks, tree branches, thorn bushes, and who knows what else growing in that filthy environment."

He paused again. "It is a blessing she doesn't have to endure this anymore."

Sam wiped his eyes. "Yes, it is." He paused, "And I'll make arrangements for her funeral."

The doctor grabbed the sheet on her lower body and pulled it over her head.

"Gentlemen, you can take pictures but then you must leave."

He pivoted to Sam.

"The Administration Office will take your information, sir, ma'am." He gazed at both Sam and Ella and attempted a brief smile.

Walking towards the door, he nodded at the Texas Rangers and quietly left.

Sam turned to the Rangers.

"Was she audible? Could you hear what she was saying?"

"Yes," Ranger Wallace answered. "We got everything on tape. She admitted guilt. The tape will be viewed by countless people of authority. It's a matter of time before the press gets word of it. Of course, it will be all over the news then."

Ranger Santos added." And… they will probably edit what she says or doesn't say; but we have the original recording…the one that counts."

Sam looked at Ella. "I'm glad we got here when we did."

Ella smiled. "Me too. I am so relieved she prayed with me and wanted to!"

Ranger Wallace continued speaking…

"And Jack Rogan will be released…he'll be a free man again."

Chapter Twenty-Nine

Ted's appointment to interview Ms. P. J. Montgomery was about to be history.

She was late.

And his law office wasn't that hard to locate in Dallas.

He glanced at her resume' for the third time.

Studied the newspaper clippings again.

Her references had checked out extremely well.

So where was she?

Ted rose from his chair and walked to the window.

"Hmm…" He frowned as a crowd gathered outside his office building.

"What's going on?" He muttered to himself.

Ms. P. J. Montgomery jerked the door open suddenly and burst into the room…turning to lock it behind her.

Out of breath, she pivoted and noticed Ted Davis's eyes narrowing as he scrutinized her.

Neither smiled.

She tossed her long brown hair back over her shoulder and exhaled loudly.

"What is happening out there? I almost couldn't get through them. I had to push my way up the steps and even push people out of my way to open the door!"

Ted shook his head.

"Please have a seat. I have no clue what that was about."

She sat in a chair in front of his desk.

He returned to his chair behind the desk.

And they briefly sized each other up…both quiet and both equally solemn.

Ted reached his hand out to her.

"I'm Ted Davis."

"Oh my gosh! You are the man I have the interview with!" She gasped and limply shook his hand.

"And you must be Ms. P. J. Montgomery."

"Yes…yes sir, I am. And I apologize for busting into your office, but I had no choice! It was total chaos out there."

"Yes, I can see it is. Believe me I don't know why."

She nodded.

"So, let's get on with the interview, shall we?"

"Oh yes, of course."

"Tell me, what does the P. J. stand for?"

Her face flushed crimson red and she hesitated.

"Well, sir, I was given a name at birth that I do not like, so I prefer to go by the initials."

He raised his eyebrows and nodded.

"That's understandable. And I am impressed with your work ethic and skills. However, if we are to work together, I need to know who I am talking to."

"Precious Jewel."

Ted could not hide the instant smile that flashed across his face.

"Thank you for that, and Ms. P.J. Montgomery it will be."

"Thank you, sir…does that mean…?

"That you are hired? Yes ma'am! Anyone who can rock an interview with that kind of entrance deserves to be hired!"

They both laughed.

He handed her a contract.

"This explains the pay rate and your duties. If agreeable, sign and I'll keep the original and give you the copy."

She took her time and did read all of the contract.

And signed it.

He gave her a copy and smiled.

"Welcome aboard."

"Thank you! I've heard what an outstanding law practice you have…and I'm happy to be part of it!"

"Good. You can accompany me to the jail to talk with a client. I was about to leave when you arrived."

"I'm so sorry about how that came about..."

He stood and strolled back to the window and gasped out loud.

"Look at that! A news crew is out there filming this very minute! No way are we walking through that mess! Come on. Follow me out the side entrance."

She stood and he handed her a clipboard and pen.

"Hold onto that. You'll need it for notes. I'll get you a smart tablet and phone later today. Let's go."

She hurried behind him and they escaped the crowd.

Safe inside his car, sitting in the back seat, she relaxed for the first time since meeting Ted.

And Ted glanced at her in his rear-view mirror and couldn't help thinking... "*Ms. Montgomery is gorgeous...looks like a professional model...and doesn't even act like it...I can already tell she isn't superficial...actually a very sweet lady...*"

She gazed out the car window at the various buildings; some indicated prosperity, but several were sandwiched in clearly shouting poverty.

Big city downtown.

Like most cities.

The sidewalks were just as crowded as the traffic winding through the streets.

She smiled at the well-manicured sitting areas with benches and assorted large pots of still blooming flowers.

Peaceful.

Calm.

Ted continued to drive.

"I'm sure there is a big difference between Dallas and where you are from…" He remarked.

"Completely! Marietta, Ohio is a college town. Has lots of older historic homes there. Tree lined streets, gift shops, restaurants, hiking trails, boating, water skiing, and it's right on the Ohio River." Her face beamed as she talked about it.

"Sounds charming."

"I think so." She laughed.

He swung the car into a parking space and unbuckled his seat belt.

"Here we are. This is the courthouse and the jail is on the fourth floor."

Ted's phone rang as he opened his car door.

He eased back into the seat and shut the door.

"Hello?"

"Ted? It's Sam. I have a lot to tell you…man I don't know where to start…"

"Is it about this case?"

"Yes, it is."

"Well, hold on. I'll put you on speaker phone. I have a new assistant, and she'll need to hear also."

Ted looked at Ms. Montgomery in the back seat and she nodded, quickly raising her clipboard in the air and sitting it back on her lap.

"Okay." Sam blurted. "Jack is about to be a free man."

"What? How can that be? I'm his lawyer and I haven't heard anything."

"The Texas Rangers are going to fill you in on everything. I just wanted to be the first to tell you since we're friends…"

"Well, I do appreciate that, Sam. What happened?"

"They found Betty. We got to see her before she died. The Texas Rangers were at the hospital with me and Ella…"

He hesitated and took a deep breath, "she confessed she did it. Said Jack knew nothing about it. He wasn't even there when she did it. And they got the confession all on tape."

"Well, Hallelujah! I mean…I'm sorry your sister passed…"

"I know what you mean, Ted. It's okay. I understand. Jack was innocent all along. He'll be released today. I think the Rangers want to talk to you and him together first."

"That explains the crowd gathering outside my office while ago…" He shook his head. "I'm at the courthouse now. Just parked the truck. Thanks, buddy, for calling to tell me. And I'll be praying for you."

Sam choked up. "Okay…and thank you."

Ted ended the call.

He turned to look at Ms. Montgomery and smiled.

"Let's go give Jack Rogan the good news."

They entered the courthouse without any unusual interruptions and checked in at the main entrance.

In the lobby, two Texas Rangers were in deep conversation with a jail Sargent on duty.

One happened to recognize Ted as he walked in with Ms. Montgomery into the lobby.

"There he is, Ted Davis! Just the man we were waiting on."

Ted's eyebrows rose in surprise and he approached them.

"I had no idea you were waiting for me. I recently received a call from a friend informing me of the latest developments…"

"Miscommunication. Sorry, my office was supposed to call you early this morning." He held out his hand and shook Ted's.

"I'm Nestor Santos and this is my partner, Joe Wallace. We're with The Texas Rangers and are assigned to the case."

Ted motioned to his new assistant. "And this is Ms. Montgomery; she is my assistant."

The Sargent joined them.

"I know Ted Davis, but I need to see your I.D. Ms. Montgomery…before you can enter the jail." He smiled.

She retrieved her driver's license and showed it to him.

"You're clear to go."

He left immediately.

Ranger Santos turned to address Ted. "We discovered Betty Baldwin did enter Mexico but not by car. She walked over the border at Eagle Pass…signing in legally. We have no clue how she left. Her documented arrival time matched the duration it would take to drive from Sam's house in East Mountain. She went to a lot of trouble running away from her arson crime scene."

Ranger Wallace added, "However, her car was later found miles away further up the border in Del Rio, Texas…completely stripped out, and apparently, she escaped and was dragged through the surrounding woods. A conductor on the railroad saw her lying in the dirt and reported her. She was in bad shape…to put it mildly."

"And at the hospital in Del Rio, Texas she confessed to her crime, and it is recorded. She succumbed to her injuries after that." Ranger Santos noted.

Ted looked at the Rangers and shook his head.

"Thank God she was discovered before she passed away. My client was innocent but had all the evidence against him." He frowned and drew his mouth into a straight line. "Betty Baldwin set him up to take the blame…and she committed the arson…"

Still shaking his head, Ted briefly looked at the courthouse ceiling, "Thank You Lord Jesus! You fought the battle for us again!"

"Amen!" Ranger Wallace replied, and Ranger Santos nodded positively.

They strolled down the hallway as they talked. An iron gate swung open as they entered the locked areas.

The clang of mechanical doors sliding shut behind them… as they passed… with buzzers randomly going off…was unnerving.

Some prisoners hummed or whistled, others grunted or panted while exercising on the floor of their cells.

Others stretched to see sunlight coming through a high window in the hallway.

And prisoner shoes squeaking or shuffling as some paced in their cells could still be heard over the chaos.

Ms. Montgomery flinched involuntarily.

They continued walking.

Toilets flushed, a harsh voice would suddenly blare over the loudspeakers, and countless prisoners were heard yelling with the guards.

Simply walking down this hallway became unruly and extremely loud.

It was no longer a civilian world.

It was the prisoner's territory.

The jail guards escorting the group stopped at Jack Rogan's cell.

He was still in solitary confinement.

A guard unlocked the steel door and Jack merely stared at the group as he sat on the concrete floor.

Ted entered the cell and stood over Jack.

He grabbed Jack under his arm and helped him to stand.

Jack was wobbly.

And quiet.

He stared at Ted and exhaled deeply.

"Good to see you, Ted. I think you are the last person I talked to…however many days ago that was…"

Ted patted him on his back.

"You are getting out of here, buddy! Right now!"

"Right now?" Jack asked incredibly.

"Yep!"

He held onto Jack's arm as they walked out of the cell.

Jack glanced at the group in front of him and rubbed his eyes.

"Jack, these are the Texas Rangers; Ranger Santos, and Ranger Wallace. They have something to tell you." Ted informed him.

Ranger Wallace stepped towards him. "Jack Rogan, we apologize for your being arrested, but all of the evidence pointed to you. However, we discovered you were set up to take the blame by Betty. She was found, and she confessed.... you are a free man!"

Jack fell on his knees. "Thank You Lord Jesus!" He cried and laughed and cried again.

"And thank you, Ted, for believing in me, and thank you Texas Rangers for keeping the investigation open!"

They all nodded at him smiling.

Jack turned to the one woman in the group grinning happily. "And you're my angel from Heaven!"

She laughed and came forward. "Good to meet you, Jack! I'm P. J. Montgomery, Ted Davis's new assistant."

"Well, you look like an angel to me! Nice to meet you too!"

They walked out of the courthouse and into the bright morning sun, exiting at the back entrance.

There was no one to bother them.

"Where to?" Ted asked.

Jack squinted at him. "Drop me off at my apartment. I can't wait to take a shower and get into clean clothes. Oh, and call Door Dash for some great, tasty food!" He laughed. "Just relaxing at home will be fantastic!"

They parted ways with The Texas Rangers.

It was such a beautiful day. The sky was blue with wispy clouds rolling by, and a slight breeze added to the enjoyment.

As the three approached Ted's parked car, a local television news van pulled in. The news team instantly recognized Ted and Jack and squirmed to get out of the van and set up their recording equipment.

Ted buckled his seat belt and glanced at Ms. Montgomery in the back seat; buckled in as well. And Jack, in the front passenger seat was seat belted in also.

"You guys ready?"

Leaning forward, Ms. Montgomery tossed her hair from her shoulders letting the long brown tresses fall down her back.

Jack had turned to hear her response and watched her instead.

She grinned, "Mr. Davis, with that T.V. crew recording us, I think the word is: action camera!"

They all laughed as Ted drove away.

Chapter Thirty

Ella flipped the switch.

Twinkling lights strung from the patio danced in the breeze.

Her first party.

And Sam was grilling.

A surprise for Jack Rogan: her homemade banner draped across the entrance.

'Welcome back, Jack!' painted red, white and blue had clusters of red, white and blue balloons tied to the patio cover… blowing in all directions from the brief gusts of wind.

Ella's masterpiece.

And so it began, a truly happy day planned for all!

Sam lit the charcoal and placed the T-Bone steaks in his special sauce to marinate while the fire grew.

Aroma filled the air as clouds of smoke drifted from the outdoor grill.

Ella sauntered over and took a deep breath.

"Oh, Sam! Nothing smells as good as this!"

"Wait till you taste the T-Bones!"

Ella raised her eyebrows. "I haven't had a grilled steak in months! What a treat!"

"Trust me. You'll savor every bite!"

"I am so ready!"

They both glanced at each other as the sudden whine of a car motor approached, then another, and instantly doors slammed as car engines were turned off.

Chatter was heard as the guests arrived.

Ella took off to greet them.

Frank and Lucille were bright eyed as they looked at the gaily decorated patio and hugged Ella.

"Well now, this beats the courthouse!' Frank bellowed.

"You outdid yourself, Ella! This looks so inviting!"

"Thank you! Come on in!"

Ella escorted them into the fenced patio area, and Lucille thrust something at her.

"What's this?"

"Her special banana pudding!" Frank bragged, smiling at Lucille.

"Well, I can't wait to try it! I'll put it on the picnic table."

"I hope you'll like it." Lucille replied.

"I'm sure I will!"

Ella placed it at one corner of the table, close to the pile of plates, napkins, and a caddy holding an assortment of knives, forks, and spoons.

Ted, P. J., and Jack suddenly walked in.

Ella looked up from the table when she heard Jack yell excitedly.

"What is this? For me? I can't believe it!"

She ran and hugged Jack as his eyes watered and the banner waved in the wind at just the right moment.

"Yes! All for you, my friend! Of course, we'll all enjoy it with you!"

He grinned at everyone as the men patted him on the back and Lucille hugged him next.

And then P.J. shyly approached him and gave him a brief hug.

Jack stood taller after that hug.

"Thank you, all of you. This means so much to me! And it will be my turn next time! Of course, if Sam agrees to grill for us again?"

"I'll be glad to! Come over here and I'll show you how it's done." Sam returned to the barbeque pit, and the guys followed him.

"Need help with anything?" P.J. asked.

"Sure! We can start bringing the food out."

Lucille spoke merrily, "Lead the way, dear."

They entered the kitchen and Ella dumped bags of crushed ice into enormous bowls and the ladies carried them outside onto the table.

The container of potato salad sat on top of one bowl of ice with a cover placed on top.

Same procedure for the container of Deviled Eggs, and the Japanese Style Green Bean and Toasted Garlic Bits stir fry.

They set the table as Sam placed the steaks on the grill.

"How do you want your steak cooked; well, medium well, pink, or what?" he asked the group.

Ted, Frank, and Lucille all replied "Pink!"

Ella and P.J. both answered at the same time, "Medium well!"

"Got it!" Sam answered.

"Go ahead and fill your glasses." Ella said. "One gallon is sweet tea, and the other is unsweetened tea. They are both labeled. Ice bucket is next to them. Help yourself and have a seat! We're about ready to eat!"

They all began milling about the iced tea area, chattering as they went, and taking their seats.

And then the moment arrived.

The crackle of the embers grew loud as the fat dripped onto the charcoal. Fat from the sides of each steak crisped tenderly.

And the aroma was mouth-watering.

It drifted deliciously across the patio with a gentle afternoon breeze.

Sam carried a platter of searing steaks from the grill to the individual's plate.

They sizzled loudly.

Bowls of food from the ice were passed family style to each guest.

Plates were filled.

Sam gave the blessing of the food.

"Heavenly Father, bless this food for the nourishment of our bodies, and our bodies for your service. We pray for safety and protection of all gathered here today. Bless them and we pray their needs be met, for our sins to be forgiven, for Your guidance and for Your will in our lives. Thank You that our friend Jack is no longer locked up, and now a free man, and we give You all the Praise and Glory and Honor and Worship. In Jesus Christ Holy name, we pray, Amen."

"Amen!" The group answered together.

"Dig in, everybody! Enjoy!" Ella grinned.

Jack cut into his steak…still sizzling…and glanced at those eating.

"I have to admit; there were days I didn't think I'd ever eat like this again."

He took a bit of the steak and moaned.

"Oh, this is so good! Thank you, Sam and Ella!"

"It's all good!" Frank added.

Sam, Ella, Lucille, and Frank sat on one side of the picnic table: with Ted, P.J. and Jack sitting across from them on the other picnic bench.

P.J. was not bashful.

"Could someone pass me the Deviled Eggs again?" She smiled.

Ted and Jack both nearly fell into the Deviled Egg platter trying to be the one to hand it to her.

Ted won out.

He graciously smiled while handing the platter to her.

Jack sat back down in his chair and nonchalantly took a bite of his potato salad.

Lucille gave Ella a brief smile and nodded toward the two men.

The meal continued with others getting seconds.

"Lucille, how does it feel having a houseful again?" Ella inquired.

"I love it! Ted and Jack have bedrooms upstairs, and P.J.'s room is next to mine downstairs. Lots of hustle and bustle going on!"

"We've been giving the tennis court a good work out!" Ted announced.

"Yes," P.J. smiled at Ted, "and you are really great at tennis, but watch out; I'm learning fast."

Ted grinned at her. "Learning? You are doing great, lady."

"Hey P.J., check out the theatre room. It's got some of the best movies… I know from when I stayed there!" Sam informed her.

"Thanks! That sounds relaxing." She remarked.

"How do you like Texas, P.J.?" Ella asked.

"Oh, I love it. Everyone is so friendly, and there is so much you can do here. I am from a small town in Ohio, and where Marietta is beautiful, and has lots to offer, well, it's just incredible here! I love to bake, and I've already discovered some specialty shops to check out."

"You like to bake?" Ella exclaimed. "So do I! We'll have to share recipes…and those specialty shops you found. I'm still fairly new here, what did you find in those shops?"

"Oh, the best variety of flour! Whole red wheat flour, and organic rye. They are both so hard to find. They also have natural spices…no chemicals!"

"We'll have to bake some loaves of homemade bread soon!" Ella suggested.

"I'd enjoy that." P.J. grinned.

"P.J., can you tell us about any cases you worked on before coming to Texas?" Jack inquired.

"My last case doesn't happen often. You can imagine how difficult it is for an older teenager to get adopted. And… well… several were months away from aging out of the system. A couple took advantage of it and were using them for free labor. That is abuse! I'm happy to say that couple is serving time now!"

Ella frowned. "Well, that's one good thing about it, but I never thought about the teenagers aging out of the system. What happens to them? Where do they go?" Ella demanded.

"They are on their own. They must get a job, and their own housing." P.J. solemnly stated.

"I didn't realize that. It seems like something could be done to help them, they don't have anyone, no family…" Lucille's voice trailed off. "Where's my phone? I want to look up some information on that, if you guys don't mind?" Lucille blurted.

"No go ahead, I'm interested in what you discover." Frank said.

The others nodded as they kept on eating.

"Well…I can't find my phone…" Lucille dug inside her purse.

"Here," Ella handed her own phone to Lucille, "use mine."

Lucille turned the phone on and got busy.

"Sam, have you heard anything else from the Texas Rangers about your arson case?" Frank inquired.

"I did. The case is officially closed. They tracked down those who stole Betty's credit cards and arrested them. It was two women. They admitted everything. And they'll never know who stripped her car. That is history!"

"I'm just glad it's over. I didn't agree with Betty's lifestyle, but I certainly can't stand the thought of her or anyone being abused or tortured." Ted replied.

"And I know I've said it a hundred times, but I'll say it again…Thank You Lord Jesus she admitted her guilt!" Jack exclaimed.

Ella chimed in. "And thank You Lord Jesus that Betty earnestly prayed to be forgiven and to have Jesus Christ as her Lord and Savior before she passed away!"

"I didn't know that." Jack blurted. "That is a great testimony."

Lucille ended her phone call and set the phone beside her plate.

She was obviously lost in thought as she continued eating.

P.J. glanced at Lucille." Did you find out anything on teens aging out in the foster care system?"

Lucille answered in a low tone," I sure did."

"It must be bad…" Ella muttered.

"It is. They have higher rates of homelessness, unemployment, and incarceration than other teens with a family. They have no safety net, no support from anyone."

Everyone stopped talking and listened.

Lucille continued. "And 7 out of 10 young women get pregnant before they reach 21 years old. Some develop PTSD. And some states do offer services to help them until they are 21, but they still feel isolated, and not ready for independent living."

"That doesn't seem fair." Jack commented.

"It's not." Frank agreed.

Ella looked up from her plate. "Maybe we could help. You know I got turned down for wanting to start a clinic here…maybe we could have some kind of housing and learning center…?"

"Yes!" Lucille yelled. "And I'll help!"

"I think that's a great idea!" Sam added.

The others nodded together.

"P. J., would you refer us to someone working in foster care?" Ella asked.

"Be glad too. They should be happy to check you out…and your motives and maybe let you interview some of the teenagers."

"Well, it wouldn't hurt to try!" Ted encouraged.

"Okay. Done deal." P.J. smiled.

They all finished eating, and P.J. suddenly stood and began clearing off the table.

"Oh no, you are a guest, let me do that." Ella declared.

"We'll help her!" Ted grinned as he and Jack gathered plates and glasses.

"Well, okay then." Ella laughed watching both men try to outdo the other.

Lucille leaned toward Ella and whispered, "It's almost sibling rivalry after her."

They both chuckled as the three entered the kitchen together.

Ella's phone began ringing and she started searching for it.

"It's here. I've still got it." Lucille reminded her.

It continued ringing.

"Go ahead and answer it for me." Ella insisted.

Lucille picked the phone up.

"Hello? Who? You want to speak to Sam?" Lucille frowned and quickly glanced at Ella.

Ella looked wide-eyed and shrugged her shoulders.

"Give it to Sam, then. I can't imagine who'd be calling him on my phone…"

"Who is this?" Lucille quizzed.

"Sybil?" Lucille blurted loudly and gave Sam the phone.

Ella jumped off the picnic bench and rushed to his side wide-eyed.

Silence swept the room.

"Hello?" Sam spoke cautiously.

He listened.

"Was it a boy or a girl?" He questioned.

"What? You want me to do what? Bring the father in for a DNA test…?" Sam snapped rudely into the phone.

He listened again.

"Okay, okay!" He commented and took a deep breath. Sam ended the call red-faced and huffing.

Ella yelled. "Sybil? What is Sybil doing calling you? And on my phone?"

"It's not what you think, Ella…" Sam muttered.

"I'll tell you what I think! Her choice to rob a bank made me live with the bad consequences. I lost my job, my reputation, and my career…"

"Ella, don't…you are wrong! Believe me, it's not what you think!"

Tears streamed down her face. "And I'll tell you something else! Now…I won't settle for a life I don't want because of her new choice to have a baby. Her decisions will not compromise my life again!"

Sam shook his head. "Ella, Ella, listen to me…"

Lucille started to speak and Frank quickly nodded to her not to.

Ella looked Sam directly in his eyes and finally calmed down.

"So, why did she call you on my phone from prison?"

"She probably got my name from the news on television, and she had your phone number."

"And it must be a boy or girl baby I heard you mention?"

"As an attorney, she wants me to bring the father for a DNA test to prove he is the father."

"Who is she saying is the father?"

Sam raised his head and looked at Ted.

"Oh no. She can't do that to me. She got me intoxicated one time…one time…" He groaned.

Lucille silently cried, and Frank rocked her in his arms.

"Don't Lucille, don't. It may not be Ted's baby."

No one else spoke.

"Well, she's not ruining our get together." Ella blurted, finally breaking the silence.

"And I want to say something to Ted and to Jack. Do not let those kind of women…and I'm talking about Betty and Sybil…do not let them change your life."

She wiped the remaining tears from her face. "We only have one life. Don't settle for less than God has for you…and that's a like-minded, God comes first in her life woman… that thinks first of God and follows His ways…and puts you before herself. Don't settle for less."

P.J. stared at Ella nodding her head yes.

"I was in jail just like Jack was…and I still intend to do something meaningful with my life. You can too, Jack. And Ted, the babies' mother…is a bank robber. I pray it's not yours, but if it is …that's between you and God."

Sam walked over to Ted and hugged him. "Man, I hate this for you Ted. All we can do is go get you tested and get it over with."

Ted looked defeated. His shoulders sagged.

"Yeah, You're right. We'll leave in the morning…so where is it we're driving to?"

"Not driving. Flying. We have a long trip. I'll get our tickets now."

He went back to the table and gave Ella a big bear hug.

"I love you lady. Don't ever doubt me or doubt that."

"I won't. It was just too much and too sudden of a shock, I'm sorry I overreacted."

He grabbed his phone off the table and looked at everyone. "Well, we're all like family now." He grinned. "Nothing to hide, and nothing to give but love."

Some smiled at him and others nodded in agreement.

"I'll book our flight." He grimaced and walked to the house.

Frank raised his eyebrows at Ella. "Well, I found out something about you tonight, young lady. I think we have the right person to mentor quite a lot of ageing out teenagers. You have the right values and principals."

Everyone grinned and Ella looked at her guests.

"Thank you, but I can only do it with all of you helping."

P. J. smiled. "I think I can speak for everyone. It's another done deal."

"Great! I love a done deal! Let's sit by the fire pit. We need to unwind after all that chaos. I'm so sorry that happened. I don't usually have outbursts in public."

"It's okay, Ella. None of us are perfect." Lucille smiled at her and gave her a hug.

They ambled to the firepit area with six Adirondack chairs circling it. The lights hanging off the patio cover seemed to twinkle lazily, and a nice breeze was blowing. Chatting about the tasty meal they had enjoyed, the evening had indeed returned to normal…regardless of Sybil.

Ted threw a few logs into the pit and got the fire going.

Sam returned to the patio and gave a sigh of relief to see everyone relaxing.

He carefully sat down in the chair by Ella and squeezed her hand.

She squeezed back.

[illegible] arrangement she'd made [illegible] Sally. She was, after all, working for Sybil now.

Complete transparency was a must.

The doctor was just as surprised by Sybil wanting a baby as Ella was.

Ella and Ted boarded the plane to Sybil's prison [illegible] flight.

Still dark outside.

The roar of engines firing up and accelerating during take-off [illegible] back to their [illegible] situation.

Their [illegible] by the window.

Most passengers on the early flight soon reclined and fell asleep.

Not Ella and Ted.

Wide awake.

Chapter Thirty- One

All arrangements were made by Sam. He was, after all, working for Sybil now.

Complete transparency was a must.

Everyone was just as surprised by Sybil having a baby as Ella was.

Sam and Ted boarded the plane to Sybil's prison. It was an early flight.

Still dark outside.

The roar of engines firing up and accelerating during take-off brought reality back to their seemingly unreal situation.

They managed to sit next to each other, Ted by the window.

Most passengers on the early flight soon yawned and fell asleep.

Not Sam and Ted.

Wide awake.

Both lost in thought.

"So, Sybil is in Atlanta, Georgia…" Ted glanced out at lit cities below.

"Yep."

"And you are now her attorney in this case?"

"I am." Sam uncrossed his legs and changed position. "On the phone with her while ago, I decided it was just a paid job, even though it was Sybil…but now…" His voice trailed off as he looked away.

"But now, even I can see what Sybil's actions have done to Ella. She doesn't deserve any further ripples in her life directly caused by Sybil." Ted advised.

"I know that now." Sam uttered and continued. "It won't happen again... I've decided to resign from the case as soon as this is over."

"You've made an important decision and a just one…" Ted nodded looking at his friend.

"I will not let Sybil come between me and Ella."

"Good call my friend!"

A loud squeal from a child suddenly interrupted the steady hum of the engines. He was about 4 years old, and escaped his mother's grasp, running down the aisle bubbling with excitement. Sam reached out to grab him for the approaching mother, and the boy stuck his tongue out boldly.

And flung his arms and legs about in the air as Sam handed to his mother.

"Not a good time for me to see childhood in action…" Ted noted.

Sam opened his mouth to speak when the flight attendants began giving instructions.

Weary, he sat patiently until they finished.

"We need to talk about Sybil…" Sam advised.

Ted gazed out the window. "I know…"

"Sybil may or may not want the baby. What if it's yours?"

"Well, Sam…" He paused. "I can't very well walk away from my own child…but I can't be an attorney and introduce everyone to my wife the bank robber!"

"You don't have to, Ted. There are other options."

"And it may not be my baby…" Ted mentioned.

"We'll soon find out. We have rooms near a hospital…and I made arrangements to have your blood work done immediately."

"Before we talk to Sybil?"

"Exactly. A rush order is already in place. We'll know if you are the father before we see her."

Ted exhaled deeply and turned his head away from Sam again.

"And then I will resign from this case." Sam continued.

Ted turned back to face Sam and raised an eyebrow.

"Ella is a special lady." Ted blurted.

"I'm going to ask her to marry me. I've prayed about it, and it will be such a blessing if she will be my wife." Sam confided.

Ted nodded.

They both stretched and tried to get more comfortable.

Neither approaching the subject again.

Silent.

Lost in their own thoughts.

Eventually, snoozing along with the other passengers.

And different levels of snoring filled the cabin.

Until an hour later.

Luggage jittered in overhead bins.

Everyone awoke suddenly.

Nervous chatter rumbled across the cabin lowly at first, then grew in volume.

And babies cried from disturbed routines.

The plane shuddered again during the turbulence, as flight attendants assured everyone, they were okay.

And they were.

The plane soon landed smoothly in Atlanta, Georgia.

Sam and Ted, tired from insufficient sleep and occasionally stumbling, prepared to retrieve their luggage.

It was an enormous airport.

And a chaotic airport, but they did get their luggage.

Eventually, they made their way with their luggage outside to the sidewalk.

Yawning, Sam motioned for a taxi, and secured one instantly.

The taxi driver was helpful. He placed their luggage into the trunk, talking non-stop as he worked.

Sam and Ted climbed into the back seat.

"Uh, we have reservations at Kimpton Sylvan Hotel Buckhead/Midtown," Sam informed the driver.

"Yes sir, I know right where that's at. I can tell you some great places to check out, if you like…" He smiled.

"Thanks, but we aren't on vacation. I booked that hotel because…besides being extremely nice…it's near the Piedmont Atlanta Hospital also in Buckhead/Midtown.…according to their ad."

"Oh, it is. And it's an exceptional hospital."

"Thanks, that's good to know."

They settled back in the seat and viewed the Atlanta traffic from the windows of the taxi.

Ted caught himself wringing his hands together and quickly stopped.

Sam appeared not to notice.

Cars honked while suddenly changing the many lanes, and vehicles sped by.

Older buildings, many renovated, were sandwiched between magnificent buildings with well-manicured lawns: all spoke volumes of the city's image.

Clean.

Organized.

And, so far, friendly.

They arrived at their destination.

And the friendliness continued.

The taxi driver was paid and tipped well.

Sam and Ted entered the Kimpton Sylvan Hotel and noticed how kind and professional the employees were.

They checked in at the desk.

All went well.

After taking an elevator with an employee, they were escorted with their luggage to their individual suites.

"Right across the hall from each other! I like that!" Ted exclaimed to Sam.

"Nice!" He continued upon entering his suite.

Sam nodded and was escorted to his hotel suite.

"See you later, buddy. I'm taking a shower." Sam called out to Ted and disappeared into his own suite.

And he did.

The hot water worked wonderers to his aching back. All his muscles responded from being cramped on the plane. Even at thirty-two years old, it took a while to bounce back from aches and pains.

Fresh and fully awoke, Sam dressed and emptied his suitcase.

Making himself at home.

"Home." He uttered and called Ella.

He stood by the windows overlooking a firepit surrounded by chairs and splendid arrangements of flowering shrubs.

"Ella would love this…" He rang her phone.

"Hello?"

"Hey lady…"

"Sam! I've been so anxious to hear from you! Are you guys okay?"

"We're fine. This is the first chance I've had to call you…I love you…did you know that?"

"Oh, Sam, of course I know that…and I love you too. And I can't stand it…what is going on there?"

"Uh, I honestly don't know what to expect. We just got to the hotel and freshened up. And we are fixing to get Ted's blood work done. We'll just sit in the waiting room until they tell us the results…they have the baby's DNA…"

Ella interrupted. "So, you will both know if he is the father of the baby, before you guys see Sybil?"

"Yes. That's the plan."

"It's great you have connections to speed up the process!"

"Yes…and I don't know why she is in a regular hospital just having a baby…she could have done that in prison…but whatever the reason is, I'm resigning from her case as soon as this is over. I don't want Sybil in your life again. Enough is enough…"

"Thank you, Sam. You don't know how happy that makes me!"

"I know that. It's something I feel strong about. And I think it's time for us…"

"Sam, I love you! And yes, it is time for us…" she emphasized in a soft tone.

"Time for us to begin…" He spoke assuring.

Ella choked back a sob. "Yes, and hurry home."

"I will, I love you."

"I love you, too."

He ended the call and took a deep breath.

He phoned Ted next.

"Ready?"

"I'm ready. I was just about to call you. I'll meet you in the hallway."

"Okay, let's go."

They both locked the doors to their hotel suites and solemnly met in the quiet hallway.

"Mom called, I was talking to her." Ted beamed.

Sam grinned. "I talked to Ella. How is Lucille holding up?"

"She said whatever happens she stands by me… whatever my decision will be."

"I knew she would. She is a great woman. Frank is fortunate to have her as a friend."

"Yep, I agree."

They took the elevator down to the main lobby.

People milled about everywhere.

Coming and going.

Some checking in and others checking out.

"Glad we're settled in." Sam muttered.

"Yeah, me too." Ted nodded.

They plodded past people and made their way outside.

The sun was blinding.

Sam squinted at Ted as they walked to the lab at the hospital.

"Sybil knows we are coming today. Wonder what's going through her mind right now?"

"Hard to say…but I agree with Ella. I'm tired of Sybil's actions affecting so many lives." Ted bellowed.

"I'm right there with you. In fact, I have to look at my late sister the same way. She could have easily ruined

Jack for his entire life! And no telling who she caused damage to by her witchcraft. That is so evil."

"I agree." Ted answered quietly.

"And they study their Secret Society manuals…be it witchcraft, or an organization…putting 100% into that and putting the God of Abraham, Issac, and Jacob after that…" Sam raised his voice.

"God says that is an abomination to Him…take no other Gods before Him. And an organization can be their god or their idol…" Ted added.

"…and some do…thinking they can do better than God…and their organization can do better than God…they are so deceived…and so lost!" Sam kicked an empty coke can off the sidewalk. "The devil comes to steal, kill, and destroy and he's been deceiving all since Eve in the garden…"

"I mean, you only have two choices. Where do you want to spend eternity? Heaven or Hell? Why would anyone choose Hell?" Ted shook his head.

"Exactly! Which takes us back to Betty. I'm so thankful Ella was able to pray with her before she passed away."

"And Sybil? I'll be all prayed up when I see her…I don't trust her."

Sam nodded. "Me too."

They advanced closer toward the hospital entrance and ended all conversation.

Once inside, Sam glanced at Ted as they maneuvered to an information desk.

"It's almost a relief to get this over with." He sighed.

Ted smiled. "Almost."

"We have an appointment at the lab for bloodwork." Sam informed one of the many employees behind the main desk.

"Which lab?"

"Uh, I don't know. The appointment is for Ted Davis."

"DNA?"

Ted nodded. "Yes."

"Go to the second floor, room 252. That's the lab you want." She smiled and turned to wait on another customer.

Ted and Sam took off to the elevator.

It was crowded but the occupants made room for Ted and Sam.

They squeezed inside.

Sam hummed a tune to himself while Ted grew quiet.

The elevator came to a halt on the second floor and the doors opened wide.

Several got off first, and Sam and Ted hurried out. A sign posted on a wall had an arrow pointing left for the lab.

They nonchalantly ambled in that direction. Sam had quit humming whatever tune he'd been enjoying. Ted kept clearing his throat at intervals.

It was clearly obvious that Ted was becoming nervous. At one time, Ted stuck his hands into his pants pockets, then instantly jerked them out. He drummed the fingers of his right hand onto his pants leg in a rhythm known only to him and stared straight ahead.

Sam remained quiet.

A window loomed ahead in the hallway with another sign stating lab registration here.

Ted eased in front of it.

An employee smiled.

"Ted Davis; blood work for DNA testing." He announced.

"We've been expecting you. Right this way sir."

She then glanced at Sam. "If you'll have a seat in the waiting room around the corner it won't take long."

Sam gave a thumbs up sign to Ted and walked around the corner.

Within ten minutes, Ted had his blood drawn, and testing would begin immediately on his DNA. Proof of his being a match with the baby…or not …was about to be known.

He came into the waiting room and sat next to Sam. The room was nearly empty except for two couples.

The T V was blaring out some game show. Loud canned laughter spilled out from the program into the waiting room.

Sam stood and scanned the room. Finding the remote control, he grabbed it from the top of the cold drink machine and lowered the volume.

And returned to his seat.

And waited with his friend.

Ted leaned his head back and briefly closed his eyes.

"Considering worse case scenarios?" Sam asked.

"No, I am not doing that. I am trusting God…there is a reason for everything…"

Sam nodded. "We're both about to have a lot of changes happen…one way or another."

"Yep" Ted answered slowly. "And me, I'm fixing to be a dad, or not be a dad. Reminds me of my own father. Have I ever told you about him?"

"No, Ted, you haven't."

"We were close. Bonded together at an early age for me. I was about four or five years old. He had been in Vietnam…had both of his legs blown off and came home in a wheelchair. He still managed to take me fishing, me and Mom. We'd just enjoy our time together. He was a Lieutenant in the Army, and I can remember being so proud of his medals. It's so important for a child to bond with his father and his mother."

"Yes, it is. So many don't experience that, and they need it to grow…both spiritually and mentally." Sam nodded.

"Right. And if I am this baby's father, I want to bond with the child." He smiled at Sam. "I can remember my mom telling my dad; Dan, Ted's face lights up when he sees you!"

"Good memories!" Sam grinned.

Silence hung in the air as both were lost in their own thoughts.

Five minutes, ten, and then twenty minutes crawled by when an employee entered the waiting room.

Ted leaned forward.

"Kyle Stevens? Is there a Kyle Stevens here?"

Ted sank back into the seat.

A couple nodded and followed the employee out of the waiting room.

More time crawled by.

Ten more minutes and the same employee entered again.

Ted squirmed in his chair.

"Ted? Ted Davis?"

He raised his eyebrows. "Yes, I'm Ted Davis."

"We have your results, sir. Right this way, please."

Ted followed her out and pivoted at the last minute looking at Sam.

"Don't go anywhere, I'll be right back…"

To be continued…

OTHER BOOKS BY THIS AUTHOR

The Running Forward Series:

Book One: *Sin, Secrets, and Salvation* (A Christian

wife endures an emotionally abusive marriage until she can no longer stay. A powerful faith and family saga of courage, redemption, and God's healing grace; awarded 1st place in Religious Fiction 2013 by The Texas Association of Authors.)

Book Two: ***River Town*** (The saga continues as Susan Penleigh starts a new life in a small Texas town. Inspiring, suspenseful, and full of real-life struggles and faith; awarded 1st place in Religious Fiction 2014 by The Texas Association of Authors.)

Book Three: ***Hidden Creek*** (The series concludes as two women and two men wrestle with the consequences of sin and the power of God's forgiveness. A fast-paced story of healing, choices, and standing firm in faith; awarded 1st place in Religious Fiction 2015 by The Texas Association of Authors.)

Lillie, A Motherless Child (inspiring life of this author's mother, born in 1928 and raised during the depression in Texas with 16 siblings. Her own mother died when Lillie was a young child; awarded 1st place in Biography 2016 by The Texas Association of Authors.)

The American Neighborhood Series:

Book One: ***Eyes of a Neighbor*** (introduction of the

main residents in the Heights: an older, historical area of Houston, Texas. Kate; a Hurricane Katrina survivor from Louisiana, also Ethan and Becky Meyers from Kansas. All residents become entangled in a murder mystery. Suspense, intrigue, inspiration and romance intertwine beginning this series.)

Book Two: ***Heart of a Neighbor*** (Hurricane Harvey

forms in the Gulf of Mexico. Size and speed are increasing. Can Kate convince her neighbors to evacuate? Who goes? Who remains, and what happens to them? Will Richard want to know Jesus as his Savior? Heartwarming. Church family bonding.)

Book Three: *Mind of a Neighbor* (Trust builds as a few neighbors leave the disaster of Hurricane Harvey together. Faith is tested as they relocate to Kansas. Locals stir up sinister rumors that develop into unexpected trouble. Gossip abounds. Can Ethan and Kate obtain God's peace that passes all understanding? Can Kate forgive an entire town? Whose faith will remain true and who is the neighbor with the evil mind? This book concludes the series.)

Tales of Texas: A Collection of True Short Stories

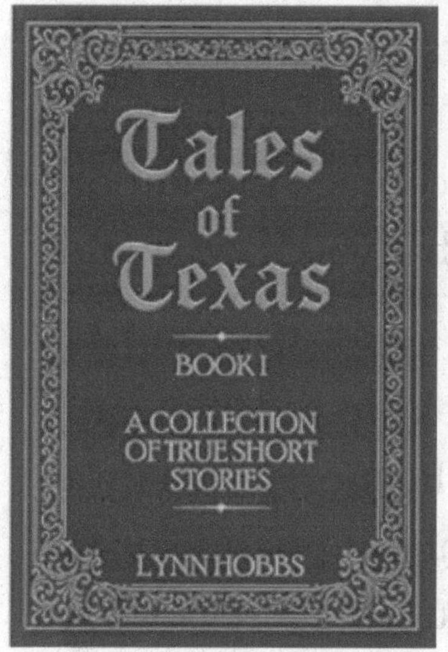

(Book 1) (In this touching collection, Texas author Lynn Hobbs shares true stories inspired by real people and real events. Ordinary moments reveal extraordinary truths about faith, struggle, redemption, heartbreak, and grace. Heartwarming and inspiring glimpses into everyday life in Texas.)

A Word From The Publisher

When you finish a book that speaks to your heart, your response matters more than you might think. Reviews are not just feedback; they are a way to share truth, encourage the author, and help others discover what you have found.

Online stores like Amazon use reviews and ratings to decide which books to recommend. The more readers engage, the more visibility a message receives. It is not about popularity; it is about reach. Every time you leave a review, you help the Word go farther than algorithms alone ever could.

If this book encouraged you, taught you something new, or helped you draw closer to Yehovah, please consider taking a moment to share that. Your honest review, even a few simple sentences, can lead someone else to find the same truth that touched your life.

Thank you for being part of this mission to awaken hearts, strengthen faith, and point people back to the fullness of who

Jesus/Yeshua is. Your voice carries farther than you realize.

How to Leave a Review on Amazon

1. Go to Amazon.com and sign in.
2. Search for the book title (for example: *The Faith of Ella Reed*).
3. Click on the book cover or title to open the product page.
4. Scroll down until you see Customer Reviews.
5. Click Write a Customer Review.
6. Choose a star rating, then share a few sentences about what you learned or enjoyed.
7. Click Submit and that's it.

It only takes a minute, but it makes a lasting impact.

Thank you for reading, for sharing, and for helping this message reach others who are searching for truth.

Thank you for being a READER!

www.ingramcontent.com/pod-product-compliance
Lightning Source LLC
LaVergne TN
LVHW030907080826
845145LV00010B/2794

* 9 7 8 1 9 6 9 0 0 4 0 7 0 *